FAIR
PERIL

Other Avon Books by
Nancy Springer

LARQUE ON THE WING

FAIR PERIL

Nancy Springer

AVON BOOKS ◆ NEW YORK

AVON BOOKS
A division of
The Hearst Corporation
1350 Avenue of the Americas
New York, New York 10019

ISBN: 0-380-97345-6

FAIR
PERIL

One

"*O*nce upon a time there was a middle-aged woman," Buffy Murphy declaimed to the trees, "whose slime-loving, shigella-kissing bung hole of a husband dumped her the month after their twentieth wedding anniversary." Striding faster through the nature park, her jeans brushing together between her ample thighs, she started to huff. "After she—had quit college to put him through law school, after she—had skipped having a life— to raise three kids with him, he gives her the old heave-ho and off he goes with his bimbo." Tramping recklessly down a hill slick with pine needles, Buffy contemplated the serendipitous rhyme of *heave-ho, go, bimbo* and brightened momentarily. She puffed her bosomy chest and raised her volume—there was nobody in the park on an April weekday, and even if there were, at this juncture of her life she didn't care. As if being heard venting aloud in the third person might be embarrassing to the normal person? Okay, then she wasn't normal. What else was new. Loudly Buffy declared, "So she, quixotic person that she is, naturally she tells him bloody fine, she can make it on

1

her own, she doesn't want a fricking penny from him, she's going to build a career as a storyteller." Yeah. Right. So far she hadn't made enough to cover the cost of her business cards. Her scutty job was what was paying the bills, not her storytelling. "The son of a bitch thinks he can pay her off and forget about her. She isn't going to let it happen. He can just keep his goddamn money and feel the guilt, goddamn it. She is so mad she . . ." Striding along a valley chilly with hemlock shade, reaching for a fiery simile, Buffy failed to come up with one sufficiently incandescent and faltered to a halt, both verbally and physically.

The mouth got going again first. "She's bloody heartbroken, okay?" Her voice hitched, and she shook her head angrily. No crying. No goddamn use. No use telling her story to the forest, either. "I talk to the trees," she muttered, "but they don't listen to me." Who had ever listened? But she told stories anyway.

"So on the first anniversary of the divorce," she proclaimed to a shagbark hickory, "she went for a long walk deep in the woods. Not a happy camper." She kicked at a jack-in-the-pulpit standing too uppity phallic near her foot, then got herself moving again, never one to follow the marked trails, squelching over damp ground topped with leaves as rotten and swampy as her mood.

"And what happened in the woods? Absolutely nothing. The end. End of story. This woman had no future. And do you want to know why? Because she was fat. Fat. FAT."

Not true. She was not obese, merely overweight. Thirty pounds. Well, maybe forty.

So, sure, just lose weight and she'd be lovable again? Like morphology was all that could possibly make her worthwhile? The thought made her want to eat somebody's head off.

A serene silver gleam showed ahead, at the bottom of the hollow. Buffy veered toward it. Why did she always do that, head toward outdoor water, even if it was just a glorified birdbath in somebody's back yard? No rational reason, but she always did. There was something about water. By all logic, a person ought to stay as far as possible from muck and mosquitoes, yet she had fallen into some sort of primordial love with the swamp hidden in the woods behind her house when she was a kid. The world had seemed more alive there—hawks, snakes, snails, cat-tails shooting out of the mud. The wet smells, like the whole place was God's bathroom. Ducks, carp, muskrats with their disgusting naked tails. She had gone there every chance she got.

But that was then, and this was now. Hard to feel the sense of wonder that kid did.

At the muddy edge of a small woodland pond, Buffy stood staring at the shivery reflections of tree branches, trying to sense a promise of salvation. Sure, it was a pretty little place, a tiny echo of Eden. Green horse-ears of skunk cabbage were pushing up along the edge. Buffy noticed bloodroot not yet in bloom, long-legged Jesus bugs walking on the water, duckweed.

Floating in a twiggy, reedy, rankly effulgent mess of trash near the edge was a dented Coors Extra Gold can some yahoo had thrown in.

So much for Eden.

On the Coors Extra Gold can squatted a greasy-green bullfrog, large compared to other frogs, but small for a bullfrog, young. It stared at Buffy with half-dome eyes the same sullied golden color as its throne.

"Can't you sit on a lily pad or a log or something?" Buffy complained.

The frog smirked. "Kiss me," it said.

Buffy felt everything stop. Her brain, her heart, her breathing, time, the world's slow turning, all hovered in abeyance. The frog—was speaking? The content of its message hung on the air, meaningless. The frog—was talking?

Then time jerked into motion again like a toy carousel. The frog—had spoken? Yes. Yes, it sure damn had. Retrieving the words from the air, Buffy heard what it had said. *Kiss me. Kiss me*, it had said, the cheeky little bastard.

Buffy was used to similar propositions from construction workers. Back when she was still riding her bike, some guy in a Day-Glo orange vest had once yelled at her to sit on his face and pedal his ears. "Kiss me" was mild by comparison, but coming from a frog, it startled her enough to jolt her free of her dismal focus on herself, which was a relief. She stood gawking.

The frog goggled back at her. "I am an ensorcelled prince," it said in a haughty baritone voice. "Kiss me, break the spell, and I will be yours to command."

Was somebody playing a practical joke, trying to make her look silly? Her ex seeking revenge by getting her on *America's Funniest Home Videos*? Buffy flashed a look all around, but the woods were typical Appalachian second growth, trees standing like fashion models, thin and boring; there was no interesting undergrowth to conceal anyone. Moreover, the frog's mouth had moved as it spoke. She had seen its salmon-colored gullet, its sticky yellowish tongue thrashing wildly to shape the words.

Because her knees felt a trifle weak, Buffy allowed herself to fold groundward and plant her large butt in the mud.

"Kiss me," the frog said with imperiled patience. Read my lips. Let me spell it out. "You kiss me. I turn into a prince."

Buffy managed to get herself functioning enough to vocalize. "This is the nineties," she whispered. "This is Pennsylvania."

"Your point being?"

"We don't have princes here. We don't even have Kennedys."

"I was stranded here by Gypsies." The frog's tone was becoming more and more imperious. "I am an ensorcelled prince. I am Prince Adamus d'Aurca. Do as I say and you will see."

Despite cold mud seeping through her pants, Buffy went hot with annoyance. This frog sounded a lot like her ex in his less endearing moments.

Her annoyance superseded her astonishment and allowed her to resume intelligent thought. And her thinking did not take long. She smiled.

"I can't kiss you when you're over there and I'm over here," she said in a wispy voice calculated to convey meekness and stupidity.

"Well, get over here and do it!"

"But I can't swim." The water was maybe a foot deep between Buffy and the frog, but why should she soak her sneakers? Let him come to her.

His Highness Prince Adamus d'Aurca complained, "God's codpiece!" then gave a kick with his powerful hind legs and plunged into the pond. One more kick thrust him to the mudbank upon which she sat, his princess enthroned in muck. Wet, gleaming a mottled, juicy off-green after his dip, he hopped past her feet and paused expectantly within her reach.

Silently she placed the thumb and fingers of her right hand around his squishy-soft middle and picked him up like an overripe banana. As a kid, she had earned a few dollars catching frogs for her biology teacher, so this was not a new experience, but were she to handle it every day of her life, she would still never get used to the tacky, humid feel of frog skin, indecently crotchy in her hand. "Ugh," she said.

Prince Adamus stretched his blunt face toward her, his

wet mouth slightly agape. His hind legs kicked and dangled, twice as long as the rest of him. "Get on with it," he ordered.

Holding him in midair and well away from her, Buffy lumbered to her feet, then groped in her jacket pocket with her other hand.

"Kiss me."

"I don't think so." Buffy pulled her knit hat out of her pocket, bent over (short of breath as her belly got in the way), and sopped it in the water at the pond's edge, raising interesting clouds of silt.

The frog's voice rose to a shriek. "You said you were going to kiss me!" More in panic than in malice, he let go a stream of unidentifiable excrement which just missed Buffy's foot. "You promised!"

"I merely *implied* that I was going to kiss you."

"You misled me!"

"Too bad."

"But I am a prince!"

"What the hell do I need a prince for?" Men. They all seemed to assume they were God's gift. "I just got rid of one dickheaded male. I don't need another one." Especially as she'd reached a point in her life where celibacy was far preferable to the terror of getting pregnant. "Anyway, what on earth do you think you're prince of? England? Monaco? Those slots are taken."

"I'm not that kind of prince!"

"I'll say." Buffy retrieved her soaked and dripping hat, carefully inserted the frog into it, then held it closed and slogged out of there, hurrying muddily back the way she had come.

"You're taking me captive!" The hat wriggled. Prince Adamus's voice issued from it muffled and hysterical.

"Think of it as role reversal," Buffy told him. "You're being swept away. Don't you read romance novels?"

"Let me go!"

Buffy did not answer. Puffing her way up the first hill, she had no breath to spare. But her thoughts were far happier, in a gloating way, than they had been an hour before. She was thinking about all the times in the past few months that she had been passed over for storytelling jobs, and who got them? Better storytellers than she was? Noooooo, people with gimmicks. A mime. A clown. A guy who did magic tricks.

"Set me free! I, Prince Adamus d'Aurca, command it!"

"That and a dime will get you a cup of coffee," Buffy panted. No, not a dime. Fifty cents. A dollar. Damn, her age was showing.

The frog's soggy voice turned pleading. "You don't believe I am a prince?"

She had not given it much thought, and she did not care to, especially not in her embittered mood. "I keep telling you, I don't need a prince or anything resembling a male of the human species," she grumbled to her hat. "What is much more interesting, and what I can really use right now, is a talking frog."

Thirteen miles away was a plastic-lined goldfish pond dominated by a large poison-green plastic frog mindlessly spouting a stream of water like pee from its mouth. Mom hated the plastic pond, the mindless plastic frog, the old lumps in wheelchairs who stared mindlessly at the frog, the nurses who propelled them to do so, herself for being as mindless as they. Strong, able to jump around, but the old gray marbles gone. Shingles flown off the roof, trump cards missing from her deck, still plugged in but didn't light up no more, out to lunch for the duration. She was Mom and not Mom. Had some other names, she knew she did, but she couldn't remember. Everything was itself and something else, including her. This place, what did you

call it, she couldn't remember coming here, all these mindless ancient people sitting in rows, boring. Pee, pee, pee
went the big frog, and a pretty girl in white walked toward
her with a plastic smile as a rickety gray man clung to her
arm. Mom knew him. He sat and twiddled his whizzer
when he didn't think anybody was looking.

Mom called out like a rain crow, "Too old! He's too old
for you!"

Tooooo old, old, old.

The pretty girl in white smiled back at her without
changing expression or speaking, a daughter, a nurse, a
bride in ugly shoes. Yes, it was a wedding, a wedding, a
wedding, silent as a funeral. Mom remembered now. She
remembered her wedding, all those solemn old people. But
the bride was just a child. The bride was just a child.

Mom stood intently still, feeling her own heart break.
Lucid moments always did that to her.

She whispered, "I am losing my mind."

Because they cracked her heart so, she let lucid moments
go by quickly. Losing her mind. Mind all gone. That was
what marrying that stony-gray old man had done to her.
Old man, all he thought about was his wiggle worm. Mom
screamed and laughed and hopped like a cricket around
the goldfish pond. Mom began to pull her clothes off.

"Shut up," Buffy told her brand-new talking frog as she
placed the soggy hat that encased him on the passenger
seat of her Escort.

"Ogress. I spit upon your nose hair."

Buffy started the car to drive her prize home, shifting
into gear rather hard. "Shut up or I'll pull your nice wet
prison off you and let you dehydrate."

"You want a talking frog, you got a talking frog. I am
going to talk till you wish you'd turn into a deaf fish. Dingdong bell, pussy's in the well, which is where the hell I

should be, in the deep dark well with a golden ball—"

"You do understand, don't you," Buffy said sweetly, "that a frog out of water can lose half its body weight in just a few minutes of exposure to full sunlight?"

"You do not frighten me, beldam. I have survived herons and owls and the foul clutches of raccoons and I will survive you, harpy. I am a prince. I am Prince Adamus d'Aurca de la Pompe de la Trompe de l'Eau. The sun is not more glorious than I am. Maidens swoon at the mention of my comely name."

Being no maiden, Buffy did not swoon. She rolled her eyes and turned on the car radio in an attempt to drown out Prince Adamus, etc. Classic rock shook the speakers.

"Aaaaaa!" the frog shrieked. "Savages on the march! Barbarians! Man the ramparts!"

It was John Cougar with his little ditty about Jack and Diane. Good one. Buffy sang along. She sang, the radio blared, and the frog bellowed imprecations, until she pulled to a stop in front of her house.

Her hovel, really; it barely deserved to be called a house. Her dumpy little hut, built out of lumber salvaged from a burned-down bra factory by an eccentric do-it-yourselfer who had eschewed the use of plumb bob and T square. A one-story cockeyed bungalow, with windows and door canted, siding slanted a different way, roofline out of agreement with any of the above, and the attached garage sliding downhill at the rate of several inches per year. Too bad; Buffy could not afford the rent on a place with right angles.

". . . piece of work is a prince," the frog was babbling. "How noble in reason, how infinite in faculty, in form and moving how express and admirable, in action how like an angel! In apprehension how like a god! The beauty . . ."

Hoping the neighbors were not at home to notice anything strange, Buffy hurried him into the house and unceremoniously plopped him from her hat into her aquarium.

"... of the world. The paragon of—blub!" Blessed silence for a moment. "Hey!" Adamus complained, resurfacing. "Land! I'm an amphibian, I need land!"

"We're gonna see how long you can tread water." Buffy laid a hefty *Reader's Digest Wide World Atlas* over the top of the aquarium to block escape.

"Air! I'm an amphibian, I need air!"

"We're gonna see how long you can breathe through your skin."

"Filthy hedgehog! Three-tongued slattern! Harridan!"

"Very *good*," Buffy approved, exiting. The frog's insults cheered her—they were so much more interesting than the ones she was accustomed to. Americans really needed to learn to swear with more flair. Perhaps she and the frog ought to give lessons. Buffy smiled as she surveyed the unkempt rectangle of real estate her landlord called a back yard. In her recycling bin she found a glass jar with a lid, and then she walked to the nearest miscelleny heap, spraddled her legs with more sturdiness than grace, bent, and started rooting. Clawing like a bear, turning over cinder blocks, she collected small red worms, sow bugs, and other creepy-crawlies. She harvested more of the same from a brick and a short length of mossy, rotting plank, then hefted those two items and headed back into the house.

The frog was floating at his ease in the dechlorinated water of the aquarium, but began to kick and thrash pitifully when he saw her. "Monster! Grendel!"

"Right." She set down her finds on a sheet of newspaper, pulled a plastic margarine container out of the dish drainer, found her scrub bucket, and started dipping water from the aquarium.

"What are you doing? Water! I'm an amphibian, I need water!"

"Would you shut up and have some respect? These goldfish are being sacrificed for your sake."

The frog did not shut up. "Aristophanes was right. We will have yet more terrible things to endure, we frogs, we will have yet more terrible things to endure."

He went on from there, lamenting the fates of frogs, Thomas the Rhymer, Odysseus, and other noble captives. Buffy ignored his monologue, emptying the aquarium until about four inches of water remained, in which three goldfish, leftovers from her younger daughter's elementary-school days, swam disconsolately. She pulled out plastic ferns, shoved some gravel to one end, and topped it with her brick and piece of planking, making a dampish platform where her frog could rest out of the water, all the while keeping an eye on him. If he tried to leap out of the aquarium, she was ready to intercept him. But he seemed dispirited. He made only a token attempt to climb the wall, then stood with his long, webbed hind feet braced against the gravel, his four-fingered hands winsomely pressed against the glass.

"Here," Buffy told him, "supper," and she transferred three beetles and a red worm from her salsa jar to her frog's glass palace.

Adamus hunkered down in the farthest corner. "Aaaaaaugh! Grubs! Maggots!"

"I imagine you prefer flying insects, but—"

"Insects? You flea-pated crone, I have been living on insects for a thousand years! Bring me roast suckling pork, quickly!"

"But if it doesn't wiggle, you're not supposed to be able to handle it."

"So wiggle it!"

As Buffy tried to think of a suitable retort, somebody knocked. Buffy rolled her eyes, slammed the world atlas down on top of the aquarium, strode to the door, and yanked it open. There stood her youngest, just sixteen, as blond and exquisite and sullen and unsmiling as a Calvin Klein perfume ad.

"Emily!" Buffy could not restrain the quick delight that always made her daughter scowl.

Emily scowled. "I was on my way to the *mall*," she stated, making sure her mother wouldn't think she was visiting on purpose, "and my stupid *car* quit, so I was walking to get to a phone and I saw you're home. Why aren't you at work?"

Buffy ducked that. "Why did your car quit?"

"Like I know?" Emily's bored, perfect eyes scanned her mother. "*Mom*, you're a mess." Emily wore a taupe silk ribbed top, a taupe-and-mauve long flowing skirt, Birkenstocks. Buffy wore mostly mud.

"Oh. Yeah, I've got to get cleaned up." Buffy stood back, gesturing to invite her daughter in. Progressing past Buffy's furniture, most of which had come from garage sales, Emily showed remarkable maturity and restraint, barely curling her lip at all. Unfortunately, she headed straight to the aquarium.

"How are my fishies? Ewwww!" She jumped back. "Ewwww, ick, what is that?"

"It's called a frog," Buffy said mildly, washing her hands at the kitchen sink. She tried not to be judgmental, but she often wondered whence this daughter had come. She had been right there when Emily popped out, but still—was this her child? Could mother and daughter be so different? Buffy habitually yanked her straight graying hair into a horse tail and fastened it with the rubber band off the newspaper; Emily spent twenty minutes every morning primping her permed bangs. Buffy shaved her legs only when she had to go to the gynecologist; for Emily, running out of disposable razors was an emergency. Buffy ate bacon by the pound; Emily was a vegetarian.

Buffy liked to stick a worm on a hook and catch a sunny; Emily marched for animal rights. Buffy killed spiders that came into the house; Emily emitted soprano screams at them.

"Kiss me," the frog said.

Emily screamed, jumped back with even more vehemence than before, and shielded her mouth with her hands.

"Please!" Adamus stood up, showing his pale underbelly, pressing his dainty hands to the glass again. "I entreat you, fair damsel, liberate a pitiful captive. I am an ensorcelled prince. Kiss me and break the spell."

Nice. She, Buffy, got the imperious treatment, whereas Emily got the soft soap.

Her perfume-ad poise blown to hell, Emily stared wide-eyed. Buffy stood with dripping hands and watched her daughter, memorizing the moment, feeling her heart melt despite her annoyance; when the brittle shell of teen sophistication ruptured, Emily was so young, so whole-hearted, so vulnerable.

"Wha-wha-wha—" Emily stammered.

"Just your generic talking frog," Buffy drawled, drying her hands on the front of her sweatshirt.

"Prithee, sweet princess Emily," Adamus pleaded.

Buffy said, "I am going to use him in my storytelling."

Instantly the brittle Emily was back, turning on her. "*Great*, Mom. Just *wonderful*."

The sarcasm was so familiar that Buffy merely blinked. "Now what did I do?" Lace-up shoes affronted this girl. The wrong brand of paper towels. Bic pens. Almost anything.

"Oh, *right*. You don't know?"

"Am I supposed to know?" Meanwhile, the frog begged and babbled, a nuisance in the background, like somebody else's baby in a restaurant. Buffy felt the beginnings of a headache. It was hard to keep edge out of her voice.

Emily shrilled, "Well, you would know if you'd think of anybody but yourself! That's what I hate, Mom—you're so selfish! You've turned into such a total user!"

Buffy sighed and pressed her lips together. Apparently "use" had been the trigger word, the one she should have avoided. When Emily had gone into hysterics and insisted on staying with her father, "use" had been a frequent word in the non-discussion. Buffy hoped that the maturity and patience that she, the mother, had shown would some-day make an impression on the girl. She had not attempted to hold on to Emily, had always loathed people who "used"—there it was again—who used children as weap-ons in a bitter divorce. Emily was entitled to love her father. Emily had always been Daddy's little princess. Moreover, Emily was accustomed to a certain lifestyle. And Emily was the child; Emily's needs came first. Buffy had put aside her own feelings and let the girl live with Daddy dear.

Buffy found herself quivering with anger.

But she kept her voice down. "Emily, I was the one who was used. For twenty years."

"Well, you're sure making up for lost time."

"That's right." They had been through this before. Buffy rolled her eyes and dismissed it. "Let's go see what we can do about your car."

"What about my fishies? They don't have enough water. That's what I mean—you get a talking frog and you don't even care what happens to my fishies!"

"Princess, you must kiss me!" The frog had progressed from vehemence to frenzy, ricocheting around the aquar-ium.

"For God's sake, take your own damn fishies!" How did moms always get stuck caring for the livestock anyway? Temper showing now, Buffy snatched Ziploc bags from a drawer and sloshed them full of aquarium water from the scrub bucket still sitting in the middle of the floor. "Go ahead, get them out before he eats them."

"Princess, Princess, Princess!" The frog bobbed and surged, standing straight up at Emily's approach. With fish dipper in hand, Emily stared at him, her young eyes like midnight-blue velvet, and suddenly Buffy felt uneasy.

"Here, I'll do it." She took the fish dipper out of her daughter's hand. The frog slumped in a corner, silent, as she scooped the goldfish out of their too-small pond.

"What does he mean, he's an ensorcelled prince?" Emily asked from behind Buffy's large mud-caked backside.

Thank modern education, the girl had probably never heard the fairy tale. Funny thing, in the Grimm version the princess never kisses the frog, just gets pissed off and flings him against the wall, and that makes him turn into "a prince with kind and beautiful eyes." Kinky. An interesting way of pussyfooting around the older versions, which were kinkier. In some of them the princess slept with the frog for three weeks before he turned into a prince.

"Nothing," Buffy told her daughter. "It doesn't mean anything. He's like a parrot. It's just something he says."

Two

Buffy was able to spot at once the trouble with Emily's car, a brand-new metallic-mauve Probe Daddy had bought her. "You have to put gas in it, honey," she said as gently as she could.

"Oh. Well, how should I know? Don't be sarcastic."

Emily's resentment was not strong enough to make her handle the emergency herself, however. Emily hated the smell of gasoline on her hands or, perish forbid, her clothing. Buffy was the one who borrowed a can at the corner Kwik-Mart, bought gas, sloshed it into Emily's tank so that Emily could drive to the pumps, paid for a fill-up, then stood on the sidewalk and waved the girl safely on her way to the mall. Roaring off, Emily did not wave back.

Emily lived for the mall. Emily would have lived *at* the mall if the place had stayed open at night. The mall was her fairy tale, her consumer fantasy, her now and her future, her all. The mall was her place to meet her friends. The mall *was* her friend. And, since the split, it was her family—the mall, Buffy thought with a sigh, was Emily's

16

mother; obviously she liked it a lot more than she did the real one.

Buffy sighed again, walked into the Kwik-Mart one more time to buy herself a consolation bag of Fritos, then munched them as she slogged home.

Hey, not all was dreary. At least she had her talking frog.

"Hey, frog."

From his brick, in the shadow of the world atlas, he ogled her sullenly, without replying. Apparently Prince Adamus d'Aurca did not appreciate her casual greeting.

"Let's get you more comfortable." Buffy thumped down to the basement, where she found some heavy wire mesh left over from the landlord's idea of fencing; she appropriated a section, took it up, and laid it over the aquarium in lieu of the atlas. There, now her baby had air. She crimped the corners to hold the mesh in place, then hustled (with portions of her bobbing) to the back yard and brought four bricks to weight the corners and keep baby safe in his playpen. Next, she positioned her Gro-Lite over the aquarium to keep baby warm, sacrificing houseplants as willingly as she had proposed to sacrifice goldfish. The beetles were crawling out of the aquarium and the red worm had drowned in the water; she removed it. "Supper's coming in a little bit," she cooed. Satisfied with herself and her mothering skills, Buffy had a shower and changed her clothes (finally), put her jeans in the washing machine, nuked herself a fried chicken dinner in the microwave, cut tender white meat off the wing, lifted the aquarium's new mesh roof, took the shard of fowl between her fingers, and offered it to her frog, wiggling it.

He bit her.

He lunged like a cornered mouse and bit her hand. It was like being attacked by a Cub stapler with gums. The two pathetic teeth in his upper jaw accomplished only two tiny drops of blood on her knuckle—a mouse would have done more damage. Yet the bite chilled her to her navel, and infuriated her. She snatched her hand, and the food, away. "You can just damn well starve!" she yelled.

"Gladly, O adipose slattern."

Letting her chicken dinner sit, Buffy stomped to the freezer for brownie-chunk ice cream.

Hunkered at the table, she attempted to soothe herself by applying the cold stuff internally. But the frog had broken his sullen silence to yammer incessantly. "I am a PRINCE give me a QUINCE when I have fears that I may cease to be were there but room enough and time the small rain down can rain fowles in the frith and fisshes in the floode Adam lay ybounden, bounden in a bond, lully, lullay, lullay, let me out you snaggletoothed hag!"

Buffy reached for a bag of Hershey's Kisses. "Shut up."

"Overstuffed knackingwench!"

"Shut *up*."

"I will not. I am a prince of the royal blood of Aurca. I—"

Buffy reared to her feet. "ONCE UPON A TIME," she roared, "THERE WAS A LOUD PRINCESS. SHE COULD HOWL LOUDER THAN WOLVES PLUS WIND PLUS THUNDER, SHE COULD BOOM LOUDER THAN A BITTERN, SHE COULD CRY DOWN GEESE FROM THE SKY. BUT HER MOTHER TOLD HER—" Buffy's voice grew whisper-quiet as the frog squatted, watching her pop-eyed. "Her mother told her that if she did not speak softly, no prince would ever marry her. So she spoke softly and smiled sweetly and a prince married her. And her mother was happy. But the prince's mother was a witch." Buffy grimaced, thinking of her own former mother-in-law. She was making up the story as she went along, but it curled her toes and she knew it was good. "One day the princess had a baby, a little girl like a pink rose. And as she lay in her lacy white bed with her new daughter, the witch said to her, 'Give me the baby,' and the princess said loudly, '*NO*,' because she did not want the witch to touch her little girl. Then, because the princess had spoken loudly, the witch pronounced a curse . . ."

Buffy paused to breathe deeply and think of the curse. The frog waited for her to go on.

"The witch cursed the loud princess that when she spoke and wished to be heard, only the birds of the air would hear her.

"And so it came to be. Her child grew, and when the loud princess said, 'I am your mother,' wrens flew to her shoulders, but the little girl could not hear her. When the loud princess said, 'I love you,' swans came and lay at her feet, but the little girl could not hear her. The little girl said, 'Who is this woman?' and her grandmother the witch told her, 'That is your stepmother.' And the little girl knew that stepmothers were supposed to be wicked and deceitful. So she took a hunk of bread and a lump of cheese and an apple in a silk kerchief and set off to find her true mother.

"She walked herself hungry, out of that kingdom and into the next, and nary a mother did she find. When she sat down in a grassy meadow to eat, the meadowlarks came and tried to peck at her bread and cheese, but she drove them away. Then she lay down where she was to sleep. But suddenly every bird in the meadow flew up and away. The little girl did not know what had disturbed them.

" 'MY CHILD! WHERE IS MY LITTLE GIRL?' "

Buffy felt a lump of pesky emotion take form in her throat, but kept going.

"The loud princess was crying so loudly that every bird in the world took fright, but no one in the castle could hear her. She searched the castle from towers to dungeons, shouting all the while, and no one answered her. She cried to her mother-in-law, 'WHERE IS MY CHILD?' but the witch did not hear. She cried to her husband the prince, 'WHERE IS MY LITTLE GIRL?' but he did not hear or care. She cried out so loudly that the stones of the castle cracked, and as she ran out the gate and shouted for her little girl, every stone of the castle crashed down behind her. And then surely the witch and the prince could not hear her, for they were dead."

Pure, sheer wish-fulfillment fantasy, Buffy thought. But it was a good story. She could feel it curling her guts. She went on.

" 'WHERE IS MY LITTLE GIRL?' " the loud princess cried, and a hawk flew down from the sky and said, 'I will show you.'

"Far away, the little girl could not sleep, and got up and walked and walked, out of that kingdom and into the next, and nary a mother did she find. She walked herself hungry, and sat down in a woods to eat, and the wood thrushes flew down and tried to peck at her bread and cheese, but she drove them away. Then—" Buffy meant to stick to the formula she had set up, because things were always supposed to happen in threes, but screw it. A person could be blabbering all day. "Then she walked until all she had left to eat was her apple. She came to a lake, and when the waterbirds tried to peck at her apple, she started to cry. 'Oh, take it,' she said, and she gave it to a swan. 'All I want is my mother.'

"But as she gave away the apple she could hear what she had not been able to hear before. She could hear what the birds were saying. A hawk flew over and cried, 'Here comes your mother.' A meadowlark flew up and sang, 'Your true mother.' A wood thrush called, 'Your true mother who loves you.' And because the birds had opened her ears, the little girl could hear the loud princess miles away, running toward her and crying, 'MY DAUGHTER, MY BABY, WHERE IS MY LITTLE GIRL?' And the little girl jumped up and cried out, 'Mama! Here I am!' "

Buffy had meant to go on, to settle the pair of them in a cottage in the woods where the birds would feed them and they could live happily ever after. But the lump in her throat made her end the story there. She sat down.

"Is that all?" Adamus asked, his voice hushed and froggy.

"Yes."

"It was wonderful. Please, tell another one."

Buffy straightened in her chair and peered at him. The pupils of his eyes glistened like black tears.

"You really liked it?"

"Yes! It consoled me. It charmed me back to when I was . . ." His voice trailed away.

The frog's emotion stunned Buffy. She was used to luke-warm reactions at best. Her husband had never listened to her stories, any kind of stories, whether stories she made up or stories she memorized and told or stories she saw in tabloids or something that had happened to her at the supermarket or the story of her life—Prentis had not wanted to listen. Her children—Marjorie, married now and living in Wisconsin; Curtis, finishing college; Emily— even before they had reached their teens, they had not wanted to listen. Kids at schools and birthday parties squirmed, wanted to play video games, listened only be-cause the adults made them, as if stories were spinach, good for you. Even the mirror on Buffy's bathroom wall listened only with a cynical glint.

But Adamus had listened raptly, with eyes that shone like the night.

Buffy did not know what to say. "Do you want your supper now?" she blurted.

"No, thank you. I do not need to eat every day. I could not eat now. Your tale is ringing in me."

Buffy sat dumb with gratification.

Adamus said, "It is not a tale I have heard before. Where did you come by it?"

"I made it up."

"You *made* that? But—but it echoes like bells no mortal should hear."

The frog's praise and astonishment were genuine, warm, yet Buffy flashed cold. Bells no mortal should hear? Overstatements like that scared her. "It's just a story," she mumbled.

"Just a story? Is 'Cinderella' just a story? Is 'Beauty and the Beast'—"

Now, wait a minute. "I am a storyteller," Buffy interrupted, protecting her turf as a pro. "I know the fairy tales, I use them in my work. But I'm not crazy. I don't *believe* them."

Silence. The frog sat like a green-mottled stone.

"They're just stories," Buffy said.

Like a chill wind through bluebells, the frog said, "Am I just a story?"

Buffy got up. It was only seven o'clock, Emily was probably still at the mall with a dozen friends, most people were just starting their evenings, but she didn't care. It had been a strange day. "I'm going to bed."

"But it is not true that you do not believe," Adamus said. "You do believe. You must. You can hear me. Many princesses passed by that pond, but you are the only one who could hear me."

Bullshit. The frog had to be some sort of gimmick, like, the government was experimenting with spy technology and she had found their escaped frog or something. What the teachers used to call a miracle of modern science back in high school, which was about the time Buffy had given up wondering how things worked. In her experience, women usually gave up their curiosity. It was no use. Wondering how the car worked, or the bank's computer system, or the State Department, would get you nowhere. For women, the world ran on lipstick and luck. Finding the right husband. Finding a talking frog.

Buffy said, "Good night."

"No. Let me out," the frog begged. "Please. I am an exile in a strange body and now you have put me in this glass prison—"

"Listen, I'll give you everything you need," Buffy told him. "Food, light, warmth, your own little wetland, vetting if you get sick—what's the problem? You're safe with me. No snakes or herons, nothing to hunt you—"

"Will you kiss me? Kiss me or let me go!"

"Good night." Buffy turned off the light. In his glass palace the frog squatted, an algae-colored lump, silent, his throat pulsing like a beating heart.

Emily drove to the mall in her new Probe, cruised the parking lot, saw no cars she recognized, and slumped in the driver's seat, reaching out to pat the stuffed bunny nesting on her dashboard to reassure herself she was not completely alone. She did not want to go into the mall if none of her friends were there. Her friends were her real family. "Mom thinks I'm a materialistic twerp," she told the bunny. Adults didn't understand that shopping was an excuse to be with other kids and also a solace for not being at home with two actual parents—stepparents didn't count—two real parents who still loved each other. Emily knew a couple of kids who had that kind of parents, the kind who got married once and stayed together. Those kids were lucky. She hated them.

Mom probably cares more about her new pet than she does about me.

Mom obviously didn't want to be bothered. Mom hadn't even gotten upset about custody or tried to keep her. Sure, go ahead, no problem, let the kid live with her father where she had to get out of the house every evening or else see her father getting all puffy-panty-kissy-face with whatsername, the new wife, walking-talking blonde joke, only ten years older than Emily, maybe twelve years, or else had some really good plastic surgery—and Emily was supposed to call her "stepmother"? No way. No way could this woman ever be any kind of mother to her.

"I'm a blonde," Emily said to the stuffed bunny, "but at least I'm a real blonde. She did it to herself. The baby goo-goo eyes. The giggle. The whole routine."

The woman was so much like her, so much like she might be in ten years if she wasn't careful, that it scared her.

"My father's a twit."

The ache in her chest made her feel like feeding her face. But she resisted the urge to go looking for food. She didn't want to get like that, like her mother.

"Let's check one more time," Emily said to the bunny, which was fading from a realistic brown to a mellow yellow from sunlight. She drove around the lot again. No, none of her friends were there. It was too early.

"Dammit." Emily expressed herself via the gas pedal and varoomed out of there.

Her father was with his bimbo. Her mother was gabbing with a talking frog.

Emily stopped thinking about her sucky parents, specifically her mother, and started thinking about the talking frog. Awesome, the shivery feeling he had given her—she was feeling it again just thinking about him. What was he? Something exciting, important, forbidden. She knew by the tingle in her spine. She knew by the way her mother had shoved her away from him and the way her mother had—

lied to her, let's face it, telling her, "Nothing," like when she was little and asking about what double beds were for.

Emily headed toward the library.

"Talking frogs," she said to the guy at the children's desk, a weird old guy if she'd ever met one, but he knew every book in the library. "Isn't there some sort of story about talking frogs?"

"Absolutely." He found a three-inch-thick volume and placed it in her hands. "They knew what was important. They put it up front. Have a look at the very first tale."

The library had an outdoor courtyard with a fountain. Emily took the fat book there, sat on a bench in the sunshine, put her feet up on the stonework rim, and opened *The Complete Fairy Tales of the Brothers Grimm.*

In olden times, when wishing still helped, there lived a king whose daughters were all beautiful, but the youngest was so beautiful that the sun itself, which had seen so many things, was always filled with amazement each time it cast its rays upon her face. . . .

Emily read on.

"What a babe! Hey, beautiful!" Someone tapped on the glass doors. Intent on what she was reading, Emily scowled at the interruption, looked up, then smiled. It was some of her friends, a few boys, several girls. She had forgotten; they had term papers due tomorrow. Naturally they were at the library.

"Whatcha doing, Emily?" They came out to the sunny courtyard.

"Nothing." She turned back to the story of the frog who was crying, *Princess, princess, youngest daughter, open up and let me in.*

Her friends surrounded her. They sat on the bench with her, they sat at her feet, they leaned over her shoulders and teased her as she finished reading. Yet, reading about the prince with kind and beautiful eyes, Emily felt all alone.

Buffy went snarling to her job in the morning. "Didn't get much sleep," she grumbled to a co-worker.

"Why not?"

"Stupid frog kept me awake. Croaking."

"Excuse me?"

"I've got this frog in the aquarium."

"You mean croaking as in, dead?"

"No, dammit." Though at 3 A.M., Death To The Frog had appealed as an option. "I mean noise pollution."

Why would a talking frog CROAK? But Prince Adamus the Articulate had made her night hell not talking, just CROAKING, resonant enough to vibrate the bungalow, like an ordinary bullfrog. Rumpled of hair and temper and pajamas, Buffy had expostulated with him repeatedly, but he had merely stared back at her, and frogs don't blink; it was impossible to outstare him. It was impossible to tell whether he was honking and quacking away as a form of psychological warfare aimed at depriving her of her sleep, or whether the so-called ensorcelled prince was truly in ranine mode, croaking for the imperative frogginess of it— swelling rhythmically, his bubble of throat puffing huge, vibrating as he emitted a sound like the combined belch of a thousand beer-swilling husbands—because it was mating season.

"What are you keeping a frog in the house for?"

"Don't ask," Buffy muttered, going about her job with even less than her usual lack of luster. When she had suddenly needed employment, she had spent a hellish week at a Trojan factory first, stroking warm latex off ranks of militarily erect, sleek steel penises marching out of the machine. Just what she had needed at that low point in her life, pricks on parade. Then she had landed this job in the

artificial-food plant, where all day she counted and pack-
aged and boxed fake fried eggs to decorate the cooktops
at Sears, fake sandwiches and dewy-fresh plastic pseudo-
lettuce to go in the refrigerators on the sales floor, fake
hyperrealistic wedges of pie and cake for the dessert trays
at Denny's and other fine restaurants. Chocolate-
marshmallow-peanut ice-cream sundaes that would never
melt. Brownies à la mode. Buffy remembered being at a
restaurant once where the waiter had actually touched the
plastic lemon meringue pie with his fingertip as he pointed
it out, totally destroying the illusion. Ick. Buffy went
through her days disgusted and dreaming of real nutrition.
Given her druthers, if she had to work at some kind of
scut job she would have held down a sales counter at a
mall, where stories would walk past all the time. She had
long since decided the food factory was not good for her—
she tended to go home and eat Twinkies by the box—but
she had not tried to find other work.

She fell asleep at her work station twice that afternoon.
Keep that up and she'd have to find another job.

Driving home, she promised herself Tastykake pow-
dered donuts instead of Twinkies.

The frog was lolling in his personal pond when she entered the house. "Listen, virago, either kiss me or let me
out of here," he began immediately. "I am a prince of—"

"Shush a minute." The light on the answering machine
was flashing. Buffy pressed the play button, and the results
startled Adamus so much that he dropped his monologue.

"It's talking!"

The opportunity for sarcasm slipped right past Buffy;
she had gone rigid. "It's *her!*" She swatted the machine to
silence it. "Jesus! She's got the incredible nerve calling
me."

"Pardon?"

"It's the Trophy Wife! My ex's little-bitty-assed gold-plated prize. I can't believe—"

"What was that she named you? Madeleine?"

Buffy stood hyperventilating, too livid to explain that all hippie-generation women with ugly and unmanageable monickers nicknamed themselves Buffy, though perhaps not all of them had proceeded to marry bastards. "She would," she muttered. Of course the Trophy had called her Madeleine. "I'm not going to listen to—I don't have to—oh, shit, I can't stand it." She rewound the tape and swatted the machine back on.

"Hi, Madeleine?" Dahling. "This is Tempestt." Her so-cool voice somehow conveyed the preciousness of the redundant *t*. "Madeleine?" Rub it in. "Emily has asked me to hire you, and she specifically mentioned, uh, your talking frog, to tell stories at her sleepover party this Saturday night. If—"

Buffy turned the machine off again. "I won't do it."

But—had Emily really asked for her? Emily wanted her own mother at her party?

"I've got to do it. But they're not gonna pay me."

"I won't do it," Adamus said.

"Yes, you will."

"Be a captive curio? Gawked at like a slave on an auction block, laughed at? I won't."

"Hate to tell you, Addie, but yes, you will."

"I won't talk."

"Ve haf vays to make you talk."

"I'll curse. I'll blaspheme. I'll shock the children and make them faint. Boogers of God!" Adamus swelled up, then jumped up, energized by his own daring. "Spittle of God! Toe lint of God! CROTCH of God!"

Buffy laughed so hard she had to sit down. Adamus deflated.

"But—you laugh at blasphemy?"

"Why not?"

"But—" The frog's wide, blotchy, mud-green face looked even more pop-eyed than normal with dismay. "But—don't you believe?"

"Not in any toe-lint sense, no." Buffy's religious beliefs were hazy, and she preferred to leave them that way. "I don't believe in Santa Claus, either. Or the Easter Bunny. Or the Tooth Fairy." The frog's ogle-eyed presence, walking-talking proof that maybe she should believe in something, discomfited her. "Of course, I do believe in fairy princes," she added sarcastically, her voice rising. "Cinderella kissed a fella, all that fairy-tale stuff. Why not? I could use a fairy godmother."

With a thud the refrigerator went dead. Simultaneously the answering machine beeped off and the Gro-Lite flickered out. A dozen anonymous household machines quit, and in dim silence the frog sat tensely, head cocked, listening. Buffy could hear it too: an unidentifiable, almost mythical sound, like distant geese flying or winged wolves or banshees wailing, far and high in the sky.

"Oh ho," Adamus said softly. "You've got to watch what you say. Now you've done it."

"Done what? It's just a power outage." Because the electricity had gone out, a person could hear things, that was all. Probably traffic. Echoing against the clouds or something.

Someone knocked at the door.

"*Now* what?" Buffy heaved herself up to get it.

There on her doorstep stood a sixtyish woman with hair dyed so stiffly blond it looked like it had been spray-painted gold. She wore massive gold circle earrings, a gold unicorn pendant, a cheap white sweater with tacky pseudo-gold dangles and beads all over it. Because of her golden spike-heeled boots, her droopy rear in its white polyester stretch pants protruded from under the sweater and her gold-draped boobs thrust forward, albeit from a rather southerly sector of her chest. She carried a gold purse the size of a Welsh corgi, somewhat battered and rubbed; brown leather showed through the golden surface. Her eyelashes were gilded with glitter mascara. Some of it had fallen off and caught in the creases flanking her mouth. The woman's middle name ought to be "Ormolu." Buffy felt dourly surprised, as always, that her former mother-in-law did not wear gold lipstick.

She felt more surprised to find her at her door.

"Fay," she said, trying not to sound either too falsely welcoming or too nonplussed. "What can I do for you?" The relationship between her and her mother-in-law had been cautiously cordial but never warm. This was the woman, after all, who had raised Prentis to be the way he was. Mama's little crown prince.

"Power outage, my sweet patootie," said Fay severely. "Power outrage, is more like it. Power scandal."

"Huh?" Buffy absorbed little of this, being hung up on the sweet patootie. I wrinkle, therefore I yam? "Sweet *what*?"

"Fairy tale is NOTHING TO BE SCOFFED AT." Fay advanced upon the door, and Buffy was sufficiently flabbergasted to back up. A white-and-golden frigate, Fay sailed into the kitchen.

In the aquarium, Adamus leaped about like oversized green popcorn, yelping, "Fairy Godmother! Fairy Godmother! Fairy Godmother!"

"It's just my mother-in-law," Buffy protested.

"Fairy Godmother!" the frog appealed like a tattling kid. "Make her kiss me. Get me out of here!"

Fay was looking around as if she saw no frog, heard no frog. "You've got mud on your floor," she said, apparently to Buffy, though she was looking at the mud. "And what's that, dead beetles?"

The unspoken message came through loud and clear: No Wonder Prentis Left You. Buffy allowed herself to be rude. "Fay, what are you doing here?"

Looking around, perhaps mentally cataloging the cobwebs in the corners and the grease on the stove, Fay did not answer, but Adamus leaped at the glass and shouted, "She has come to rescue me!" Leap. "I am Prince Adamus d'Aurca!" Leap. "You warthead, don't believe in anything, how do you think I talk?" LEAP leap. "A frog can't talk. A frog has no ribs. But *I* have ribs." The frog ricocheted wildly, splashing water out of the aquarium onto the muddy floor. "A frog has barely any brain. But *I* have access to the biggest brain there is. I—"

"Sit, you ninny," Fay told the frog. "Rescue, my sweet patootie. This Murphy person summoned me, that's all."

"Huh?" Buffy said.

"But how should she have access to the Pool? I am the archetype!" Adamus caromed yet more crazily, splattering water onto his putative fairy godmother. "I am the handsome Jung prince! You must rescue me!"

"Would you stop it?" Being showered by eau de frog, stepping away, Fay slipped on the freshly slimed mud and lost her temper. "SQUAT!" she bellowed.

Adamus squatted instantly, silent and motionless except for the throbbing of his throat.

The gilded godmother turned on Buffy. "And you call yourself a storyteller," she barked. "You should be ashamed of yourself. Are you going to kiss him?"

"Hell, no!" Aside from being irritated by the uncanny presence of this whatever-she-was, fairy godmother-in-law, Buffy felt heartily annoyed that Adamus had actually obeyed Fay. Whose frog was this, dammit? Fay had always tried to take over everything, and Buffy had always put up with her bossiness, but no more. Been there, done that. Buffy squared off, hands on her considerable hips. "I am not going to kiss him and nobody else is going to kiss him."

"May I ask why not?"

"He's mine. Like I would kiss the goose that laid the golden egg?" Ow. Bad metaphor. But Buffy forged on. "He's my lucky frog." And she deserved some luck, dammit, after Prentis. "He's gonna help me quit the day job."

It would have been nice if Fay had argued. But Fay merely became suddenly disappointingly calm. Fay caressed her own golden hair with golden fingernails and contemplated both Buffy and the frog with glittering indifference. Did they make golden contact lenses? The woman's eyes looked strange.

She coiled her metallic tresses into a bedspring curl around her forefinger. "You know what you're getting into, of course," she said to Buffy with irony coiled in her tone. "You know there's nothing cute about fairy tales. You know about the fair peril and the punishments. You know that everything is itself and something else as well. You know about the resonances. You are, after all, a professional storyteller."

"I am a professional storyteller and I don't have a clue what I am getting into and I don't care."

"Really." Fay's golden eyes narrowed to shining slits. "You summoned me here. What do you want?"

Clueless, as she had said, Buffy could think only that she wanted nothing from Prentis's mother, nothing, not a thing more than she wanted from Prentis himself. Sarcastically she asked, "Can you fix the refrigerator?"

"For heaven's sake." Fay lifted her enormous purse and swung it as if disciplining a mugger, thwacking the hulking white mass of the fridge. With a submissive whimper it chugged back on. Simultaneously the Gro-Lite flickered into glowing life, an anonymous borborygmus started somewhere in the basement, and the answering machine beeped to attention. Fay rolled her eyes and minced toward the door.

"Uh, Fay, wait." Buffy began to feel, queasily, that she was in trouble. "Listen, how do you know this frog? What's he talking about, access to the Pool?"

"Fairy Godmother! Don't leave me with her!" Adamus quavered at the same time, breaking his terrified silence.

Fay gave them both a bored aureate glance and walked out.

Three

Captive, Adamus thought, quivering to his heart, gulping to force air into his lungs. *Hostage. Prisoner.* Again. Still. Odd, how the unbearable had become familiar, therefore comforting, and how the familiar had become ennobled to the dignity of a doom, a fate. Was he fated never to be free? It seemed so. Ever since the beginning, even in that first life, that pitifully brief life, he had been a captive. At the mercy of his mother, at the mercy of his father, and then there had been the dungeonlord dreadful and kind, the prisoner's heart quivering with terror and love—

Here she came now, the doomster, the storyteller, here she came toward him after locking the door, here she came with her sad, vehement, symmetrical face and her wild silver-black hair and her footsteps like thunder and her thoughts like flowers and lightning and her body a harshly clad, cream-colored, world-sized warmth that he both feared and craved.

Even in that first brief life, the dungeonmaster had betrayed the love; Adamus had looked for an adoptive father and found a doomster. Then, in that next, uncanny life—

at the first fiery touch, the brand of eerie lips on his fore-head—captive again. At the mercy of the unseelie mother. Quivering with love and terror again. And then—doom anew. Life anew. Terror anew. Captive in the body of a frog.

To be a frog was to be loved by no one.

To be a frog was to be soft of belly. To be a frog was to be cold. To be a frog was to be always naked. Always afraid.

She was walking toward his glass prison. She was moon and sun in one. He could not bear it. His dogged, imbecilic heart shook anew, looking for a goddess, a true love, a mother—but he knew the fate. She would be his doomster.

God, if there is a God for frogs, help me.

To be a frog was to be—helpless when the urges came. The seasons. The necessity to burrow in the mud, or emerge from the mud, or sing and fall in love.

To be a frog was also to be smooth. To be quick. The naked have their ways of covering up.

Was it useless to fight fate? Was it useless to try to escape the doom? Perhaps. But Prince Adamus d'Aurca was not yet finished with fighting.

"What the hell does Fay have in that purse?" Buffy asked no one in particular.

Naturally, no one answered her.

She focused on her talking frog. "What does she mean, I summoned her?" she demanded, perforce assuming that he knew more about fairy godmothers than she did. "How did I summon her?"

"Ribbet," Adamus said.

Buffy scowled. Aside from being imperious and arrogant, the frog was a smart-ass. He was not croaking, but saying "ribbet." He precisely enunciated the word.

"Stop that," Buffy commanded. "Answer me. What is the Pool?"

"Ribbet," said Adamus in bored tones. "Ribbet, ribbet, ribbet."

"Talk, dammit!"

The frog ogled her in mock terror and started gabbling at once. "What a fool to school in a pool, agog I slog through a bog; dreams must explain themselves and a soul has to cast a two-legged shadow, go west Jung man and learn to distinguish between a frog and a fairy tail; in a word, it's absurd when a bird—"

"Oh, for God's sake." Buffy jabbed the TV's power button to drown him out. Cable news blared on.

Adamus screamed.

Buffy had heard that sound once before, when she was just a kid, just another feral thing prowling the swamp, and she had one day witnessed a frog being speared by a bittern. Since then she had forgotten how a frog in extremis screamed like a human child. The sound, the wild despair of it, shook her so much that she jabbed at the buttons six times and succeeded only in turning the volume down; the TV did not click off. What made it worse was that the politician on the screen, confabulating sincerely, was her ex, Prentis Sewell, wannabe state representative.

In the aquarium, Adamus had squashed himself into the farthest corner, his throat palpitating. Buffy cried, "Adamus, what's the matter?"

"Wha-wha-what—"

"The television?"

"A—a visitation," Prince Adamus said, tremolo. "A manifestation, an epiphany. With a voice as of ten thousand chariot horses bugling. Shining brighter than the sun."

"For God's sake, it's just my husband," Buffy complained. Husband? The slip made her irritated with herself.

"My ex." With the volume down, Prentis's voice was a distant quacking as he promised, maintaining eye contact, that he was going to change things. "I'm the storyteller!" Buffy burst out. "I'm the storyteller, and there he is on cable telling political fables."

"Make it go away!" Adamus begged.

"Gladly." Annoyed now and therefore calm, Buffy shifted her finger to the correct button and turned Prentis off. To hear him tell it, she had been turning him off for years. An actual mind in a woman will do that to some men. But closer to the truth, or perhaps another way of saying the same thing, Buffy thought: Prentis had dumped her in favor of politics. A mind makes a political wife a liability; what if some reporter asked her something and she actually, God forbid, said what she thought? Besides, she was not decorative enough. He had tried some image enhancement on her, but ineluctably, Buffy's idea of dressing up was to throw on a denim skirt.

"I'm surprised the Trophy wasn't with him," she muttered. The Trophy was an asset. Decorative and docile. With men, that was. With Buffy, she was the cat who had called her Madeleine.

Better goddamn take care of returning that phone call while she was thinking of it. Buffy turned to the phone and stabbed her finger at the buttons. She knew the number by heart. It used to be her own.

"It—it talked," Adamus said, quavering. "It was full of light. Was it—was it a god?"

"Prentis? I used to think so." The hausfrau—make that haus slut—had picked up. "Hello, Tempestt? This is Buffy. Congratulations." She poured on the honey. "On the first anniversary of my divorce. Don't you remember? That made it legal. So you and Prentis could go out and get married instead of just shacking up together . . . goodness, I didn't *mean* to offend. I just called to let you know I'll be there for Emily's party on Saturday; what time? Fine. No, no charge, I'm doing it for Emily. No, absolutely not, I will not accept money from you. Congratulations again. See you Saturday. Don't call me Madeleine. Bye."

She hung up. "I feel a sudden profound need for lasagna," she said to the frog. "You hungry?"

He squatted, trembling, in his corner. He whispered, "The god—the god in the box of light—is your husband?"

What? Oh. The TV. For God's sake. "Adamus, forget it," she told him. "It's just a machine. Aren't you hungry?"

He did not answer, but she went ahead and made the lasagna anyway. En-Cor, frozen, in a cardboard pan, in the microwave. When it was ready she offered the frog a share and he ate it, sitting up on his tautly muscled haunches and stuffing noodles into his wide mouth with the pinky fingers of both dainty hands. He ceased trembling; his sleek green flanks relaxed. She offered him more lasagna. He ate more. He ate almost as much of it as she did. She offered him Italian bread and he ate that too. Lettuce-carrot-cucumber salad with garlic croutons? Yep, sure, you bet. Dessert? Some chocolate silk pie, some ice cream, some Nilla wafers? Yes'm. He ate.

When he had finished his meal, in lieu of an after-dinner mint he took a great gulp of air, swelled himself even more than he was swollen already, split his skin, stripped it over his head and down his torso with his clever little hands, stepped out of it like a blasé lover stepping out of his trousers, wadded it up, stuffed it into his mouth, and swallowed it.

"Ewwwww!" exclaimed Buffy, suddenly wishing she had not eaten so much.

Glistening in his fresh green skin with cream-colored underbelly, a half size larger than before, Adamus lounged seductively at poolside, smirking at her. "Kiss me," he invited.

Searching her mental database for a sufficiently down-putting retort, Buffy discovered that there simply wasn't any.

She did the dishes. Didn't want to turn on the TV, not if it was going to scare the frog to death. The radio made a poor substitute. With nothing to do except housework, and who the hell wanted to do that, she sat around for a while and then went to bed early again. She was tired. Hadn't gotten much sleep the night before.

But once more, as soon as the lights were out, Adamus began his ranine serenade.

Buffy yelled, "Your royal Princeness, please shut up!"

He did not shut up. Nor was the word "croaking" sufficient to describe his virtuosity. He wonked, he honked, he bawled, he boomed, he tooted like a tuba and groaned like a bassoon, he sang like a donkey, he mourned like a dove, he moaned a bass melody, he bellowed like Bruce Springsteen with a head cold, he roared out his aria of froggy yearning. He had grown even louder and more resonant than the night before. Buffy could not even feel sure that he heard her shouts. She tried cotton in the ears, head under the pillow—no use. With each sob he vibrated her bed.

Sob? She must have been dozing, dreaming.

It was 2:37 A.M. by the curtly precise readout of the digital clock on her nightstand. Buffy sighed. As she turned over, Adamus let out a lamentation so intense that it shook the cobwebs loose from her ceiling and showered them down upon her. She thumped out of bed and padded forth to remonstrate with him.

"Dammit, Adamus." She clicked on his Gro-Lite to see if he had thrown himself upon a sword or something. No such luck. He sat in the shallows staring back at her with eyes like golden amulets, mystery symbols, pagan rings.

Sleep deprivation and the deep of night do strange

things to a storyteller. Buffy found that she was no longer angry at all. Rather, gazing fascinated into those black-and-golden orbs, she felt a sense of great echoing distance, then a rush of sudden insight, almost a vision—of a time when the nights were bottomless shadows lit only by fire, a time of tiny villages isolated amid leagues and leagues of primordial forest, a time when children who wandered off were never seen again, a time when a traveler rode out of the woods maybe once a year to tell new stories to help the old ones hold the world at bay—the time a little boy, Prince Adamus, was born into.

Awed, she whispered, "Addie. Tell me your story."

He stared back at her.

"I mean it. What is your story? Tell me all about it."

He did not speak, but in his silence and the night, she knew well enough: in order to deserve his story, she had to give him one.

She stood barefoot in her dirty kitchen, facing him, yet she knew herself to be the minstrel visiting his palace. His regal gaze upon her was the same color as the torchlight; she felt her own shabbiness, her clothes worn from years of travel, her thoughts worn and shabby, so that nothing in her repertoire of stories—shaggy-dog stories, folk tales, ghost stories for children's parties—nothing in her shopworn supply was good enough to offer him. She knew she had to offer him something deeply true. In order to deserve his story, she had to give him her own.

"Once upon a time," she told him softly, "there was a little girl named Maddie."

His pale throat throbbed like a white heart. His golden eyes watched her.

"And Maddie looked like most little girls, round pink cheeks and wise eyes, but there was something odd about her. Maddie looked at the sky and saw stories about wind angels. She looked at the sea and saw stories about wild horses in the waves. She looked at the hills and saw stories about stone giants. She thought in stories. The world was made of stories to her. Some of the stories came to her easily like sunshine and some were dark and difficult like stormy nights. But any kind of story, all of them, she gathered like bright chewing-gum wrappers and ladybugs and dandelions to carry in her pockets and keep in her room and heap in her bed at night when she slept."

Buffy paused, collecting the pieces, because this was one of those difficult-in-the-night stories. She was coming to the hard part, when one day, she couldn't say exactly which day, some wind shaped like her mother had blown into her room and said, "What is all this mess?" and swept all the stories away.

It hadn't happened exactly like that, of course. She wasn't going to be able to tell it exactly the way it had happened. But that didn't matter. Her story would not be accurate, but it would be true.

"Each day Maddie would offer a bouquet of stories to her mother," Buffy said, "and her mother would say, 'That's nice, dear,' and drop it in the trash can. So she carried a story in her cupped hands to her father. But he said, 'Go do the dishes.' So she brought stories to the other children. But they said, 'Let's play something else.' In school she was always watching for stories, for truth, not for facts, so the teachers thought she was stupid. When she grew to be a big girl, not a little girl any longer, the boys she dated wanted her to give them access to her anatomy, not stories. When she grew to be a very big girl and got married to a man who said he would take care of her, he did not want her stories, either. He did not like them cluttering up the bed. So Maddie gave up gathering stories anymore."

Buffy hesitated again, because she did not yet know how the story ended. Though she did know—she had given up her stories, but they had not given up on her.

"But the stories would not let her alone. The wind angels whispered in her ears. In her dreams the wild horses ran out of the waves and up the beaches and carried her away. The hills called to her, the stone giants told her stories that rang like stone hammers in her mind, dark and difficult. Once upon a time there was a girl named Maddie, the stone giants said. Maddie was a storyteller. Now Maddie was dead. She threw away the bright chewing-gum wrappers and the ladybugs and the dandelions and she grew up into a fat, boring person named Buffy. Maddie the storyteller was no more."

The frog gave a sudden leap to sit at the apex of his brick-and-rotten-board throne, staring at her.

"So she . . ." Buffy's voice began to misbehave, and she found that she could no longer maintain the storyteller's distance and tone. She was losing it, damn it. "So I'm trying very hard to bring her back to life, you see." In a pathetic whisper, not at all like a professional minstrel, she said, "I'm trying." Damn it, she was screwing up. What was going on?

"Addie," she appealed.

His throat swelled like white bubble gum. He resonated with a tremendous froggy burp. The glass of the aquarium rattled.

"Oh, for God's sake." Shaken loose from her—reverie, whatever it was—Buffy could have smacked him. Stupid frog. What was she doing standing there spilling her guts to a stupid frog? She clicked off the Gro-Lite and went back to bed.

The next morning Adamus was even larger than before. Excluding legs, and compared to a shoe, he had achieved about size 7 ½. Women's, that is.

Buffy went to work and fucked up mightily from lack of sleep.

This could not go on. If the frog kept growing at the rate he was, and if he kept his pricky attitude, she was not going to be able to handle him. She needed some input.

Over lunch hour Buffy went to the public library to see her good buddy LeeVon in the children's room.

LeeVon was one of those rare people who was so emotionally transparent that you had to like him even though he was incomprehensibly weird. He had a skinhead haircut, multiple piercings, and thick, black-rimmed Sartre glasses that seemed to serve some purpose other than to correct his vision; they had non-functional lenses. He wore black leather to work every day of the library year, rode a Harley with similar regularity, and had a tattoo of Peter Rabbit on one arm and Mr. McGregor on the other. When LeeVon flexed his biceps, Peter hopped and Mr. McGregor shook his hoe. The children adored the tattoos and LeeVon. Buffy had gotten to be friends with him through Storyteller's Guild—he was a stellar storyteller, better than she was, but so lazy about self-promotion that his talents were largely confined to story hour at the library, where he had been a fixture since forever; the place might have fallen into rubble without him. A college dropout hired in more liberal days, back before degrees were de rigueur and parents started to look for child molesters under every peculiar haircut, he was now so firmly installed that even the protests of paranoid newcomers could not dislodge him—perhaps because no one else would have worked for the salary he continued to accept. Whatever. There he was, fingering his nostril rings and munching an egg salad sandwich on pumpernickel, his combat-booted feet up on the desk, when Buffy walked in.

"Buffmeister!"

"Hey, LeeVon." After her mostly sleepless night, she could muster only tepid enthusiasm.

"How's it going?" Being LeeVon, he really wanted to know.

But life was too weird to talk about, even to LeeVon. "It's going okay."

"How's your mom?"

"I went to see her a week ago and she didn't even know me."

"Alzheimer's is hell," said LeeVon with clean, satisfying sympathy.

"What makes it worse is she hasn't changed all that much."

LeeVon's eyebrows levitated.

"She's been a mess practically since I've known her," Buffy said. "Dad made her crazy."

"Have I ever met your father?"

"I hope not. He's dead." Buffy changed the subject. "I'm looking for a rather specialized book about frogs." Never mind that this was the children's room; in this library, when you needed the right book you went to LeeVon.

He sat up and beamed at her, his face angelic above his black leather collar. If you could see past the nose, lip, and eyebrow rings and all the rest of it, you had to notice that LeeVon was a beautiful man, ergonomically designed and porcelain-skinned and ageless even though he had to be as old as she was. He drawled, "Waaal, paint me green and call me Kermit! That gold-plated mother-in-law of yours was in here yesterday looking for books about frogs."

Buffy felt cold, incorporeal fingers run up her spine.

LeeVon swung his feet down and peered at her more closely through his thick glasses. His delight faded. "What's the matter, Best Beloved?" LeeVon called everybody Best Beloved, as in the *Just So Stories*. He adored Kipling, though if asked, he would explain that he had never kippled. "Something wrong?"

"Nah." Just lack of sleep. It was a free country; why shouldn't Fay study up on frogs if she felt like it? "I've got this bullfrog at home," Buffy said, "driving me crazy. Talking. Keeping me awake at night."

"Really? What's it saying?"

"Huh?" Buffy was feeling more than usually hazy. "At night he says, 'Ribbet.' The rest of the time he mostly says, 'Kiss me and I'll turn into a prince, you potbellied, snaggletoothed hag.'"

LeeVon laid the remains of his egg salad sandwich to one side, positioned his elbows on his desk and his chin on his interlaced hands, and studied her. Then he said the only safe thing. "You are not snaggletoothed."

"Damn straight I'm not. He can be quite rude. I need some sort of how-to-train-your-frog book. Sort of the *No Bad Dogs* of frogs."

Carefully LeeVon said, "I did understand you to mention that this is a talking frog, Best Beloved? As in, uh, a frog that talks?"

"Right. One of those kiss-me frogs like in the fairy tale." Buffy saw the look LeeVon was giving her and her voice rose. "C'mon, LeeVon, it's not like I *believe* he would turn into a prince. But he does talk."

"In English."

"Absolutely in English. Look, I figure there's a logical explanation."

"Of course. You are a logical, rational person, Best Beloved, which is why you won't accept alimony from your rich-lawyer-politico ex." The sarcasm was gentle. "May I ask at what pet shop you acquired this remarkable animal?"

"Prentis? He came from the pound."

This quip amused Buffy far more than it did LeeVon.

While she yawped and hooted, he merely sighed and waited, chin on hands, brown-eyed gaze steady, for her to quiet down.

"Sorry," Buffy said, subsiding into chuckles.

LeeVon shrugged. "Every conversation has to bottom out." He straightened and stretched. "I have no frog-training books," he said. "Frogs are not like dogs. Frogs are not known to come when called. I do, however, have this." He reached down and pulled a fat green tome out of the cubbyhole at his feet. A wide, mischievous smile jingled his various facial rings. "I will have you know I did not offer this special volume to Fay," he said. "That woman gives me the horrors."

"LeeVon, how very unprofessional of you."

"Thank you." Aglow with humble pride, he passed it over.

Buffy took it in both hands, then found that she needed only one; it was oddly lightweight for so sizable a volume. On the plastic-sheathed cover, a large frog in a green evening suit and creamy waistcoat ogled back at her. The title shone in ornate letters of embossed gold: *Batracheios*. No author.

"You are not going to be able to train your frog," LeeVon said. "I wouldn't try it. But this may help you to *understand* your frog a little better. What's his name, by the way?"

"Adamus."

LeeVon looked thoughtful.

"Prince Adamus d'Aurca. To hear him tell it."

"Huh. Well, you gotta watch those princes. Be careful, Best Beloved."

After she thudded out the door, LeeVon got up from his desk and stalked to the window, looking out. Watching her stride away.

"There she goes," he muttered.

Behind him, a carbuncular kid who probably should have been in school was asking for a book about birth control. LeeVon ignored him.

There she goes, and she has it and she doesn't know what to do with it. But me, I know all about it, and I don't have it.

I don't have anybody and I probably never will.

Another lonely weekend loomed ahead. The same useless mating games. The same crowded bar.

The pimply kid was getting plaintive. LeeVon said, "Just a minute," and watched Buffy disappear around the corner, her large buns pumping under her teal-blue work slacks. There, she was gone.

His friend. He liked the Buffmeister about as much as he liked anyone. But sometimes friends were no damn help.

The carbuncular kid was becoming frantic. Probably in danger of getting his girlfriend pregnant. LeeVon said, "All right, okay," and returned to his chair. Once there, he tried to focus his attention on the kid. Just a normal, nice kid, he sensed. Well intentioned, a little dense, thought he was invincible until he got in trouble and then he panicked and didn't know what to do. More responsible than most. LeeVon said, "A book on birth control. It so happens that I have one right here." He reached under his desk, where he kept a stack of blank books he bought heavily discounted at various remainder stores, most recently Ollie's Outlet, Good Stuff Cheap. Chintzy flowered covers. Pulpy blank pages.

LeeVon passed his long hands over the top one, and it was neither flowered nor blank anymore.

"Here." He passed it to the importunate kid. "This will give you everything you need."

When the kid had left, LeeVon went to the staff bathroom and looked at himself in the mirror. A foggy old mirror. Everything seemed dark in it, including his own reflected face.

"A little too goddamn weird," he muttered.

Driving home after work, with the green book called *Batracheios* lying on the car seat by her side, Buffy listened to a woman on talk radio describing how she was going to fill her ex's convertible with tapioca pudding. It sounded like a wonderful idea. Too bad Prentis didn't have a convertible; he hated tapioca.

But unexpectedly, her thoughts veered with rueful insight to Adamus: was a pissed-off paramour what had happened to him? Was he some vengeful ex-girlfriend's idea of joke's-on-you? Was he really a man in a green skin, turned into a bullfrog by a maddened mistress? All the fairy tales ever said was that a wicked witch had cast a spell. They never said why. Wicked witch; was that male chauvinist folklore code for "angry woman"? Angry with a reason?

Or was Adamus a victim, a scapefrog, an innocent?

A thousand years. Either way, a thousand years was an awfully long time.

Not that she believed any of this.

She had to find out his story; she just had to. When she got home, perhaps he would ask her to tell him a story. He liked her stories. God bless him for liking her stories. If he did not ask to hear one, she would offer. And she would think of one that would prompt him to tell her his.

She smiled. It was a plan.

But when she walked into her skewed little dwelling and looked to the aquarium, he was not there.

Four

The wire mesh top was knocked clear off the glass prison and lay on the floor, bricks and all. One brick had taken the Gro-Lite down with it to sprawl on the linoleum like a corpse made of twisted metal and a shattered glass bulb; the aquarium hulked dark. At first Buffy thought Adamus might still be in there. Classic denial. She turned on the ceiling light and thundered over to look.

No frog.

Where was he? Had somebody broken into her house and stolen her frog? No, the evidence pointed to an escape. A kitchen cabinet door hung open. An empty Cheerios box lay prostrated amid oat dust. Hungry frog. Oh, poor baby. He had probably leaped at the top of the aquarium until it fell off. Strength of desperation.

"Adamus!" Buffy called.

There was, of course, no answer.

"Addie, I'm sorry, I'll fix you breakfast from now on." He'd better damn well like Pop-Tarts. "Where are you?"

No answer.

Could he have left the house? Buffy checked the doors

and windows, feeling cold and afraid for unexamined reasons—there was no time to analyze her emotions; she needed to find Adamus.

The windows were locked, the doors likewise. He had to be still in the house. She didn't see how he could have gotten out.

"Addie!"

Nothing.

She searched, forced to assume that he was hiding from her—but where? She tried watery places. The toilet—thank God he wasn't in there. The bathtub—no. The laundry tub and washing machine in the basement—no. The kitchen sink, then under the kitchen sink—nothing.

Then she started over and simply looked every place she could think of. In the deep, dark, dirty corners of kitchen cupboards. Under tables. Behind furniture.

Three hours later, Buffy had made her third full sweep of the house. She had moved every piece of furniture. She had emptied every cubbyhole large enough to hold a frog. Years' worth of quiet, peaceable dirt had been disturbed and now aspired to the status of dust in the wind, agitating her sinuses. The place looked like somebody had turned it upside down and shaken it; even the attic dirt was on the move. Buffy hadn't had her supper and what was worse, she didn't want any. And she hadn't found Addie.

He just wasn't anywhere. He was gone. Just plain gone. Somehow he must have found a way out of the house while she was at work.

It was dark outside.

She gave up, sat her hunkers on a kitchen chair, and stared at the darkness outside the window as only an exhausted middle-aged woman can stare. Adamus. Gone. Now she was never going to know his goddamn story.

Now he would not listen to hers anymore.

Damn it, for all that he talked and talked, he was the

only one who listened to her. Talking frog, hell, what she
needed was her listening frog back again.

Why did everybody have to go and leave her?

She stood up. "I'm going to bed," she muttered, although there was no one to hear her or care. She walked
to the desolation of her bedroom—it looked as though a
bomb had dropped in there—pulled some clothes off,
crawled onto her cheap mattress, and huddled under her
blankets. At least she would get a good night's sleep for a
change. There was nobody around to bother her.

Story of her life.

She wept.

Never in her life had Buffy learned to cry with any mod-
icum of dignity. Once, when she was a child of about ten
years old and she was crying and being annoying, her
mother had ordered her to look into the mirror and see
how ugly she was. The twisted redness of her own face
had shocked her, and ever since then she had resisted crying and was therefore all the more fated to cry unaesth-
etically. Some women could cry graceful, silent Audrey
Hepburn tears; Buffy was not one of those. She wonked,
she honked, she bellowed, she quacked, she bawled, she
roared. Her own noise humiliated her and made her cry
louder. She traumatized the house to its foundation with
her crying. Definitely not a princess. Who cared; there was
nobody to hear her. Nobody gave a damn.

Buffy cried her pillow wet, blew her nose on it, then
turned it over, gave a few final yawps, and slipped into
sleep.

Bent over like a fishhook, Mom picked at the lawn. It
was not dignified or seemly for a woman outside, where
people could see her, to get down on her hands and knees
like she was scrubbing a floor, so Mom bent from the waist
to pick the bits of twig and maple wing, oh those messy

maple trees, to pick the leaf stems and the litter the inconsiderate squirrels and chipmunks and birds had left behind, half-gnawed acorns, seed husks, scraps of eggshell. She had bent from the waist this way so long and so often that this was her body's shape now, like the crook of somebody's cane. Her hands had grown crooked too. She didn't like it. Her back hurt, and her legs. She sniffled to herself; there was nobody else to hear her. Everybody else was in bed, but she had to get it done or he would be angry at her. She had to pick up all the mess off the lawn. It wasn't fair. There wasn't enough light for her to see properly, even with all those tall lamps on poles all over the place, but she still had to do it. Her trembling hands groped deep in the grass for leaf trash, separating the brown from the green. She had to get all the brown out, or he would be angry. She had to get every little bit, even though her back hurt and her legs hurt, too, and her hands were dry and crooked and sore, caked with brown, the skin of her fingertips cracking, rubbed open. Her bare knobby feet, too, they were getting sore. But she had to get the lawn clean. He would be angry if she didn't.

"Mrs. Murphy!"

Bent over, Mom had only a peripheral sense of something white moving, a person walking up to her.

"Mrs. Murphy! What are you doing out here? It's nighttime."

It was one of those nice young women, nurses. Mom felt herself start to cry as she turned to her, unable to straighten as she held up the evidence. "Look at my poor hands!"

"Yes, I know."

"Look what he's making me do. I have to pick up all this."

"Your husband? He's dead, Mrs. Murphy. Nobody's making you do anything."

"He'll be angry if I don't get it finished soon."

"It's time to sleep."

"No, I can't. He'll be angry."

Her back hurt. Her legs hurt. Her hands were cracked and seeping. And the nurse, trying to lead her away, still didn't seem to understand. Nobody had ever understood, except maybe that other little girl in white, what was her name, somebody's daughter, wide bride, got married way too young, what *was* that poor child's name? Mattress? Madness? Maddie?

Sometime later in the night, Buffy awakened to the touch of chilly hands slithering up over the edge of the bed. "Heard ya calling me, baby," whispered a throaty voice.

Buffy's eyes popped open to encounter pop-eyes at close range. Huge, glistening golden eyes. She was so startled that she could not move or scream; she just gawked.

"What a babe." He hoisted himself onto the mattress with a grace perhaps owing to years of mounting lily pads. "You lay the eggs, baby," he said in a voice froggy with emotion, "and I'll squirt the milt on them."

Buffy yelped, thrashed her way out from under the blankets, and grabbed him.

"Addie?" She hoisted him by the armpits. It took both hands to lift him. He was as big as a year-old baby. How had he gotten so large so fast? But it was indisputably Prince Adamus d'Aurca; she would recognize that green-lipped smirk anywhere. "Addie!" She was so glad to see him that she almost kissed him, which would not have been a good idea—but then she realized where he had placed his clammy four-fingered hands. "You grabby little creep!" Reacting with more force than forethought, she thrust him away from her, throwing him against the wall.

"OW!"

Buffy gasped, terrified that she had hurt him and equally

terrified that he would turn into a prince with kind and beautiful eyes. The latter she need not have worried about. He merely plopped to the floor, where he sat, green and not at all symmetrical.

"Addie!" Buffy lurched toward him.

He cowered, whimpering, "Mercy, voluptuous one."

"Well, don't grope me!" She knelt beside him. "Are you all right?"

"I—I sneer at wounds," he said shakily. "I am a prince of the house of Aurca."

She saw no damage. He seemed fine. Already getting his attitude back. "Prince, my patootie," Buffy grumbled, saggy with relief. "You're still a frog. I always knew that throw-him-against-the-wall thing was a euphemistic crock." The sleep-with-the-princess version had a lot more of the knell of truth about it. It wasn't the prince who was supposed to get knocked up.

"Try it again," he said with apparent sincerity. "Harder."

What was this, S and M? "No, thank you. You sure you're okay?" Gently she picked him up, holding him at a safe distance from herself. "Nice to see ya. Where you been keeping yourself?" His skin was slimy-wet and smelly. "Ew!" She stood up and headed toward the bathroom, plopped him into the bathtub, and hit the light switch.

In the sudden glare he cringed again. "Mercy, massive lady."

"Mercy yourself." Now she could see that his smooth jade skin was dewed with punky water and smeared with a reddish clay she knew she should recognize. She did recognize it. "Oh, for God's sake, you were in the *sump hole?*"

"Princess, prithee kiss me. Your song in the night has enslaved me."

"Give me a break." Buffy reached for a washcloth.

"Your power turns my bones to jelly, but I know that your soul must be as generous as your flesh. Kiss me and let me cling to you, let me cling to you for a week and make milt."

"Addie," said Buffy sternly, "this is sexual harassment, and I hate to tell you, but you're not worth it; all you've got is a cloaca. Knock it off." She twisted the spigots, turning on the bathwater.

"But—but that is wonderful. You make the silver pizzle pee in the white pond. Ow!"

"Too warm? No, too cold. Poor baby." Buffy knelt by the tub and started sloshing water over her dirty frog.

"Don't! Don't wash it off."

Buffy held off with the washcloth but wrinkled her nose. "You've got to be kidding." Evidently clay that smelled like rotten mushrooms was perfume to him, like ripe, dead, road-killed ground hog to a dog.

"You don't like it, sweet lady?"

"Nooooo, why should I not like it? You just stay here and be stinky. I'm going back to bed." It was no use trying to put the frog back in the aquarium, as big as he had grown. Buffy snapped off the light, leaving him in three inches of water in the bathtub, and closed the door on him to keep him there.

No sooner had she positioned her head on its pillow than the croaking began. Ribbet, Adamus sang, riiiibbet, oh RIIIIIBBBETT RRIBB RRIBBB RIIIIIBBET. And if aquarium-sized Adamus had been able to vibrate the house, bathtub-sized Adamus sounded capable of launching it right through the pearly gates.

Buffy smiled. "Music to my ears," she whispered. She stuffed her forefingers into her ears, thrust her head underneath her unsanitary pillow, and went peacefully to sleep.

* * *

The first thing the next morning, Buffy faced a moral dilemma: what to do with Adamus while she used the bathroom, for which her need was urgent. "Turn your back, please, your Princeness," she told him.

He did not turn. With a blank, suffering look on his broad face, he whispered, "I'm hungry."

"I don't know whether I should feed you!" She stood jiggling her legs and biting her lower lip; more damn problems. Her food seemed to have an alarming effect on Adamus. He was discernibly larger than he had been the evening before. If this didn't stop, he would soon be human-sized. And what if he didn't stop then?

"I'm *starving*, puissant lady!" Buffy heard a catch in his voice. "I can't help it. I am not trying to grow so greatly."

"It's not your idea?"

"No!"

Maybe it was the damn additives, chemicals strange to his medieval body. Damn processed food. Nothing she could do anything about.

"If I promise to make you waffles, will you wait outside the bathroom?"

"Yes."

He flopped wetly down the stairs after her, and she stuck some Aunt Jemimas in the toaster. Shuffling around in bathrobe and cow-nosed slippers, she cleared a patch of plastic tablecloth for Adamus to squat on. She set a plate in front of him, and one for herself, then brought on the waffles and the strawberry syrup. They ate—he used knife and fork, which at first she didn't even notice, eerily unsurprised. They ate rapidly, silently, and single-mindedly. Two of a kind. Sometime during the second batch of waffles Buffy realized that she ought to be getting ready to go to work, and sometime during the third batch she realized that she had no intention of doing so. The plastic-food people needed her and she needed their money; nevertheless, she was not going. For reasons unrelated to logic, conscious choice, or her storytelling career, she could not bring herself to leave Adamus home alone. Suppose he got out of the house; suppose she lost him? She couldn't risk it.

The realization made her peevish. Realizing they need someone has that effect on some people. While Adamus finished his fourth batch of waffles, Buffy sat back, swung her feet onto an empty chair (her cow-nosed slippers, upright, peered at her stolidly), picked up the large green book LeeVon had given her, and leafed through it.

"*Batracheios*," she read aloud; she knew that reading aloud was an annoying habit, had always pissed the hell out of Prentis, and she was doing it for that reason. "Subtitled, 'A Compendium of Froggery.' "

Adamus ate doggedly, or perhaps froggedly, ignoring her.

"It says here," she remarked, "to cure rheumatism, roast a live frog and apply it to the sore area."

Gumming a soggy waffle, Adamus missed a mastication.

"To cure warts, rub a live frog over them, then impale it on a thorn to die."

The frog stopped chewing, set down his fork with a clunk, and stared at her.

"To cure whooping cough, place a small frog in a box tied around the sick person's neck. As the frog decays, the cough will go away."

"Stop it," Adamus said.

"Oh, beg pardon. Let me see what else is in here." She flipped through the pages, some of which were pulpy and covered with print and some of which were glossy with bright pictures of various famous frogs—frogs who went a-courting; Beatrix Potter frogs; Jim Henson puppets, which Adamus would probably loathe; others—interspersed among quotations and verse, the latter being mostly bad, doggerel (froggerel?) except for the poetry of Anne Sexton, which was frightening and sublime. Buffy forbore from reciting the poetry, leafing past it to a section devoted to technical esoterica. "Izaak Walton on how to rig up a live frog as bait for bass—"

"Stop it!"

Buffy had sufficient mercy to desist, but continued to read silently, then reread, fascinated: *Thus use your frog: put your hook through his mouth and out at his gills, and then with a fine needle and silk sew the upper part of his leg with only one stitch to the arming wire of your hook, or tie the frog's leg above the upper joint to the armed wire; and in so doing, use him as though you loved him.*

It made her shiver. Thus use your frog. Use him as though you loved him. She read the passage a third time.

Was she really a user, as Emily claimed?

Speaking of Emily. "Tomorrow is Emily's party," she said to Adamus.

"Good. You go. Have a nice time." He had given up on finishing his fourth waffle and was sitting lumpen on the table. Nothing sits quite as lumpen as a frog.

"You're invited, remember? She specifically asked for you."

"I am not going to be made a show of."

Buffy read, "To secure a reluctant lover, catch a frog, wrap in white cloth, put onto an anthill after sunset. The frog croaks in agony as ants eat it—"

"Stop it!"

She realized that she was being as offhandedly cruel as Izaak Walton, but could not seem to help it. Adamus had kept her up at night. Adamus had frightened her. Adamus had left her and made her cry. Moreover, this was too good. "—and the lover suffers the pangs of love. Finally all that is left of the frog is a small bone in the shape of a hook. Fasten it to the clothing of your reluctant lover, who should cleave to you, suffering like the frog."

"Lady," said Adamus in a trembling voice, "you can make me suffer. And you can make me go to your daughter's festivity, and you can humiliate me, and you can make a show of me. But you cannot make me speak."

His eyes, rings of ancient gold floating on black pools, black wells as deep as time—seeing herself reflected in those eyes, Buffy experienced a sudden, slewing disorientation as her point of view skidded out of control and did a 180. She closed *Batracheios* and held it in her lap, looking into her frog's wide, distraught, lichen-colored face.

She said softly and slowly, waiting for the right words, "Once upon a time—there was a prince—who was turned into a frog—and forced to go from his bright palace to live in a dark swamp in a rank and wildering forest."

Addie stared sullenly at her.

Buffy found more words. "There he shivered in peril of everything from snakes to otters to men who hunted him with spears for the sake of his meaty thighs. Fishes in the water and foxes in the forest and ospreys in the sky all prey on frogs, for frogs are small and thin-skinned and sweet."

Addie, no longer sullen, had lifted his heavy, dewy head to gaze at her intently.

"But the frog prince became clever; he survived. All alone he lived there for a thousand years.

"Then one day a small girl like a sunbeam came toddling to the dark pool where he was hiding. He rested on his log and looked at her, unafraid because she was merely a babe, like the babies in their long white christening gowns he remembered from his princely palace—but he underestimated her. She reached for him all too quickly and caught him in her questing hands, as dainty as a raccoon's hands. She lifted him and kissed him, but because she was so young and innocent, her kiss had no effect; he remained a frog. Yet from that moment he became her baby, for even though she was only a baby herself, she was as much larger than the frog prince as the other humans, her family, were larger than she.

"So she took him home in a pocket of her apron and dressed him in baby doll's clothes and gave him a doll's cradle to sleep in and mothered him the way her mother mothered her. And he lived in terror of her love, for her power over him was immense. She was his goddess. At any time she could have killed him with a hug."

Adamus's golden eyes glittered like beer-bottle caps flattened on a black road.

Buffy said, "Yet he survived. And he had hope, for if he could live with her another thousand years, until she grew less than innocent, then one day she would kiss him and he would transform, and she who had been his mother would become his bride."

There was a long pause as Buffy waited for the rest of the story to come seeping out of her and Adamus waited for Buffy to tell it.

Buffy said slowly, "One day the frog crept out of his cradle to see the sunbeam girl, his goddess, all swaddled and smothered in a dress of white lace as if in a rain cloud, veiled in white lace, weeping bitterly. Also in the room stood a personage three times as tall as she, all draped in black lace, and this was her terror, her mother. And the mother took the child by the hand and led her out of the room and away.

"Then the frog was smitten with fear—for himself, for her—and with a sense of what it means to be a prince. He followed, leaping along the hallways. He saw her sitting small and white and veiled in a carriage, and he leaped to cling and ride along as the strong gray horses pulled it away.

"The carriage rolled faster and the gravel flew up and pelted him where he clung until he knew he would have to let go and fall and be killed, a frog lying small and flat and brown on the roadway—but he did not let go; he hung on. The dust choked him until he knew he would have to let go and fall and be killed, a frog lying dry and dead in the weeds beside the road—but he did not let go. He clung until finally the carriage slowed and stopped at the tall stone entrance of a great palace the frog recognized from long ago. His heart pounded in his frail chest, for the sunbeam girl had brought him home.

"Then she descended from the carriage, her glow all veiled in cloudy white, weeping like rain.

"Her mother draped in black led her into the palace by the hand, and the frog followed, leaping like a shadow behind her. Surely, he thought, they had brought her here for some religious rite, a baptism, a communion, to enter into a white-clad cloister, perhaps—for he knew she was far too young, too innocent, for that other white-clad rite. She had kissed him only that morning, and he had felt her innocence like dawn dew upon her lips. She remained nothing more than a girl child, and he remained nothing more than a frog.

"Still, his heart pounded hotly in him, for deep in his belly a thought squirmed like a hookworm, that she might be meant for him. This was his home.

"Then he saw the bridegroom awaiting her. A man four times her size, harsh and gouty, like a toad."

Buffy stopped abruptly, realizing with a shock what she was doing, whose story she was telling. The toadlike man—it was her father, whom she remembered with more ambivalence than affection. She carried his picture clearly in her mind as she spoke, as clearly as if he lay in his coffin before her. There was no mistaking him.

The child bride was her mother.

Nobody had ever told Buffy in so many words, but families have their own ways of conveying stories. She knew well enough: they had made her mother marry him. A bride at the age of fourteen. Given away by a widowed mother to a man who promised to take care of the child and give her everything she needed.

By the standards of the day, he was a good man. A good provider. He had provided his wife with a nice, hot kitchen, a new baby once a year, a whack on the mouth if she talked back.

What that wedding night must have been like.

"The mother let go of the girl's hand," Buffy said in a low voice to Adamus, "and the bridegroom seized it, and he took her away to the inner sanctum, and when she came out, she was not a sunbeam girl anymore."

Buffy ended the story there, folding her hands on top of the green book in her lap.

"But the prince, the frog!" Adamus exclaimed. "What happened to him?"

"She could not see him anymore. The tears had washed all the light out of her eyes. She no longer talked to him or sang to him or rocked him in her arms. She would never kiss him. So he went back to his pool in the forest."

Taut and quivering, rearing on his fingertips, Adamus stared at her. "You are two people," he said nearly in a whisper. "I do not understand you."

"*I'm* two people?" She spoke gently. "You should talk."

"But—but you are a woman."

"So?"

"How can these thoughts be in you? How can you be like me?"

She contemplated several levels of meaning to that. "Addie," she said sweetly, "go jump in a lake."

"How can I? You hold me a prisoner here."

So that she would not have to listen to him any longer, she opened *Batracheios* again, but something had changed: instead of the usages of frogs, a list of punishments confronted her. "The evil mother was brought before the court and put into a barrel that was filled with boiling oil and poisonous snakes." "They put her into a barrel studded with nails on the inside, hammered on the lid, and rolled it down the hill into the river." "In the red-hot slippers she danced until she fell down dead." "Burned at the stake until she was ashes." "And the pigeons pecked out her eyes." Sickening punishments. From the fairy tales; Buffy recognized this Grimm stuff. And it was always a wicked mother/stepmother/witch who was getting the business. How come? Why not a wicked father once in a while? Sexist folklorists.

Hastily Buffy turned the page.

She was rewarded. An interesting headline caught her eye. She read silently. Very interesting indeed.

All that day between baby-sitting her frog, she read her swamp-green book, and the more of it she read, the more there was. Like Adamus, *Batracheios* seemed larger each time she looked, and harder to understand.

Five

"**P**ickle-faced scant-hearted prickmedainty thick-necked ogress," Adamus hissed snakelike between his gums.

"I can't make you speak, remember?" Buffy rang the doorbell of the house that used to be hers, trying not to wonder what sort of personality defect caused her to be there. Trying not to think how idiotic it felt to be standing on the doorstep of that big pseudo-Tudor house, listening to the door chimes sounding inside—she had always loathed door chimes. Dingdong bell, pussy's in the well, whoa, contemplate that. Come to think of it, the really bizarre thing would be to move back into this overwrought faux-genteel mansion. Come to think of it some more, the most bizarre thing of all was that she was standing on the doorstep with a forty-pound, two-foot frog in a rented mini-tuxedo standing erect and volubly outraged by her side.

Emily opened the door, sweet and regal in a wheat-colored tunic and leggings.

"Hi, tootsie. Happy unbirthday." Emily's birthday was

not until August, when she and all her friends would be away at various camps and resorts; she always had her party in the spring. Seeing the unbirthday girl, Buffy felt a warm upheaval swell her ribs and tried to snag the kid in a hug. Whenever she was around Emily, child, daughter, her chest ached for contact, her arms ached. She reached out. But with a quelling glance Emily eluded her. Preserve that teenage cool.

"*Mom*," Emily protested, "I wanted you to bring the real frog."

Buffy tried to salvage some of her own cool. "Define 'real.' "

But Emily had no patience with ontology. She gave her mother a blank stare. "You know what I mean. Your frog frog, not some sort of a puppet."

A quintessentially froggy voice quoth, " 'Tis I, Princess Emily." Adamus swept her a bow.

"Oh!" It was such a childlike gasp that Buffy had to smile. Emily's hands flew to comfort her mouth, which seemed uncertain whether to shape delight or fright. "How, uh, how—"

"Steroids," Buffy said. And the girl would probably believe her and think, Ew, gross; my mom, what a user. "May we come in?"

"Uh, sure." Emily regained her poise. With a toss of her honey-tressed head she turned, leading the way past a vast parlor and a glassy dining room to the informal living room, where a group of teenage girls clustered in front of the large-screen TV. "You're going to have to wait until we watch the end of this movie," she told Buffy.

Thumping along behind her, Adamus lifted his head, saw the image of Winona Ryder flash before him, and screamed. Simultaneously, several of the girls turned bored heads, saw him, and, no longer bored, screamed as earnestly as he did. Some of them scrambled away from him, but as far as Buffy could tell, he did not notice. Squatting on the Oriental carpet (a tax shelter) in his tux, he was staring raptly at the screen as Winona, in charming dishevelment, closed in on her lover.

"That's just my mom's frog," Emily said. For just a nanosecond Buffy heard a hint of little-girl approval in those two important words "my mom," and she was so touched that—standing there in her clownish storytelling outfit, pigtails bow-tied with fluorescent-pink shoelaces, black sweatshirt puffy-painted with dancing pigs, wide black pants edged with multicolored braid—she glowed like the ever-ingenuous Winona. Her child had smiled; her frog, like a two-year-old in front of Sesame Street, was temporarily pacified; life was good.

Right on cue to pop her bubble, Tempestt came flitting in, carrying snack mix and drinks on a lacquered tray.

Tempestt, in a froth of curls and a ruffled silk romper. Even if Buffy hadn't detested her already, the romper would have done the job. "Oh, good, Madeleine's here!" Tempestt announced, dulcet to the max. "This is Madeleine Murphy, our storyteller. Such an interesting puppet! Are we all ready for some stories?"

"Sure," one of the guests responded in tones of existential ennui.

"Spiffy-diffy," added another equally morosely. The movie had ended. Sluggishly the kids rearranged themselves in a semicircle on the carpet, facing Buffy sullenly.

It was Emily's party, Buffy reminded herself. *Smile. Be good.* And tell one hell of a good story. But not for the first time she wondered, why had Emily invited her? Storytelling as entertainment was not Emily's style.

Give it your best shot.

She told them the one about the ghost of Toad Road. Did the voices, the sound effects, the gestures, the thrilling scream. They listened with reasonable attention and clapped politely when she was finished. But before she could begin her next story, Emily asked, "But what about the frog? When does he get to talk to us?"

So that was it. Emily didn't really want a storyteller at her party. She wanted Addie.

Damn.

"Is he going to tell us a story?"

Clueless in that regard, Buffy said, "Ah, uh, ah, he, uh—"

Emily leveled her midnight-blue eyes at Adamus and asked him directly, "Are you the frog from the frog-prince story? The one with the golden ball?"

Adamus looked back at her. Then he stood up and walked forward on his long, green hind feet. And despite the fact that he was a mere two feet tall, he advanced with such presence, such statesmanship, that Buffy stepped back. He took her place and faced the damsels fair, his courtiers clad in denims from the Gap.

"Sweet Princess Emily," Adamus addressed her. "Lovely maidens. I am not a frog. Or, I was not always so. I was born a prince. I am Prince Adamus d'Aurca de la Pompe de la Trompe de l'Eau."

The damsels did not all appreciate the solemnity of this moment. Most of them giggled or sat stolidly. But, seated on the carpet at his feet, Princess Emily gasped and gazed.

Tempestt laughed and clapped. "Oh, how clever. It really looks as if the puppet is doing the talking!"

"Shut up," Emily whispered without shifting her gaze from Adamus.

"I am a fairy-tale prince," Adamus continued. "I have been a prince for over a thousand years, yet I have never led a charge into battle, never met with advisors, never sat at the head of a banquet table, never pronounced judgment or ordered an execution. I have never wooed a lover, married, or sired children. I have never in a thousand years danced for joy; I have never in a thousand years grieved. I am immortal, yet it has been a long, long time since I have lived. I have no more soul than an angel.

"But it was not always so. I was born a mortal prince, fourth son of a minor Austrian royal in a chilly castle along the Danube."

Tempestt tittered. "Madeleine, I never knew you were such a ventriloquist. Excuse me." She fluttered out. But Emily's blue-velvet gaze never strayed from Adamus's blunt green face.

The frog's quiet baritone voice went on. "The first ten years of that life were much as might have been expected. Feasts and fasts, games, friends, teachers, lessons, thrashings. I remember those good years when I was a mortal boy as if they were a bright dream. So long ago. They came to a swift end. My father's ambition had led him into war with a neighboring principality, and he was bested. There was a meeting, a treaty, and I was sent to live in the enemy king's castle as a hostage to ensure my father's promise of peace."

This was, Buffy realized, a true story. Starkly factual. But even beyond that, deeply true. It curled her toes.

"Truth to tell," Adamus continued, "he was kinder to me than my father had ever been, that king. He was a gentle enemy. For a winter he was kind, and I began to hope—but then in the spring my father's armies came and surrounded his stronghold and besieged it. Then—no more kindness. He thundered with anger, and seized me, and ordered me to be bound so that I would not flee or hide, and bespoke my father from the ramparts. 'You have betrayed your word of honor,' he roared as I lay trembling on the stones. 'Withdraw at once, or I will use your son as a missile to hurl upon you.'

"And I heard my father's voice for the last time, cool and clear on the dawn air: 'Do with him what you like. I have the hammer and the anvil still to make better ones than he.' "

Emily gasped and murmured, her wide eyes dark with stormy emotion.

"So they took me and placed me in the sling of the engine of war—" Adamus spoke slowly, hesitantly, as if this part were causing him some difficulty, even after a thousand years had gone by. "They placed me bound in the ballista, and I felt its great muscles clench and spring and hurl me high, high over my father's army. My terror was so great that I wished I would faint, but I did not. And then there was a moment of soul-sickness at the height of the arc. And then even greater sickness unto death as I began to fall."

He paused. There was not a sound in the room. Emily's lips had parted, flower-soft. Buffy stood stricken by the story, the cruelty, the danger—she was beginning to sense the danger. Yet she did not move or speak.

I wanted to hear his story. I am hearing it.

"The angels were too appalled, I think, to save me." Adamus paused again. "But the Queen of the Realm of Fair Peril happened to be driving past in her chariot of air. And she saw fit to take me. I do not—I do not think I died. I think I fainted. And when I awoke, I was lying in her hard white arms." Adamus spoke more easily yet more low. "And she kissed me like fire and put the mark of her lips upon me." He touched his forehead. Above his eyes— or in back of them, as he was a frog—Buffy saw a brown mark she had not previously noticed amid his other mottlings, a dark smudge like a brand. The place where eerie lips had burned? Buffy was not convinced. The smudge was shaped somewhat like a lipstick mark—but then again, people were always getting on the front page of the Life and Weirdos section of the newspaper by digging up potatoes shaped somewhat like Elvis.

"And so I became a prince of Fair Peril, the place that is not a place, where everything is itself yet something else."

"Fairyland," Emily whispered.

"In a sense. When I was a mortal boy, I listened to fairy tales, I shivered, and now I know why: they are such tales as the unseelie folk would tell if they had the heart to understand mortal longings. But for a thousand years I heard no such tales. The people of Fair Peril do not tell them. Mortals do."

Buffy felt her own eyes going as wide as Emily's.

Adamus said, "In mortals there is a dream and a reality only story can tell. I became such a quiddity in such a story. I will live almost forever. As long as there are people mindful of the tale. And I will never grow old." Adamus tilted his heavy head. "Another name for the Realm of Fair Peril is the Realm of the Ever Young. Princes and princesses do not grow old there. They do not grow at all." He spoke quite softly. "The Queen's kiss made me a comely youth fit to serve her, but after that—nothing. I did not change."

Emily leaned toward him. "But—but you're a frog now."

His golden gaze focused on her, calling upon her to understand. He said slowly, "The Queen of Fair Peril is a jealous majesty. As beautiful as the dayspring and very jealous."

"You—she—"

"It is hard to explain." His voice grew more intense. "There were no chains on me, yet I had no freedom. In that place it was all mist rising and talking trees and silver lilies and gray steeds galloping, it was lovely, I had everything, yet—I had nothing."

Like a lovely, expensive house, provided by an expensive marriage. *I had everything*, Buffy thought, *yet I had nothing. I had no selfhood. I had no freedom.*

Her toes curled tighter. Today the frog was a better storyteller than she was.

"Or, I had only myself," Adamus said. "No more soul than an angel. Body was all I had, all I could call my own. So when the Queen demanded the usage of my body, I refused her."

This time it was Buffy who spoke, quietly. "La Belle Dame Sans Merci thee had in thrall."

"No, she didn't." He turned to her, his golden eyes glittering with defiance. "I am no one's chattel. I cried out to her, I told her, 'Send me home, I want to go home, send me back.' Back to the earth from which she had taken me, even if I were only rotting bones or a foul semblance of my former self—for, you know, in Fair Peril wishes have a way of becoming punishments. But still, I risked it. I wished to breathe changeable air again, feel the chill of winter, the sweat of summer." Adamus turned back to the damsels in denim, toward Emily. "I wanted to know mortal transience, mortal joy and grief, mortal love. And the Queen said to me angrily, 'I will grant your wish—if you can find a mortal willing to love a frog. Otherwise, may you remain a prince in green breeches forever,' And I became as you see me."

"Oh, poor prince," Emily whispered. She stretched out her hand to him. Then she rose to her knees to reach for him with her hand. And with her mouth. And, apparently, with her heart.

So seductive was the spell of the frog prince's tale that Buffy nearly did not react in time. For a moment she stood mesmerized, looking upon a tableau suspended in fairy-tale timelessness: Emily, as lovely as a lily, with her soft lips parted to kiss, and Adamus standing in holy rapture, his homely head tilted up to receive her.

"No!"

Buffy yelled just in time, and sprang. Just before they could touch, she leaped forward, knocking them apart, sending both of them sprawling. Her daughter gawked up at her from the rug. Buffy turned on the girl and, on the cusp of the moment, shouted the most stupid, childish utterance she could possibly have offered to Emily and the world.

"*My* frog!"

At that moment something top-heavy, wrinkled, and garishly golden walked into the room: Fay. Catching the ex-daughter-in-law at her very worst, of course.

Simultaneously Buffy saw a green, tuxedo-clad blur hurtle up from the rug: Adamus, launching himself toward Emily like a missile. He'd had practice, but Buffy had bulk. She blocked his leap, then pounced as he fell. "Fairy Godmother!" he bawled to Fay, squirming fiercely in Buffy's two-fisted grip. "Fairy Godmother! Make her let Princess Emily kiss me!"

"Grandma!" Emily wailed at the same time to the same person, "I want to kiss him! Tell her to stop interfering!"

What made them think Fay could tell her to do anything?

"Let go!" the frog demanded.

"Grandma!" Emily whined.

Emily's friends had formed a front row, watching the entertainment with a lot more interest than they had shown for the storytelling.

"Fairy Godmother, make her let go of me!"

"*Grandma!*"

"Good God, she's not a fairy godmother!" Buffy snapped. "And, Emily, this is not a fairy tale. This is real life." Yeah, right. There she was, down on the floor wrestling a forty-pound frog who was trying to bite her. "Stop that, you toad!"

Adamus went rigid in her grip. "I am not a toad!"

"You can call me an ogress, I can call you a toad."

"I AM NOT A TOAD!" He swelled enormously in his indignation. With a shriek of polyester, his rental tuxedo split and fell off him. Buffy gawked, too startled even to worry that she was now going to have to pay for the ruined costume. Too startled to speak. Primal silence gripped the room as everyone gawked at the naked frog.

Everyone except Fay. She spoke with annoying calm and condescension. "Ms. Murphy. As this is not a fairy tale, why do you seem to think that something untoward will happen if Emily kisses the frog?"

"I don't want her kissing *anything* till she's twenty-one." Buffy wedged Adamus, who felt rather like an inflatable doll from the Porn Corner, under one arm, then lumbered up and reached for her prop bag. "We're leaving."

"But what's the harm?" Fay asked with honeyed malice. "You don't believe those silly stories."

Emily was getting up from the rug. "You're a mean witch," she told Buffy, so passionate her young voice shook. "You're a total user. Ogress."

"Sweetie—" Buffy meant to tell the child that she was trying to protect her. It was true, she was trying to protect her.

But from what? A talking frog?

"Fairy Godmother!" Adamus yelped, deflating so suddenly that Buffy nearly lost her grip on him. "Help me!"

"You wanted mortal love," she told him, folding her gold-clawed hands serenely atop her enormous purse. "Live with it."

Love?

But there was no time for Buffy to think. Emily was in her face. "Get out of my house. Don't you ever come near me again." Emily, like a spear, pale and defiant—Buffy hadn't thought there was that much passion, that much spirit, in the child. "You're not my mother. Go."

This was a bit much. Buffy protested. "Honey pie—"

"You've got *your* frog. Go away."

Oh, for heaven's sake. The youngster would get over it. Buffy took her frog and went.

"Addie," Buffy tried to explain, "I couldn't let her kiss you. I just couldn't. She's too young."

Adamus did not answer. Slumped in the kitchen sink (Buffy had made the silver pizzle pee in the silver pond for him), not looking at Buffy, he had not spoken since Emily's party. It's hard to read a frog's facial expression, but to Buffy he did not seem to be entirely sulking. Rather, he seemed defeated.

"She's my daughter," Buffy said. "I worry about what might happen to her." All right, damn it, apparently she did believe—something. Something might happen. And she did not want Emily to make the same mistake she had, expecting Prince Charming to take care of her. And to lead the same hellish life her mother had, wed way too young, enslaved body and soul to a well-respected tyrant of a man—what was a so-called prince if not a tyrant? Addie seemed sweet at times, but hadn't her father been sweet, too, when he wanted to? And Prentis? Until he got what he wanted? Even nice men were raised to be pricks. And that was today. Addie had been raised to be a *medieval* prick—if Buffy could believe what she was thinking.

She said to him, "I want Emily to have a life. Have some freedom. Not buy into some fairy tale. Not give herself away when she's still just a baby, when she's too young to know what she's doing."

Adamus gave no indication that he was listening. Buffy sighed.

"Do you want something to eat?"

"No."

At least it was speech. A monosyllable.

"Can you understand? At all? If she went to kiss a boy from her school, I wouldn't worry so much, I'd figure it was something she could handle. I'd trust her judgment. But when it comes to this fairy-tale thing—"

Okay, damn it, Fay was right. Fairy tale was potent, puissant, inconceivably powerful. You didn't mess with it.

"You have an unfair advantage, Addie. A fairy-tale prince, for God's sake."

Silence.

Timidly Buffy suggested, "Would you like me to tell you a story?"

His head swiveled heavily; he gave her a hard golden stare. "No." Sluggishly he swung his head toward the TV. "Make sing the box with shining gods in it."

TV instead of her stories? If he had bitten her to the bone, he could not have hurt her more.

But he had a right to want to hurt her. Silently she got up and turned the boob tube on for him. It looked like it was Kevin Costner and some babe in the Saturday Night Movie. Adamus rested his chin, or the part of him that should have resembled a chin, on the edge of the sink to watch. His body softened, his sleek green flanks relaxed, his gaze grew rapt.

Damn him. He was just like all the rest. Buffy muttered, "I'm going to bed."

She left her frog lolling in the sink, mesmerized by Hollywood dialogue. Didn't have the heart to shut him in the bathroom. It wasn't like he was going anywhere. He was stuck with her and he knew it.

Although she felt bone tired, she found it difficult to get to sleep; Adamus was not croaking. The silence, broken only by bursts of ominous music when nasty-bads came on screen, oppressed her. But after a couple of hours she dozed off.

Some very dark time later, she was awakened by the glockenspiel crash of breaking glass.

"Addie?" Her first thought was that the frog was flouncing around the house and had bumped into something or knocked something over. Maybe he had cut himself. She had to go see if he needed help. But a cynical, motherly inertia kept her from getting herself moving real fast; as the mom of three, she had been awakened out of a sound sleep a few times too many, and no kid had died on her yet. Her reactions had slowed proportionately as her age and mass and angst had increased.

"All right, I'm coming," she mumbled as she heaved herself upright, nudged her feet into their cow-nosed slippers, and shuffled toward the bedroom door.

The intruder, in brief, was a lot faster than she was. A quite fetching intruder dressed with cat-burglar élan in black, butt-hugging jeans, black turtleneck, and an utterly charming black velvet French hat.

Emily.

Trust Emily to do this thing in style. Emily, who had smashed a window even though she should have known the spare key was right there by the bushes in a hyper-realistic plastic dog-poop key hider Buffy had brought home from work. Emily, swooping like Ms. Musketeer through the night, buckle that swash. Emily, frog-rescuer and savior of an ensorcelled prince.

All of this Buffy comprehended afterward, when she had time to feel ruefully proud of the kid. In the actual event, her attention, from the moment she waddled around the corner into the kitchen, was entirely taken up by the tableau.

Emily, embracing Adamus tenderly, kissing him.

Prince Adamus d'Aurca. Standing there in human form.

Over six feet tall and buck naked, with the sheen of supernatural glory on every consummate inch of him. Sleek ballet-dancer legs and bunched buttocks exquisite with muscle, tapered torso, broad shining shoulders—he lighted up the kitchen with the glow of his transformation. Though his bare, beautiful feet touched the floor, he did not seem to stand; rather, he manifested, too perfect and otherworldly to be quite human, too lusty to pass as a naked angel lacking wings, much too sweetly flesh. Emily—even though the spell was unmistakably broken, Emily was still kissing him.

Buffy stood struggling for breath at the sight of him. Then she found it and screamed.

Shrieked, rather. An embarrassingly Victorian ululation, useless except that it startled them apart. She caught a freeze-frame glimpse of their two faces, Emily's rose-colored gasp as she noticed her prince's unclad midsection, Addie staring back at Buffy with no more expression than a wild thing and with beauty that threatened to stop her heart. That old Queen of Fair Peril sure knew what she was doing when she shaped him. Wide pagan mouth. Greek brow. Golden eyes—she saw them from across the room, those glittering gold-dust eyes pooled with midnight black. Addie: she would have known him anywhere.

Standing there with the brand of faerie lips hot on his brow.

The next instant the two of them, Emily and Adamus, fled like a pair of deer.

Hand in hand, they darted out the door into the night. Buffy screamed again and stumbled after them, getting to the door just in time to hear the car roar away, speeding God knew where. No, probably God did not know. God had no place in that amoral kingdom. And Buffy could tell herself and tell herself that she would call the police, the National Guard, the President, and Oprah, that she would do whatever it took to get Emily back, but in her heart she knew: she was talking all the king's horses and all the king's men. No use. Emily belonged to the Realm of Fair Peril now.

Six

*F*ree! By all the gods and little red devils, how joy to fill a million hearts ensouled that one simple word. *Free! She set me FREE.* How the power had filled him, the power of a paradise of angels in her kiss. With awe, adoration, joy, Adamus gazed upon her as she sent the mechanical chariot scudding at dizzying speed through the night. Such power. This, then, at last, was his fated princess. Princess Emily. How beautiful she was in the half-light that kept flashing past from the tall lamps. Up until the moment she had lifted him in her hands, when the touch of her soft lips had flashed through him like lightning and turned him inside out, up until that moment he had not known, he had not understood—she had been just the daughter to him, the pale shadow, the second choice. His focus had been all on the mother, the thunder woman who fascinated and appalled him. But now—

She felt his gaze and glanced at him, the soft contours of her face shaky in the changing light.

"Princess Emily," he said, his voice shaky also.

"Shhhh." She turned back to the large dark glass, the

speeding lights. "I've got to concentrate or we'll wreck."
But she kept talking. "I can't believe it." He could hear the
delight and terror in her voice. "I mean, I believe it, but I
can't believe it. You're real."

Did she mean he had a soul now? Could this be? Possibly—because the potency of her kiss was like lightning
and larksong, like nothing he could have expected, like
nothing he had ever experienced before. The transformation from hostage child to faerie prince did not rival it. The
branding fire of the kiss that had made him a servant of
the Queen of Fair Peril, that was only a bad dream by
comparison. Even the rigors of becoming a frog did not
compare with the shock of this metamorphosis. Even the
helplessness of falling to death was as nothing compared
with this helplessness, this—this naked falling, this becoming a—a hostage to her. This falling in love.

Her kiss had made him her captive.

Not free.

The realization put a keen and painful edge on his joy,
but joy remained. He adored her. His terror and unhap-
piness ran through him like wine. He whispered again,
"Princess Emily."

"Shhhh. I can't look at you. We have to find you some
clothes before the cops stop us."

He said, "I love you."

"Hush. Please." Her voice trembled. He saw a shivering
smile. He saw her rosebud chest heave.

She must not have meant, Adamus decided, that he had
a soul, because a soul was a constant, was it not? It did
not seem possible that he could have a soul when everything about him could be transformed so quickly and completely. When he had been a frog, his thoughts had been
green and watery, his dreams informed with algae and the
flitting of winged insects, his lusts founded upon the lay-
ing of eggs. But now that he was a prince, his thoughts

had transformed as much as his body. Just the thought of her small, round breasts under the thin cloth made his—made him cover a salient part of himself with his hands. And his thoughts had a new texture. Blue velvet in them, and smooth bedsheets, and the whisper of silk on skin. And that wine-red heat in his heart, his blood. And the color of gold, her hair. The weight of gold in his thoughts. Crown. Circlet. Wedding ring.

He loved her. He loved her. Heady joy. Yet—how could he say he loved her? He knew he did not yet have a soul.

Only one thing seemed constant: he was still in thrall.

"Nine-one-one."

"Yes, my daughter just ran away with a naked fetch."

"A naked what, ma'am?"

"Fetch. Frog, fairy-tale prince, stud muffin, crotchthrob frog fairy—"

"Name-calling won't help us, ma'am. You say his name is Tayell Prinz?"

"No, his name is Prince Adamus d'Aurca, and he just took off in the altogether with my daughter!"

"And your daughter is how old, ma'am?"

"Sixteen."

"And how long has she been gone?"

"About a minute and a half now."

The dispatcher's tone of professional boredom never varied. "Call us if she hasn't come back in twenty-four hours, ma'am."

"But she's likely to do anything! She broke my window, stole my frog—"

"She broke a window? I'll send an officer to take a report, ma'am. Your name and address?"

Buffy hung up without answering, her thoughts reserving a hot spot in hell for people who considered that a broken window was more important than a missing child,

Emily, who had already been gone for two minutes. God damn it that time had been wasted. Buffy grabbed her car keys and headed for the door. Her slippers slowed her down; broken glass be damned, she kicked them off and ran out barefoot into the night. The Escort, with the nearly supernatural perversity routinely demonstrated by inanimate objects in times of stress, stalled the first three times she tried to start it, then bucked as she backed down the driveway and shimmied like a belly dancer when she pushed it to sixty before the first traffic light. Goddamn car. But at least no cop saw her run the light. Buffy accomplished a one-car stampede to the edge of town, back Main Street to the commercial strip at the other end, and around the bypass before a cop stopped her. Speeding. Driving without a license. A ticket for $297. He did not ticket her for hysteria, driving barefoot and in a nightgown (cerulean-blue flannel with glow-in-the-dark stars, planets, and crescent moons), or asking goofy questions. No, he had not seen a metallic-mauve Probe with a teenage girl and a naked fetch in it.

Forty-five minutes later, Buffy, still barefoot, flannel-gowned, and hysterical, stood at the door of the Prentis Sewell stately residence, pounding and leaning on the loathsome door chimes.

After an inordinate interval, Prentis opened the door a crack and peered out with his cute little dresser-drawer weapon in hand. Prentis, in sweats, jaw set, trying to look tough on crime, as if there might be a TV crew on his doorstep at three in the morning. Turning his hair-implanted head slightly so that the light caught his best angle. Seeing his ex, he opened the door fully yet seemed not at all sure he might not need the gun. "Buffy, for God's sake—"

"Emily's missing."

Prentis puffed his chest and scowled. "I hear you ruined her party."

"Better than ruining her life." Could he think of nothing but taking potshots in the post-marital war? At least she had been *there* for the party. "Suction the wax out of your ears, Prentis. Emily is missing. Gone. She's run away." Prentis belonged to the old boys' network; he might be able to get the cops to do something.

"She's got a right to run away after the trick you pulled."

Dear God, what was it going to take to make him get the picture? Buffy had thought he might be able to see past their personal differences long enough to focus on helping their youngest child. Silly thought.

"Prentis," she said between her teeth, "may I draw your attention to the fact that your garage door is hanging open and the Probe is gone."

His stare shifted and his scowl turned to a frown. "Hey." He swiveled and bawled into the house, "Tempestt!" After waiting for a short while, he raised the volume. "Pestt!"

It was a measure of Buffy's agitation that learning in this way of Tempestt's uncomplimentary nickname failed to cheer her.

"Pestt! What's Emily gone and done with the Probe?"

A sleepy soprano response wafted from upstairs.

"She's not there? Did she wreck the car and not tell me?"

"For God's sake," Buffy exploded, "forget the damn car! We've got to find Emily!"

He turned back to her and gave her his what's-the-big-problem look. "Emily? Hell, she's a kid, she's probably out cruising with her friends. Snuck out without telling us. I'll give her what for when she gets back."

Buffy said, "She's out cruising with a—" How to explain this in terms even a politician like Prentis could understand? "She's with a young man who is entirely too old for her."

"*Is* she!" Prentis crinkled into his most charming running-for-office grin. "Well, she's sixteen. She's legal. That's about the age I liked them when I started screwing them."

It knocked Buffy's breath away. He might as well have punched her in the gut. She staggered back. It would not have hit her as hard if she had thought he was being boorish on purpose to hurt her—but she knew better. He was being Prentis.

"Just joking," he said.

"You are a toad," Buffy managed to whisper. "A total, odious toad." She turned her back on him and ran, her bare feet colder than the pavement, colder than the April night air.

Driving around feverishly till dawn, talking to the kind of people who hang out on street corners all night, Buffy did not manage to track down Emily or Adamus. Instead, outside a bar that echoed the neon glow in the east, she found LeeVon. She would probably not have noticed him, as she was not in the habit of scanning what came out of bars, except that he was serenely standing there watching for sunrise in his underwear.

"LeeVon?" She pulled over and took another look. It was him, all right. Black-rimmed eyeglasses. Mr. McGregor on the left arm, Peter Rabbit on the right. T-shirt with holes in it. Bullwinkle-print boxer shorts. Well, of course, she should have known; what else would a guy like LeeVon wear under his black leathers? Bullwinkle shorts. Bony knees and wrinkled orange socks.

"Buffles!" He smiled like the dawn, delighted to see her, not at all concerned about being seen in his underwear, and alcoholically unimpaired as he bent beside her window to talk with her. "Mercy heavens, Best Beloved, what are you doing here in your nightgown?"

"You should talk. Strip poker?"

"Nah. Nude dude needed my clothes."

She jumped so hard she rammed her head against the Escort's ceiling. "Ow! Adamus?"

"Are you okay?"

"Compared to what! LeeVon, help me out, come on, my daughter has run away with my frog. The naked guy, was it Adamus, dammit?"

His mouth came open and hung that way, showing the stud in his tongue. It had never made sense to Buffy how that thing didn't click against his teeth when he talked.

"LeeVon!"

He stammered, "The—the cinderella in the car, was that your little darling? It was! But—but I didn't recognize her. She was changed somehow. Different."

"When!" Buffy barked.

"Pardon?"

"When were they here? Just now?"

"Oh, no. Hours ago. I went back inside and played Candyland."

"Great. Just lovely. Wonderful." Buffy jammed the car into gear. "So now the handsome prince is running around in your black leathers."

"Black jeans, actually, and a leather jacket."

"Only you would give him your clothes."

LeeVon seemed surprised at her comment. "Well, he needed them."

"Right. LeeVon, get in."

"Pardon? My bike—"

"As if you can ride home on your motorcycle in your BVDs? Get in the car."

He did so, complaining, "Nobody better take my bike."

Stamping on the gas, Buffy veered off at a reckless vector, trying hard not to hate all men. She didn't want to be that way. She actually did know some nice men. Knew some people with good marriages, too. Women her own age, even. She managed to keep her volume down when she said, "My daughter is missing and all you can worry about is your bike?"

"No, my bike is *one* of the things I'm worried about. Tell me what is going on with Emily."

He knew her name? Points for LeeVon. Not everybody remembered the names of other people's kids.

Buffy told him about it in full, amphibious detail, slowing down almost to the speed limit as she became absorbed in the story.

"Emily's an idealist," LeeVon said once she had briefed him. "I mean, a lot of kids are, teenagers, more than most adults like to give credit—but Emily has always been completely committed to the fairy tale. Whom did you name her after? Emily Dickinson?"

"No. I loathe Emily Dickinson." Weird old witch; every poem Emily Dickinson ever wrote could be sung to the tune of "The Yellow Rose of Texas," and most of them sounded better that way. "I just named her." She had always liked the name Emily. It sounded pretty.

"There's poetry in her just the same. Elinor Wylie. Not so much Sylvia Plath."

She forgave him completely. Good God, Emily was an individual to him, a person, not just somebody's kid. A lot more a person than she was to the cops or her own father.

"The idealism is what worries me. When it comes to a cause, Emily's unselfish." Buffy found herself pulling into her driveway.

"What are we doing at your place?"

"I have no idea." Buffy only then realized that she had given up for the time being. The initial search was over, and unsuccessful, and it was time to regroup. She led the way inside—the door swung unlocked and open, the way she had left it. "Watch the broken glass."

LeeVon hunkered down and started cleaning up the shards of her window.

"I can do that." Buffy stepped into her slippers.

"Well, I know you *can*, Best Beloved, but let me help. Do you have a piece of cardboard that will fit the orifice?"

She found some and got it taped in there, then brought LeeVon the dustpan and whisk broom, then made coffee. LeeVon finished with the floor and sat at her kitchen table in his Bullwinkle shorts. She served coffee, sat across from him, and sipped. Outside, birds were piping like flutes. The refrigerator hummed, matronly. The pseudo-satin-stitch daisies on the plastic tablecloth lay soothingly white under the fluorescent light. Everything seemed very calm.

"All you can do, I guess," said LeeVon, "is wait."

Buffy did not answer. Too tired. Idly she flipped through *Batracheios*. Wait? LeeVon was right, there was nothing else to do, but she was afraid for Emily; Addie was the enemy now, yet she missed him, she wanted him back; in the too-damn-early dawn, after a night of driving at top speed to nowhere, she felt adrift, borderless, disoriented. LeeVon the librarian was her buddy and he had given her this book and she was looking for something to point out to him, but she couldn't quite remember what. The book had grown and changed since the last time she had read it, and she could feel the green cover alive and warm and flexing in her hand. The glossy pictures of frogs in green suits and creamy waistcoats winked at her. "Here it is," she muttered, happening upon the headline that had interested her. "Transfrogrification. One part wrath added to two parts perverted sense of humor. Coddle the mixture over medium heat." She had that part under control. Wrath, heat? Just think of Prentis. The sense of humor was her own. No problem. "In appropriate garb, repeat the following gibberish: gimme an F, F! Gimme an R, R! Gimme an O, O! Gimme a G, G! What's it spell? FROG! What's it smell like? A FROG! What—"

The dawn hush was rent by a startled and distinctly ranine scream. Buffy looked up and LeeVon was not there.

"LeeVon?" She saw his black-framed eyeglasses lying on the floor. What was going on?

"Graaaah!"

She stood up and leaned across the table to look. A medium-sized bullfrog sat amid a muddle of cotton underwear on LeeVon's chair, a frog with miniaturized rings crowding its nostrils, lips, eyebrows, and the edge of the flat circle that passed as an ear. A frog with miniaturized tattoos, including an interesting one that Buffy had not previously seen, on its butt.

"*Nice* tat! Who is that naked kid? Mowgli?"

"Buffy, unfrog me!"

"Well hung! Kipling would be proud."

"*Buffy!*"

"All right, okay." Denial, also known as delayed reaction, had always been one of Buffy's strongest qualities; she was just beginning to mentally process the most recent calamity. "Did I do that? Okay, okay!" As LeeVon emitted an indescribable vocalization, "All right, just chill out a minute. Let me find the instructions."

There was a difficulty, however. Adrenaline had jolted her wide awake and snapped her out of her floating sense of not-quite-self; consequently, *Batracheios* presented itself as bookishly normal to her, a coffee-table volume of annoyingly cute pictures and bad poetry. Buffy spent a full hour going through it page by page and could find nothing on how to turn a man into a frog. Nothing at all. And certainly nothing on how to unfrog him.

"LeeVon," she said finally, "let me pick you up. That's a buddy." She did so. "Now don't panic, but I'm going to put you in the aquarium for the time being, to keep you nice and moist."

"Graaaaah!" The stud in the end of his four-inch, front-mounted tongue thrashed in the air, catching the light.

"I said, don't panic!"

"Graaaaaaaaah!"

The frog's distress, combined with everything else that had gone wrong, affected Buffy with a degree of existential desperation she had never previously attained, angst beyond tears, a despair that smashed right through her armor of cynicism. Woe afflicted her, desolation sufficient to make her stand in the middle of her kitchen with a hyperventilating frog in her hands, throw back her head, and bawl, "Fairy Godmother-In-Law! Fay! Get your droopy patootie over here!"

Fay never swore. She prided herself upon never swearing. She might not be a lady by some people's standards of wealth or style or status of birth, but, by gosh and golly, she could, and would, be a lady in deportment.

However, when that Murphy person's summons yanked her out of her chair and hurtled her streetward like horizontal bungee jumping, it just slipped out. Fay said, "Damn!"

Then she detested Murphy worse than ever for making her do that.

Fay knew herself to be a pro, a minor but longtime practitioner in fair, perilous power. She knew the Murphy person to be an immensely talented amateur. At first, years ago, Fay had been pleased and proud that her son had recognized that talent, had married a woman so much like his old mother. But very shortly she had come to wish he had married Little Bo Peep, a sheep, anything else. It is hard for an old pro when an amateur possesses the untrained power to boss her around. No matter what other considerations might arise, Fay's goal in dealing with the Murphy person had for years remained focused and simple: to protect her own niche and status, achieved through a lifetime of hard work and political maneuvering (Prentis had learned most of what he knew from her) and sucking up to the Queen.

Driving faster than she liked toward the unlovely and out-of-whack Murphy residence, Fay thought about all this and said, "Damn," again—it just slipped out again—which made her furious. Mad enough to commit an act of rebellion. She stamped on the brakes; despite the power of Murphy's summons wrenching her innards, she wrestled the Eldorado to a stop at the curb. "All right, just a minute," she grumbled. She wanted to check her purse.

Hastily she dumped the contents out of her massive gilded bag, then repacked it: all four of her marriage licenses, divorce papers, death certificates. Mirror, lipstick, mascara, eyelash curler, cellulite cream, nose-hair remover. Several sexual hang-ups in the latest decorator colors. Her son's fraternity paddle. The papal encyclical on birth control. A sheaf of newspaper clippings about various child abuse cases. An inferiority complex, pink. Birth and First Communion certificates for her children. Prom corsage. Emergency-room rape kit. The swimsuit issue of *Sports Illustrated*. Checkbook, credit cards, press-on faux fingernails. A box of baking soda. A religious tract on the evils of masturbation.

Fay frowned. It did not seem like enough, not if she had to defend herself, considering the mood Murphy was in. She glanced around the interior of the Eldorado.

Some people's cars are best conceptualized as mobile stereos. Fay's was not one of those. Fay's car was a mobile closet.

Fay smiled. From a stack of old newspapers she selected the one with the article about Murphy's mother refusing to testify that her husband had assaulted her. That went into the purse. She also jammed in a can of Ultra Slim-Fast and an aerosol dispenser of Strong-To-Last breath spray.

There. Nothing like emotional baggage to pack a wallop.

The strength of Murphy's summons was scrambling her intestines. Necessarily, Fay started the Eldorado and rock-eted off again.

She wondered what the h—Goodness. This had to stop. She wondered what in mercy's name Murphy wanted. Probably something to do with that twerp Emily. Now, there was another one who bore watching and needed to be put in her place.

Whatever the problem was, Murphy could just—Murphy could expect no help from her.

Some people liked to say yes. Some people liked to say no. Fay knew herself to be, as befitted a lady, one of those who liked to say no.

Speeding toward the Murphy residence against her will, Fay was not ashamed of this trait. She cherished it. It and her purse were going to save her.

Buffy had forgotten it was Sunday morning. Not that it mattered, but it startled her and blinded her momentarily to see Fay dressed for her weekly glory competition, a.k.a. church: Fay wore a gold acetate, elastic-waisted dress with a gold-on-gold brocade jacket in a fleur-de-lis pattern; she wore gold button covers shaped like butterflies and match-ing gold earrings; she wore gold mesh nylons and gold spike heels. And, oddly, a white hat. "I would like a por-tion of respect," Fay complained as Buffy opened the door. Fay was not pleased.

"I'm a little out of sorts right now," Buffy said.

"Sorts or no sorts, I expect a proper mode of address."

"Fine, your Aureateness." Buffy stood aside to let Fay through.

"And for heaven's sake, get out of that dreadful granny gown."

"Never mind the nightgown for right now. I've got two problems. Number one, Emily—"

"My problem first!" LeeVon squawked from the aquarium. "My problem first!"

"Okay, LeeVon first. I turned him into a frog by mistake. How do I unfrog him?"

Fay gave her an expressively blank golden-eyed stare. "Kiss him."

"Oh, for God's sake. *Duh*." Feeling furiously stupid—as Fay probably intended her to feel—Buffy grimaced but turned immediately to the aquarium and picked up LeeVon. "Pucker up," she told him.

"Turn your back," he begged.

"How, for God's sake?" She kissed. "Bleaaah." But aside from a green taste of aquatic slime on her mouth, nothing happened.

"That's odd," Fay said with the puzzled frown of a hausfrau confronting a cake that has failed to rise. "That ought to have worked. Try it again."

"You try it." Buffy thrust the frog at her.

"No, thank you."

Buffy rolled her eyes and approximated her lips to LeeVon's once more. Nothing. LeeVon's throat quivered and he whimpered, jangling his rings.

"Never mind, sweetie," Buffy told him. "I'll get you back somehow. I promise."

"Yeah, well, I'm due at work tomorrow morning!"

"You can go," said Fay in bored tones, "but I don't think they'll want you manning the desk. I'm late to church." She turned toward the door.

Buffy called, "Fay, wait, wait! We have to find Emily."

"Are you saying she's lost?"

Yes, of course, that was what Buffy was saying.

Thoughts of Emily kept making her feel cold. Emily, another body in another smashed car. Emily, another victim of another mugging, or worse—Emily, another bludgeoned and violated young female body reported in the morning paper, a corpse with golden hair, baby-fine, softly shining—so different from this woman's metallic coif. Buffy knew the fears were silly; Emily was with Adamus, she should be safe, right? Wrong. Emily was with a man from an era when men owned their women like chattels. When a man was a person and a woman was something less and a girl less yet. Emily, another battered girlfriend with nowhere to turn for help. Emily, lost and alone.

Buffy felt so cold with fear that she could barely speak. "She's run off with Adamus."

"So?"

Jesus, Buffy thought. Emily, seeing things she should not yet see, doing things she should not yet do. *I know where Prentis gets it.* "So she's your granddaughter! Help me get her back."

"Why?"

Good *God.* "So she doesn't end up married to a lout at the age of sixteen!"

"I was married to my first husband when I was sixteen," Fay said. "Didn't set me back any."

Actually, that explained a lot about Fay. Didn't set her back? That was debatable, as was any comparison between Emily and this garish golden sweet potato on feet. "Emily's not like that."

"Thanks so much." Fay grasped the doorknob in her gilded claws.

"Fay, *wait!* Do you know where she is?"

Her fairy godmother-in-law gave her a glittering look, hefted her purse in a very decided manner, and walked out.

Seven

"**T**his just absolutely sucks," LeeVon said. Somehow he had regained his composure and a bleak sense of humor. "Every time I hop, I jingle like a tambourine."

Sitting at the kitchen table and poring over *Batracheios* again, Buffy had to laugh, tried not to, got her insides sloshing like an off-balance washing machine, and started to hiccup.

"Never mind, Best Beloved." Atop his eminence of damp brick, LeeVon squatted placidly as only a ranine philosopher can, warmed by the reading lamp Buffy had rigged up for him. "I know you didn't mean to do it. You know what I think the problem is?" Now that LeeVon had calmed down, he sounded like himself again, only froggily sheepish. "Why kissing didn't work, I mean?"

She focused her hiccuping attention on him.

"I think I need a guy."

Since she had known LeeVon, Buffy had been so preoccupied by the exigencies of her own private life that thoughts of his had never occurred to her. What LeeVon did or dreamed in his off time was sublimely none of her business. It wasn't that sort of friendship. Moreover, LeeVon was—was LeeVon. All such thoughts of him seemed irrelevant. LeeVon, librarian of mythic proportions, with a sexual preference? What he was saying startled the spasms right out of Buffy's diaphragm and affected her voice like helium. "You gay?" she squeaked.

"Yes."

"You serious?"

"Yes. Absolutely."

The friendship had moved, Buffy realized, into a new level. He trusted her. Look what she had done to him, yet he trusted her.

"Consequently," he added, "it can't be just any guy." His voice turned coy. "I like them young and cute. And, of course, he has to be one of my kind."

She started to laugh again, this time with relief. "Well, that's the answer, then. It's gotta be. So who can I take you to? You got a, uh, a steady?"

"No." His voice had quieted. "No, I wish I did."

"Is there, uh, anybody?"

"Not really." He was speaking so softly she could barely hear him. "This town isn't the best place in the world for a guy like me to meet somebody, Buffles. Not the kind of dude you want to take home."

He was telling her, she realized, that he was lonely. She didn't know what to say.

He said, "There's the Pony Ride, and that's about all. Queens and quickies."

The bar in front of which she had found him standing in his underwear, he meant. "So what do I do, take you back there?"

"Yes." He brightened. "Excellent idea. Any decent God-fearing queer who could go for me, or vice versa, is going to need some alcoholic fortification before he agrees to kiss me."

"Sounds like a plan. Tonight."

"No, it's Sunday, dammit."

The bar would not be open. Blue laws. "Shit. Okay, tomorrow night. You can last that long." Buffy felt expansive with hope that LeeVon would soon be back to—"normal" hardly seemed the word, but anyway, would soon be back. "You want a sandwich or something?"

"No, thanks. Not hungry. You?"

She shook her head and leaned back in her chair, staring. There was silence. It was no use to offer to tell LeeVon a story; he was a better storyteller than she was. As talking frogs went, she found him not nearly as satisfactory as Addie. He bellowed no endearing insults at her. He undertook no ranine posturings. Probably he wouldn't croak at night, either. How boring. Another fifteen minutes had to pass before it was time to go to the phone again. Every hour on the hour Buffy had been calling the Sewell home to ask whether anything had been heard from or about Emily. Nothing so far. On the chance that she might have to go someplace or do something, Buffy had taken a quick shower and dressed—sweatshirt, jeans, running shoes. Other than that, she did not know what to do. Go out and collar people on the street, ask them if they had seen her daughter? But what if Emily called or came to the house while she was gone, what if Emily needed her? After today she could call the cops again and insist that they do something. But the waiting was hell.

"That witch Fay knows where Emily is," she said softly.

"Watch what you say, Best Beloved. The air has ears."

The warning was so gentle that Buffy did not bristle. "I don't care," she said. "She knows. I swear she does."

"I agree."

"I detest that kind of adult."

"Pardon? The polished-surface kind?"

"No, not so much that. The kind who says, 'What was

good enough for me is good enough for my progeny forevermore.' "

"An interesting form of selfishness." LeeVon's voice had gone feathery. He hadn't thought about it before. He didn't have kids.

Being LeeVon, he probably didn't have parents, either.

Buffy said, "That Brasso bitch. I've got to come up with a way to get her to help me."

"Good luck."

"Yeah. The only way I can think of . . ." Buffy did not vocalize her thoughts, which were dark, intriguing, and not yet fully actualized. "So what's it like to be a frog?" she asked after a short while.

"Frightening. It's terrifying to be so small and portable. Why?"

"Portable," Buffy muttered.

"Best Beloved, what are you contemplating?"

"Prentis." She got up, grabbed her car keys, and strode out.

Prentis considered that his ex did not understand him, and he was right. The key to Prentis, which Buffy had never imaginatively grasped, was that Prentis had been raised by Fay.

Part of the reason Buffy did not understand, of course, was that Prentis never talked about it. But that was no excuse. She should have understood anyway.

Prentis never talked about it because talk about personal terrors was not manly. Prentis barely thought about it for the same reason. Terror, not manly. By an interesting circular sort of entrapment, or perhaps a torment more in the shape of a Möbius strip, Prentis's chief terror was exactly and precisely that of not being manly. Not muscular enough, not athletic enough, not aggressive enough, not upstanding enough. Sons of mothers like his, he knew from sixth-grade health class, sons of dominant mothers, mothers whose glare bore physical force, mothers who could turn almost anyone into a quivering jelly of apology with a single whack of the emotional baggage, mothers to whom the word "witch" was not an insult—sons of forceful mothers were likely to turn out not manly. Early in his teens he had learned to be constantly on his guard against an incipient lack of manliness. At any time some sneaking, effeminate emotion might turn him into a sis. He could not let that happen. He studied the masters, James Bond, John Wayne, Humphrey Bogart. (With a name like that, the guy had to hang tough.) He learned that masculinity involved total control, and he learned to be in control of himself and those around him, an obsession which led him naturally into politics via the law. Control became his identity, his livelihood, and his armor.

Only at three in the morning, when his always-and-forever insomnia would not let him sleep, was Prentis likely to admit even silently, to himself—

No. No, dammit, it was not some kind of sissy fear that sent him pacing around the downstairs in his terry-cloth robe at this obscene hour; it was anger. He was pissed, dammit. At women. Women in general, such as his mother with her killer purse and Emily who used to be his sweet little daughter but now seemed to be turning into a bitch and a whore just like the rest of them, out running around, and Tempestt asleep upstairs, not knowing he was awake and pacing—not that she'd care if she did know. Just as long as he kept the money and the perks coming in, she didn't care. And Buffy. Specifically, Buffy. God, was he angry at Buffy. Angrier than he was at anyone, because at one point she had actually seemed to love him.

Tick tock tick tock tick.

The secret, cat-footed fear was that no one would ever—

No. No, he was damn not going to think about it. He was pissed.

The door chimes donged.

The sound jangled Prentis like a buzzer, freezing him where he was.

Nerves. Okay, damn it, nerves were always there, right underneath the armor. Partly because of what his mother might do to him—that hag didn't need her bag of baggage; she could make him wet his pants in public with merely a pensive and affectionate smile—but mostly because he knew who it was. He knew just who was standing on his doorstep. Another one exactly like Fay, only more so—wasn't that what always happened, that a boy tried to get away from his mother, then ended up marrying her?

Prentis knew who was the only person in the world loony enough to be dinging his dong at this hour.

The chimes sounded again.

Goddammit. But Prentis knew he had no choice. With his face under iron control, reminding himself that he was not a lonely boy any longer but now a lawyer and a statesman, he got himself moving warily toward the door.

Buffy was leaning on the chimes for the third time when Prentis opened up.

"If you keep harassing me like this," Prentis said, blocking his front doorway with his Health Club bod, "I'm going to have to get a restraining order."

"Your daughter's missing." Buffy considered that she was giving him one last chance. "I just want you to do something. What about that Honorary Member of the Association of Sheriffs thing you bought? Make your friends find her."

"Hell, she's probably already pregnant, what's the point?"

This time his boorishness didn't shock Buffy's breath

away. This time it merely hardened her. He had done it, he had gone too far; he was doomed. Buffy said, "I was mistaken when I called you a toad, Prentis."

He turned on the Reaganesque charm. "Well, we all make mistakes."

"Damn straight. You're not a toad, you're a frog." Wrath was simmering. Buffy stirred in the perverted sense of humor and started her incantation. "Gimme an F, F! Gimme an R, R! Gimme an O, O! Gimme a G, G!"

Prentis's attempt at charm had blinked off. He was flinching back from her, uncertainty wavering on his face. "You're nuts."

"What's it spell? FROG! What's it smell like? A FROG! What's it look like? A FROG! What's it quack like? A FROG! What is it? A FROG!"

Unfortunately, it still smelled, looked, and quacked like Prentis. "You're psycho!" he quacked in his flat, central-Pennsylvania accent. A trifle pale under his salon tan, he ducked back into his pseudo-Tudor lair and slammed the door.

"Damn!"

Buffy drove home in a deep indigo funk. What had gone wrong? It had seemed like a straightforward enough plan: transfrogrify Prentis into a portable batrachian form, grab him and hold him hostage until his mother cooperated and vouchsafed information, then find Emily. Then, once Emily was safely home, let the Pestt or somebody kiss Prentis to give him back his gonads. Nobody would call the cops; as a politician, Prentis certainly would not want the sort of publicity that centered around having become small and green, and anyway, there's no law against keeping a couple of pet bullfrogs. It had seemed like a certain, simple, and invulnerable plan.

"You were going to put *that* in here with me?" LeeVon exclaimed when she told him about it. "A testosterone-prone hetero running for office? Thank God it didn't work."

"Look, it should have worked." Buffy slumped over the table and laid her head on her cushy forearms. She mumbled to the tablecloth, "Everything's wrong. Emily's gone and nobody gives a damn."

Silence. Then there was a tambourinelike jingling as LeeVon hopped forward. "I've been thinking about her."

"Good." Buffy did not move. "I'm glad somebody besides me can spare her a thought."

"Now listen, Best Beloved. This is not directly about Emily, but just listen. You asked me what it is like to be a frog. I'll tell you. It is very strange. I see everything differently. I am looking straight at you, but you are not you; you are bigger."

"Oh, *thanks*." She burrowed deeper into her own arms.

"No, listen! By bigger, what I mean is mightier, stronger. More primal. A black-haired conjurer in a spangled gown—except it's just the Buffles sitting there in blue jeans after all. . . ." His tone grew wry and tender, yet uncertain. "I don't know how to explain it. Everything is canted, slanted, shadowed differently, haloed in a golden light."

That jolted Buffy upright. She sat stone straight and peered at him. His eyes were shining golden. Of course, frog eyes always did.

"Like in a dream," LeeVon said. "Have you ever had a dream of your own house, but in the dream it is somehow familiar and strange at the same time? Your house, yet not your house?"

Buffy barely nodded. "Maybe a frog's eyes see things differently."

"Maybe. But you are not a frog. What was it like when you were looking at that book?"

The memory made her uncomfortable, yet seduced her like the call of wild geese in the sky. "Very strange."

"Like you were in a dream?"

"Not a dream exactly. More of a—a different reality."
Different and therefore more exciting.

"Like there is another place? Only it isn't a place. It's a
trick of seeing."

"I don't know, LeeVon." She felt dead tired, too tired to
think. "What are you saying? Spit it out."

"Emily is with the prince." LeeVon spoke slowly. "And
he is a prince of Fair Peril, what most people call fairyland.
He's a fairy-tale prince. So Emily is in fairyland, right? Just
as I am at this very moment, since I have been turned into
a frog, which is not a possible event in the world we know.
So I am in fairyland, like Emily." LeeVon's cautious voice
had gone so soft Buffy could barely hear him. "But fairyland is not a place."

Dead tired, Buffy still could not sleep, not while Emily
was still missing. Sometime after midnight, she lay stark
stony awake, forearms resting on her forehead as she
stared at the dark ceiling, stared as if the night could tell
her something. Stared as if staring could help her see the
stars through all the barriers between them and her. Stared
past the fake, greenish-white phosphorescent stars span-
gling her own nightgown sleeve.

"Good heavens," she whispered, and then she sat
straight up, banged herself on the head, and yelled it.
"Good heavens!"

"Graaah!" In the aquarium, LeeVon was startled awake
by her shout.

Buffy rampaged out of bed. "Good grief, it was the stupid nightgown!"

"What? Best Beloved, what are you saying?"

"I forgot about the goddamn appropriate garb!"

Only a few minutes later, Buffy stood at the security-
lighted front door of the Prentis Sewell residence in sneak-

ers and her stars-and-planets nightgown. The way the spell read, a cheerleader's outfit seemed to make more sense (and Buffy winced from imagining herself in one), but hey. This would work. It had worked before. Buffy pounded gleefully on the door. "Prentis! Get your vote-grubbing butt out here." She played joyful rhythms upon the door chimes. "Prentis! I've got a treat for you."

This time he came to the door in silk pajamas. Two ways you can tell the essential truth about a man: how he acts when he's drunk, and what he sleeps in. Prentis was a wimp, though he yanked the door open with an impressive show of energy.

"That does it," he declared in a voice that attempted movie-stud manliness but skidded too high. "I'm calling the cops."

He'd call the cops on her, but he wouldn't call them to make them find Emily? Screw him. Ire and perversity at the ready, Buffy gabbled rapidly, "Gimme an F, F; gimme an O, O; gimme a G, G!"

"You are a total fruitcake." Wary-faced, Prentis was retreating. Buffy jammed her foot in the door so he couldn't close it.

"What's it spell—" Suddenly, *DAMN I messed up*, Buffy realized what it spelled, but inertia carried her onward. "FOG! What's it smell like? A FOG! What's—"

Prentis thinned, dislimned, and vanished. A dense and malodorous six-foot miasma, however, hovered over his doorstep.

"Prentis?" Buffy whispered.

No reply. Her ex had never been one to hold back in times of stress. If he had been able to talk, Buffy decided, she would have been hearing some impassioned comments from him. But as all she heard was a swampy silence, it seemed that a fog, unlike a frog, couldn't talk. No mouth.

No kisser.

How was a person supposed to bring Prentis back, supposing she wanted to? Which Buffy most certainly did not, but still . . . she felt kind of bad.

Already the fog was starting to swirl and dissipate in the April nighttime breeze. "You'd better get inside before you get wafted away," Buffy said. Forget taking Prentis hostage; the fog did not appear particularly portable. "Can you do that? Can you move around?"

Apparently so. The fog withdrew. Buffy called, "Okay, well, so long, see ya," and closed the door, shutting Prentis into his own home so that he would not become a dissipated person. Uh, effluvium. Just call him *Mist*er Sewell. Ha-ha.

Cheered by her pun, Buffy got into her car and drove off sedately, thoughtful. She felt sure that Tempestt was not smart enough to figure out that the odor in the bedroom was her husband, but she hoped Fay would not catch on too soon. Her dealings with Fay, she decided, were going to have to take place largely on a basis of bluff.

It was exactly twenty-four hours since Emily had disappeared. Buffy went home and called the cops.

Fay came shooting in like a gilded yam hurtled out of a potato launcher as Buffy was sucking at her second cup of morning coffee. The bored cop who had taken her report had left hours before, but Buffy had not been able to get back to sleep, or rather, to get to sleep at all. Paradoxically, therefore, she did not feel awake. She was just working herself up to ask LeeVon whether frogs slept, and how they did it with no eyelids to close, and whether their chinless heads ever nodded until their proboscises drooped into the water, when Fay came crashing in.

"Murphy!" Fay shouted quite loudly for a woman her age. "What have you done with my son?"

Sluggish, Buffy did not respond. Let Fay rant awhile first. Jeez, it wasn't hard to tell who rated. It didn't matter what happened to the granddaughter, but touch the son and whoa, baby.

"Murphy!" Fay screeched. "Answer me!"

Buffy gave her no more than a bleary stare. It hurt her eyes to try to look at Fay at that hour. What a way to start the morning. Buffy would have summoned Fay after her third cup of coffee, maybe, but meanwhile, here she was, the bitch of glitz, and it was beginning to occur to Buffy to wonder how she had gotten herself into this situation. Okay, sure, she had picked up a talking frog in the woods, but did that mean she had to end up in a pissing contest with the ormolu ogress?

"I know you've got him here somewhere." Fay checked the aquarium first, gave LeeVon a scornful glare—*You call that skinny thing a frog?*—then rampaged through the rest of the house. Buffy watched. She'd never been able to understand how some women could sprint in high heels, glitter-gold Wal-Mart heels yet. It was an ability she grudgingly had to admire. She got up and poured herself her third cup of coffee.

"Where is he!" Fay shrieked, reentering the kitchen.

Buffy sat down with her coffee and put her slippered feet up on a chair. "Where's Emily?"

"Emily, Schmemily! You tell me where Prentis is right now or I'll call the cops."

"Go ahead. May the cops help you as much as they've helped me."

"Yaaaaah!" Fay lifted her golden-clawed hands in the manner of a witch who has been pushed beyond her limited patience. The gesture actually woke Buffy up, because OUCH. She felt it. Felt it physically, felt it rip into her as if her shirt had disappeared along with her common sense—Fay was not touching her, yet somehow those metallic fingernails were tearing her skin.

It hurt, ow, ow, OW. But stubbornness or sheer weariness kept Buffy from vocalizing what she felt. She sat like a frog on a log, stoical. "I'm missing a child, too," she pointed out, "and I didn't notice much sympathy from you. Where's Emily?"

"Eeeeyaagh!" Fay stamped her resplendent feet, then lifted her hands again, more collectedly this time. "Gimme a—"

"Changing me into some damn thing won't help you find Prentis," Buffy said. "Besides, I doubt you can do it." In actuality she felt the quick sweat of severe fear trickling down her ribs. But being married to Prentis for twenty years had taught her how to play poker. And she had some basis for her bluff; she knew she had the power to summon Fay, whereas Fay had not thus far shown the power to summon her. For whatever obscure reasons—and Buffy was not sure she even wanted to understand them—for whatever reasons, the supernatural pecking order seemed to have placed her above Fay.

Fay knew it, too. She lowered her hands, and this morning she was a gold-and-crimson person, her face flushed with frustration. "Oooooogh!"

"Where's Emily? C'mon, Fay. I'm supposed to be at work."

"So am I," LeeVon put in morosely from the aquarium.

Fay flung up her hands again, this time plunging them into her own brittle, glittering coif and traumatizing it into astonishing disarray; she now resembled either Phyllis Diller or a supernova. "Where the heck do you think she is!" Fay shrilled. "She's right the heck where you'd expect! *Where is Prentis?*"

"Right where you'd expect," Buffy said, and it was true. Prentis was at home.

Fay's claws attacked the air again. Once more Buffy felt their magical impact slashing at the tender skin of her chest and belly. Once more, with the assistance of pride and perversity, she managed to sit without showing that she felt anything.

"Eeeeyaagh!" Fay's frustration rocketed her right out the door. Buffy let her go. She listened, heard Fay's Eldorado squeal away, then took a deep, shaky breath and slumped in her chair.

Her frog du jour asked, "Are you okay, Best Beloved?"

"I think so." LeeVon was a friend; Buffy did not mind peeking down her own shirt in front of him, for the first time in her life glad that the size of her frontage required her to wear an industrial-strength bra. Red welts covered the parts of her that it did not protect. "Ow. That bitch. You should see what she did to me."

"I can imagine."

"Damn her." But even though it hurt like hell, the skin was not broken. Buffy let go of her shirt with a gesture of dismissal. She sat where she was and tried to think what to do next. "Well," she said, not as steadily as she wanted to, "that did not go quite as expected."

"Like anything ever does?"

"Yeah, yeah." Duz, schmuzz, buzz my cuz. Missing work again, gonna get fired, okay, find a different job, but who's gonna hire. Buffy couldn't think. Her mind felt as foggy as Prentis's entire insubstantial quiddity, and once more she was so tired that she might as well have been floating on air, even though her hunkers rested firmly on her kitchen chair. She kept her eyes open yet saw nothing that made sense. The ceiling shone like water. The aquarium seemed to drift up and turn to haze. Kiss me, miss me, yeah, yeah, a frog is not a dog. Where the hell is Emily, right where you'd expect her to be—

Buffy sat bolt upright, suddenly and sublimely lucid. "Oh, for God's sake," she said to LeeVon. "She's at the mall."

Eight

"*T*here's her car."

As LeeVon could not see out the Escort's window from his nest of soggy paper towels on the passenger seat, he could not confirm this. Anxiously Buffy drove closer to the metallic-mauve Probe.

"It's hers, okay. There's her SAVE THE RAIN FOREST bumper sticker." Buffy veered with more fervor than accuracy into the nearest parking space. Made it without hitting anything.

"Don't get your hopes up," LeeVon said.

Without replying, Buffy hurried around to his side of the car, picked him up along with some damp paper towels to keep him comfortable, and cradled him in her hands.

"The car might have been there since yesterday."

"I don't care. I know she's here." Huffing along at her fastest thunder-thighed stride, Buffy carried LeeVon into the Mall Tifarious.

It was a gargantuan new mall designed to put shoppers into an ambience-induced euphoria in which they would buy, buy, buy. Sunlight streamed down through three tinted-glass domes into circular courtyards six stories high, each of which featured a fountain culminating in a pedestal upon which rose a fairyland-themed sculpture incorporating a lot of gilded filigree: a rearing deer with lacy wings; a frilly-dressed girl with a garland of golden roses; a heavyset, toadlike, verdigris-mottled frog with a fussy filigree crown and butterfly wings that looked way too delicate to support his bulk should he ever want to fly. Nonsensical but evocative verbiage was inlaid around the pedestals in gilded mosaic tile: "Maypoles, hollyhocks, white snakes, soul cakes." "Wishing hearts, coltslip, nightspring, a gold ring." Et cetera. Translucent oriflamme-cut banners trailed down from railings painted white and pink and lavender blue dilly dilly. Curving stairways of the same dilly-dilly ilk connected the six levels of shops, but never in such a way as to facilitate efficient passage from bottom of mall to top or vice versa; the goal, rather, was to send the consumer wandering in a disoriented daze past as much merchandise as possible.

"There's no damn sensible way to do this," Buffy complained to LeeVon after attempting a comprehensive scan of the first and second floors. The placement of the escalators was staggered. The elevators were hidden in the penetralia of the anchor stores. "This place is annoying." Buffy had never been a happy shopper or a mall enthusiast. If she absolutely had to buy something, she preferred to go to Wal-Mart and get it over with. New clothes to her meant bringing home two packets of pastel-colored cotton panties from the supermarket; home decorating was prissy-print toilet paper. The Mall Tifarious was wasted on her. "Everything's plastic," she grumbled, though the potted trees, four stories tall, were real. "Where's Emily?"

LeeVon was ignoring her. "James the butler!" he exclaimed with delight that jingled his face like wind chimes. "Now, *he* could unfrog me." The object of his approbation was a carved, wooden, rather two-dimensional effigy snootily holding a tray outside The Bombay Company. "I *love* Anglos."

"That's a pseudo Anglo," Buffy grumped, "outside a pseudo-Brit store." No Emily. They moved on.

"Santa Fe store!" LeeVon liked faux cowboys too, and the Santa Fe store had plenty of those, along with faux-sandstone statuettes of howling coyotes and coffee-table baskets made of synthetic mesquite. No Emily.

"Plastic!" Buffy burst out. "Everything's fake, everything's plastic, just like those goddamn fake pies where I work. Fake British, fake Southwestern, fake Colonial, fake Native American, fake Oriental, just like every other goddamn mall in the whole goddamn country, full of plastic, homogenized multiethnicity."

LeeVon ogled her, pop-eyed. "What do you mean, Best Beloved? It's wonderful! Fuchsia trees, hootoo birds flying everywhere—it's not like any other mall I've ever seen."

Buffy stopped walking and looked down at the frog in her arms. His eyes, the metallic rings of his irises, seemed to pulse and glow like gold straight out of the smelting fire.

Uh-oh. Buffy said, "You're seeing things."

"I'm seeing what's *there*, Maddie!"

"That's what I mean." They made plastic key lime pie to make you believe that real key lime pie existed. Which it did. Bizarre thought. Following it, Buffy barely noticed that LeeVon had called her by her childhood name. "Let's go down to one of the fountains."

"Good! But don't let the bearcats get me."

Bearcats?

At the fountain's (probably fake) marble verge, Buffy placed LeeVon in the water and watched him skim away with graceful thrusts of his ballet-dancer legs. How could frogs sit so much like beanbags, or like husbands during football season, yet swim so much like Baryshnikov flying? Watching LeeVon, Buffy found it hard to remember that the frog had been a man, but felt vaguely willing to believe that he would be a man someday, as if being a talking frog were kind of a tadpole stage for being a certain kind of man.

She realized that she was very tired. Not thinking too clearly. Unfocused, she sat and stared blearily, without blinking, at the coins lying in the fountain. They were mostly pennies. Kind of golden. Underwater. Circles, circles, rippling, magnified, big, bigger than pennies, gold circles, gold ripples, gold rings. Interesting, how a pool of water made everything look different. Buffy dipped her hand into the water, then lifted it and watched the drops fall like liquid light from her fingertips. She watched them splash and make rings. She put her hands into the water, both of them, then dabbed water on her face, her eyes. She expected cold, to wake her up, but it was not cold, not at all; it was as warm as transparent blood, soaking into her skin as if it were a part of her. She shifted her glazed gaze to the statue atop its pedestal, the deer, rearing. A stag with antlers of gold, filigree wings. She stared and waited, so exhausted she knew what would happen.

It did.

The stag moved, flexing its muscular neck to rear higher, leaping away from its pedestal. It soared on real golden-eagle wings instead of silly filigree, and looked down on her with eyes so wise she had to look away. She lowered her gaze and saw the bearcats lolling on breasty boulders around the pool, sunning themselves, their fuzzy tummies turned fearlessly to the sky. A dense and convoluted forest rose all around, lavender green dilly dilly, a mazy, layered, intertwined, up-down-and-sideward forest, not at all like the thin and boring vertical Pennsylvania forest where she had met Prince Adamus d'Aurca. This was the Forest Multifarious, a living labyrinthine complication so tall that the sky showed only as a tinted dome far overhead. Birds called, invisible. The air smelled like hollyhocks.

A splish-splash plashing made her look down as an eight-inch, dark torpedo shape swam up to her. She blinked. For a moment the frog, gleaming wet, had been not quite a frog.

"LeeVon?"

"Yepperdoodles." He was really a very nice guy. Could have said sarcastically, "Who else did you think it might be? You know a lot of frogs with nose rings and tattoos?" But LeeVon hardly ever seemed to get sarcastic.

"Don't mind me," Buffy said. "For a moment there, you were looking kind of phallic."

"Why, thank you, Best Beloved." LeeVon hopped out of the water to perch on the stone beside her, puffing proudly, with his head up like a—Buffy blinked again at the phrase that came to mind, drew back, and gave him a hard glance askance.

"Uh, LeeVon. This pool got a name?" She was thinking that Adamus had said something about a pool. LeeVon was a superlibrarian. He would know.

He did. "I believe they are all inclusively named the Collective Unconscious."

"Oh. I see." Buffy didn't quite see, but she did have all too firm a grasp—mental grasp—of one concept. "Well, I apologize."

"Pardon?"

"I apologize. Apparently turning a guy into a frog is kind of a hands-on way of calling him a prick."

"Hands-on?"

"Shut up." She turned away from the sleekly throbbing frog with gold rings in its nostrils to look around. So this was the place. The Forest Multifarious. Hootoo birds. A wise-eyed deer circling overhead on golden wings. A white snake rippling past.

Buffy breathed deeply—now the air smelled of coltslip. She felt good in this place, better than she had felt in a long time, certainly better than she had ever felt in any ordinary shopping mall. She did not feel at all tired anymore. She said to LeeVon, "We ought to be able to find Emily now."

Prince Adamus turned his head from side to side upon the petal-soft pillow but did not awaken. His sleep was made of gossamer chains as whisper-strong as the Queen's touch. He could not awaken, not yet. To awaken would have been to grieve, perhaps to act—thoughts unbefitting a fairy-tale prince. Therefore, until it was time to dress in fine garments and return to court, it was better for him to sleep and be beautiful.

Beautiful, he slept.

As befitted a medieval prince, he slept naked between sheets that smelled of coltslip and amaranth. His shoulders flexed, and he dreamed not of the flowers but of Emily. He slept naked and alone.

He lay on a bed quilted out of sweet rushes and silk, smelling of bluebells and asphodel. The bed was cupped in a bower braided thick with briar roses. The bower grew out of the bight of a great white wych oak tree taller than a tower. The tree swayed in a dark wind. In the treetop the bed swayed.

Adamus stirred in his sleep and moaned. He arched his back as if in pain. He whispered, "Emily . . ."

Where was she?

His dreams were dark and troubled, though he did not awaken. Of her own accord she would not have left him. What had they done with her? Where had she gone?

* * *

"It's getting dark," LeeVon said.

"Your point being?" Balancing her way along a horizontal limb far above the ground, or floor, whatever, Buffy spoke sharply—but since searching the upper galleries of the mall for Emily now meant climbing around in the forest canopy, she felt entitled to a little edge in her tone. Needing both hands free, she had stowed LeeVon in her bra, specifically in her cleavage, where he had become annoying. His wet feet tickled. He talked too much. She wished he would just stay quiet and allow her to forget about him and concentrate on not breaking her neck—but he insisted on squirming around and poking his head out of her shirt and making useless comments.

"My point being, we ought to be heading back. I have to get to the Pony Ride."

"Back" seemed so far away that for a moment she did not know what he was talking about. "The Pony Ride?"

"The bar where we hope to get some sexy guy drunk enough to unfrog me."

Buffy had forgotten about LeeVon's agenda for the evening and his life. Even under normal circumstances she would have found it a bit of a strain to escort a frog to a gay bar—she had never felt comfortable in bars, gay or otherwise, and did not usually go into them—and at this point she felt like she couldn't deal with it. Her surge of energy had worn off, or playing Ms. Tarzan had taken it out of her, and once more she felt exhausted. Had not eaten or slept in far too long. Drifting in a state beyond exhaustion. Go to the Pony Ride and party? Somebody had to be kidding.

As her mama had raised her to be nice, she hedged, of course. "I don't think I can find the way out of here anymore." One of her childhood nightmares had involved getting separated from her mother in a big store and getting lost and being locked in the big dark store overnight with all that spooky merchandise. The nightmare had made her hate big stores for years. She still hated them. But nightmares can be useful sometimes.

"You found the john," LeeVon pointed out.

This was true. The odd thing was, the mall was still a mall. Walls still rose, or rather, trees rose like a wall. Needing to pee, Buffy had managed to part the lavender-green foliage long enough to find a real ladies' room, apparently in Nordstrom's.

LeeVon said, "It's not like there's only one way out of here, Best Beloved. This is a mall. It has lots of entrances."

"So?"

"So there are lots of ways out of here."

"Not necessarily. People get into here lots of ways, that's all." Into this place that was a place yet not a place. Where everything was itself yet something else.

"Maybe so, Best Beloved. But you can get us out." LeeVon spoke with a calm certainty that was more than cheerleading, more like faith in her.

Undeserved.

Silently Buffy balanced her way to where she could brace her hands against a tree trunk. Then she stood still and spoke the truth. "Maybe I could, but I'm not. No way am I leaving here without Emily."

LeeVon lost his calm. "Buffles, you promised!"

"I didn't exactly promise; I intended. Look, things change, plans change. With any sort of luck I can get you to the bar tomorrow night."

"You said! That counts as a promise."

"Not really."

"In this place it does." LeeVon's voice shot from a childish whine to a low . . . threat? Was it anger Buffy was hearing, or concern? She could not interpret. "They're serious about promises here."

"I can't help that. I'm not leaving without Emily." Buffy

added hastily, "Look, LeeVon, I'm sure we can find somebody to kiss you here."

"Oh, *right*. Like I'm going to hop up to some guy and say, 'Kiss me and I'll turn into a librarian.' "

Buffy leaned against the tree trunk and closed her pulsing eyes.

"It's risky enough going up to guys when I'm *human*," LeeVon grumbled.

Buffy pressed her hands to her eyelids.

"Oh, for God's sake." LeeVon sounded peevish but resigned. "Just get me to a fountain. I'm all dried out." They had ditched the paper towels someplace. Maybe in the Disney store. Talk about plastic. There was a place that took soul cake from all over the world and turned it into sugar and celluloid. Even seeing lavender green, Buffy could not make Disney come alive. Mannequins said, "May I help you?" in there.

Soul cake?

Fountain. The immediate problem was a fountain for LeeVon.

Buffy found a spiral vine to take her down to the understory, then a leaning trunk the rest of the way to the ground. To find a pool she followed the sound of splashing water. A hootoo bird flew right by her head, flashing its crazy grin. A ferret or something slipped into the underbrush. Must be passing the pet store. On the floor, growing right out of the tiles, bloomed flowers so yellow they seemed alight. Coltsfoot? Primrose? Cowslip? Coltslip, that was the word, coltslip.

Bright round stones wavered in the bottom of the pool. No, coins. Pennies and things. Fountain. Buffy sat on the stone rim and watched LeeVon leap in with that distinctive froggy *ker-plop*. Watched him scud away. Watched the ripples and the pennies reflecting the fading light. Looked up. This was the fountain with the statue of a girl on the high pedestal. A very beautiful girl with her golden hair pulled straight back Alice-in-Wonderland-fashion above her serious golden eyes. She had a garland of golden roses and she had a golden ball in her dainty white hands, but no one to play with. Lovely girl. She had to be lonely up there, thirty feet above the water on her narrow tower. Now Buffy noticed the golden star shining on her forehead, very bright against the night gathering in the glass dome.

"That's a princess," she said aloud.

LeeVon popped his head out of the pool. "C'mon in," he called to her. "The water's fine."

"No, thank you." Swim? She felt more likely to fall asleep in there and drown. Trying to keep herself going, forgetting that the pool was not chilly but as warm as a womb, she leaned over and splashed that limpid water on her face and eyes.

When she looked up again, the princess on the pedestal was Emily, scowling down at her.

Buffy lunged to her feet, clambered up, and teetered on the rim of the fountain, hands stretched toward this princess presence that was ineluctably her daughter. Her mouth moved, but only croaking noises came out.

"What are *you* doing here?" Emily asked icily.

"Graaah—graah—graa—"

"Found yourself another talking frog to lord it over, I see."

"Looking for you!" One exchange too late, Buffy finally got it together in regard to vocalization. "Honey, are you all right? Have you been keeping warm? Are your allergies bothering you? Do you need your inhaler?"

Where did you sleep? How much of yourself did you give to him?

Emily rolled her eyes and did not answer either the spoken questions or the unspoken ones.

Is there any of you left for me?

"Are you all right?" Buffy demanded, neck cranked all the way back to look at her daughter.

"Sure. Why wouldn't I be?" But Emily's tone had thawed marginally. She flounced her creamy lace-festooned skirts out of the way, sat on the edge of her plinth, swung her slippered feet, and peered down. *"Mom,"* she decreed from on high, "that shirt doesn't match your jeans at all. Not even close."

For God's sake. It was Buffy's turn to scowl. "Get down from there," she commanded.

"Like how?"

Buffy opened her mouth and shut it again, feeling her eyes getting froggishly large.

Emily spoke quickly to revise her spontaneous response. "It's nice up here," she declared. "I like it."

"Yes, heaven forbid your mother should think you need help."

"You shouldn't be here, Mom. It's dangerous here." Emily said this with smooth-faced bemusement. Fair Peril meant nothing to her personally; she was young and therefore certain that nothing irreversible could happen to her. But it surprised her to see her mother venturing there.

"You should talk. I'm not the one imprisoned on top of a—"

"It's not a prison!" Emily flounced to her feet, glaring.

"No?"

"No. It's a, um, a great honor. Because I belong to Adamus, you see." When Emily mentioned the name, her hard young face softened into a starry-eyed smile, her chest swelled, her voice lilted. "He's so sweet. He adores me."

"So he put you on a pedestal."

"No, Mom." But Emily lost her smile, looking unsure. "Anyway," she added loyally, "it's an awesome view."

"Does he come around to *feed* you?"

"Of course that would be what you'd think of." The golden star on Emily's forehead blazed with the force of her youthful scorn. "Like I need to eat?"

"Of course you need to eat." Buffy felt panic begin to pound in her temples. She had to get Emily down, had to get her down, there had to be a way—why hadn't she paid more attention in physics class, damn it? Think. Think. Okay, maybe she could run cables down from the trees— no, across from the galleries—no; if she broke the statue, then Emily would be in pieces—

A distant but insistent noise kept trying to demand her attention. It was like somebody was talking at her from a building next door through a garbage chute or something. With her focus thoroughly on Emily, Buffy barely noticed the interruption—but then a large, forceful hand grabbed her upper arm.

Buffy spun around, nearly toppling into the pool. Ogres, two of them! Blue ogres a head taller than she was and about twice as wide. She gasped and fought to break free, threw herself from side to side, tried to flee, but one had a dragon grip on her and the other one snagged her other arm. She struggled wildly.

"Come with us, ma'am. You're only making it worse."

Cops?

Damn.

The sudden change in her perception staggered her, and the cops took advantage of her discombobulation to get her moving. They whisked her toward a mall entrance, and Buffy had never considered herself a very whiskable person. Son of a bitch, this new fact of life, that things were themselves plus something else, could be a pain in the butt. "I was just trying to talk with my daughter," Buffy protested. "Emily!" She lagged, sagged, dragged her feet, making herself as heavy as possible, trying to look back over her shoulder, but all she saw was mall—Waldenbooks, people, SALE signs, and railings—as they hustled her along. "What did I do?" she appealed. "Is there a rule against standing on the edge of the fountain?"

"You're wanted for questioning." The cop sounded so utterly bored that Buffy knew he had told her this before. It was humiliating how bored the cops were after the fight she had put up. It was embarrassing how people were staring.

The other cop said, "You are Madeleine Murphy, correct?"

"Buffy."

"Yes, ma'am. You're wanted for questioning concerning the whereabouts of Prentis Sewell."

Tempestt sat in the middle of the thick parlor carpet, sorting through decorator magazines and waiting for the phone to ring. The cops were in the other room, by the downstairs extension, waiting right along with her. The cops seemed to think that the phone should ring, somebody should call to state a political manifesto or demand ransom or something. Tempestt didn't think so. No reason; she just didn't think so. She had no theories, didn't like to overwork her brain, but she expected that, wherever Prentis was, he would find a way to get home soon enough. Meanwhile, she was worried about him, of course, but she could not honestly say she missed him. It was nice to be able to sit and look at her magazines without Prentis wanting her for something. Prentis could be a real ass-hassle when he was around the house.

As Prentis's second wife, Tempestt had recently achieved that uncomfortable point in the marriage where she was beginning to understand why the first marriage had failed. The simple truth was, while Prentis put up a huge ego front, he had to be the most insecure man on the unhappy face of the planet.

Always stewing about something. Always anxious about something else. Always wanting to know where she'd been, what she'd been doing, who she'd talked with. Jealous. Always jerking his chin up in the air and looking at her narrow-eyed, like he'd never believe her no matter what she did or said.

Well, so much for the honeymoon. No wonder he thought everybody cheated; he had cheated on Buffy, hadn't he? With her, Tempestt. And now that he was married to her, he would probably cheat on her too. Fine. Whatever. The minute she found out he was fooling around, she would stop going to bed with him, but she was going to stay married to him, and she wasn't going to let him drive her over the edge like Buffy. Poor Buffy. If the woman wasn't so nutso, Tempestt would have liked to have lunch with her. They could have a lot of fun comparing notes about Prentis.

It was so great having the place to herself, with Emily gone too. That girl was a major pain in the ass. Miss No-Meat Superiority with her special menus.

Tempestt found a vanilla-raspberry-pistachio color scheme she really liked, dog-eared the page, then looked up with an unfocused gaze. A thought had just occurred to her out of nowhere: suppose Emily's absence and Prentis's were connected somehow? Like, bad people had both of them?

Nah.

She turned back to her color scheme and found another one on the next page that she liked even better, lemonade-apricot-whortleberry, but looked up again, frowning; there was that damn smell. Some sort of heavy swampy odor had gotten into the house somehow—probably Prentis would know what it was. That was the main thing men were good for, knowing about houses and cars and stuff. Tempestt would ask him about the smell when he got back. It was kind of annoying that she couldn't figure out where it was coming from. Like, it seemed to move around. She would go into a room, and it wouldn't be there, and then it would. Sometimes she could swear it was following her.

Well, hell, let it smell. In thirty seconds her nose wouldn't notice it anyway. That was the way noses were built. Which was a good thing when families had to share bathrooms. Tempestt flipped back and forth between the pages, comparing the vanilla-raspberry-pistachio room to the lemonade-apricot-whortleberry one.

The phone rang.

Tempestt jumped up to get it, pausing until the cop in the doorway gave her the nod so both she and the cop on the extension picked up at the same time.

"Hello? Oh, hi, Amber."

It was not a kidnapper, just a friend with whom she chatted happily. "Nuh-uh, nothing yet. I figure he's just trying to make me worried. Huh? Sure. Like, testing me. He doesn't trust me. Well, what do I expect, I was the other woman . . . huh? No, he's not all that great in bed. I'd have an affair in a minute, but why risk it? I'd rather have money than sex anyway. Yeah, it's more fun and less trouble. Huh? Yeah, I'm okay, except I've got this headache from this stupid smell." Which seemed to be getting ranker and pissier by the minute. "Yeah, there's this awful kind of locker-room odor in the house."

And sometimes, swear to God, she felt like something was watching her. Like Prentis was right there watching her with his reassure-me eyes. But whoa, Tempestt did not mention that part. She did not want to go over the edge like Buffy.

"He went back into the house and I left," Buffy said for the sixth time.

"You went there to ask him to 'do something' about finding your missing daughter."

"Yes." Buffy had gotten tired of talking to these cops. They didn't really listen. Gave the impression that they didn't believe her.

"At three o'clock in the morning."

"I couldn't sleep, so why should he?"

"In your nightgown."

"I was upset."

"And he said he was going to get a restraining order, told you your daughter was probably already pregnant, went back inside, and closed the door."

"Yes."

"And you simply left."

"Yes. I went home and reported Emily missing, and then I tried to get some sleep." This was most certainly the truth. Buffy had told them basically the truth, omitting only the part about having turned Prentis into a fog. Though she was too tired to feel any guilt—moreover, Prentis was such a slime-enhanced primitive life form that he deserved whatever happened to him—still, she saw no sense in trying to explain Prentis's transfogrified condition to these cops when they were not even capable of understanding that Emily was imprisoned in statue form on top of a pillar at the mall, as she had repeatedly told them.

"Do you have any idea where your ex-husband is now?"

"If he's not in the house, then I don't know." Enough of this crap. "He hasn't been missing for twenty-four hours yet, has he?" Buffy's tone conveyed some feeling. "How come you're looking for him, hauling people in to question them, the whole Dragnet routine, but when I call to say my sixteen-year-old daughter has run off with a naked frog, they tell me I have to wait for twenty-four hours before I report her missing?" It stunk that a politician was perceived as worth more than a young girl was.

The cops were watching her steadily. There were three of them in the little room, two standing and one seated, just like on every cop show she had ever seen. "You're upset now," said the seated one, who was doing the honors. "The way you were upset when you last spoke to your ex, right?"

"Damn straight I'm upset!"

"And did I understand you to say 'frog'?"

"Yes. Well, I meant—oh, my God." Buffy sat straight up in her chair, having just remembered something. "LeeVon."

"What's that?"

"I left LeeVon in the fountain at the mall."

"LeeVon?"

"LeeVon Trubble. He's a librarian. Well, actually, right now he's a frog, but you can tell him from the other frogs because he has rings all over his head and a tattoo of Mowgli on his butt. That and, of course, the fact that he talks." Buffy started to rise from her chair. "I've got to—"

A large though not ungentle hand on her shoulder constrained her to keep her seat. "Ma'am," the seated cop said, "there's a nice, clean, comfortable facility on the other side of town, and we are going to take you there."

"Huh?"

"I want you to go in for psychiatric evaluation, ma'am. It's strictly voluntary, but I want to explain that if you don't go, I will have to arrest you for beating up on these officers here."

One of the silent cops, not the one with his hand on her shoulder but the other one, unexpectedly spoke. "Uh, Chief. Something that jingled did crawl out of that fountain and bite me on the ankle. Felt like a goddamn stapler, only it was alive. I—"

The chief swiveled in his chair and glared. "Don't you start now."

"Oh, poor LeeVon." Buffy struggled again to stand up. "I've got to get back. I can't just leave him there."

"Ma'am, you're not going anywhere except to the smiley-face ward."

Nine

*B*uffy fell asleep in the cruiser on the way to the hospital. Being a passenger in a vehicle of any sort often had that effect on her. And once she started sleeping, she couldn't stop, she was so beat-to-meat-dead-on-her-feet exhausted. She fell asleep again during admission. She walked in a narcoleptic trance to her room. "Looks like there's no need for sedation," somebody said. From other rooms came bizarre humanoid noises, but Buffy didn't care: this place was more sane and under control than her life was at the moment. She slept.

She zonked through the night and napped through the next day, between meals and shrinkly evaluations. The food sucked. As for the shrinks—well, it was wonderful to have anyone listen to her with as much interest as they did. If the food had been a bit better and if it hadn't been for Emily and LeeVon, Buffy would have been tempted to stay. She enjoyed herself. When the shrinks asked her questions, she told them stories—the one about the goose girl and the talking horse Falada, whose severed yet speaking head hung under the gateway; the one about the youngest son and the toad and the treasure; some others. Between stories, she told them about Adamus and about turning Prentis into a fog by mistake when she had really only meant to turn him into a frog. They listened quite attentively and nodded greatly. Buffy liked them, and they assured her that they liked her too. A lot. They were probably going to want to keep her there forever.

Getting out was no problem, however. Buffy phoned a co-worker who owed her a small favor and asked the woman to stop by her house after work and bring her a few things—if she was going to stay in the kookiehouse for long, she needed a few things, right? Right. So the friendly co-worker used the house key kept in the hyper-realistic plastic dog poop and brought Buffy, as requested, her toothbrush and toothpaste, some spare socks and underwear, and her nightgown. Specifically, her star-spangled nightgown. With the obsessive insistence that is humored in those who have gone gaga, Buffy had instructed the woman to bring her that nightgown and no other. "Appropriate garb," she had babbled. "The rules are quite strict, you know."

At about two in the morning, when there was nobody around except the graveyard shift, Buffy lay clad quite naturally in her nightgown, which was appropriate garb for sleeping, but she was not sleeping. Having slept half the day, she was wide awake, silent, and waiting. When the la-la ward seemed quiet enough for her purpose, she heaved herself up, put on sneakers and socks instead of slippers, and headed out of her room and down the hallway, toward freedom.

The young man behind the desk said, "Can I help you with something, Ms. Murphy?" All of the staffers in this place were very polite with patients who remained non-violent. He did not say, "Where the hell do you think you're going in your nightgown?" And he would chitchat a minute or two, making friendly noises, before he ordered, "Okay, Ms. Murphy, it's time for you to go back to your room now."

Buffy told him, careful to spell it right this time, "Gimme an F, F! Gimme an R, R! Gimme an O, O! Gimme a G, G!"

He watched her in the same bored, smirking way that the cops had watched her. In the face of that sense of superiority, it was easy to coddle anger over medium heat.

"What's it spell? FROG!" Then Buffy did not have to cheerlead any further. She walked around the desk, extracted the enfrogged staffer from the muddle of his clothes lying on the carpeting, then found his keys—they were what she wanted; enfrogging this poor guy was just a way of making him small and portable enough for her to handle. She fished the keys out of his trousers pocket and unclipped them from his belt. Meanwhile, she held on to him so that she would not step on him by mistake or lose him. "Where's my stuff?" she asked.

"Graa—graaa—" He seemed distraught.

"Oh, never mind." She had spotted the bank of little drawers, like safety-deposit-box drawers. She found the one with her name on it and used the little key to open it. Wallet, car keys, everything was there. Fine. Using the big key, she unlocked the ward door. "Don't tell anybody about this," she warned the frog gently, "or they'll want to dissect you." Then she kissed him, a businesslike smack. Lucky thing he was a guy, and—yes, he seemed to be hetero. Human again, but almost as bug-eyed as a frog, he stood naked and dumbfounded, attempting to cover the most interesting part of him with his hands. Buffy figured he would want to get his clothes on before he did anything about her escapade. Still, she did not have much time. She resisted the urge to take a good look, instead catching only a glimpse as she waved good-bye and twinkled down the corridor.

Twinkled quite literally. She glowed in the dark, or her stars and crescents and planets did.

"Hey!" yelled a security guard in a startled and unprofessional tone. Buffy yanked the nightgown up above her knees and ran.

Like a rhinoceros, Buffy didn't have world-class acceleration, but once she got her mass moving, then inertia kept her barreling along quite fearsomely. She found a door, ran outside—alarms went off. She ran some more, across the too-damn-big parking lot, then into a bewilderment of alleys. She ran until it was close to heart-attack time, then ducked behind somebody's garage and leaned against its cinder-block wall gasping for breath, rasping and coughing and trying to listen; she couldn't hear a thing above the thundering of her heart.

As soon as she could, she walked on, trying to keep to the shadows even though she shone like a constellation. Briefly she considered ditching the nightgown; nakedness would have made her no more conspicuous than a five-foot-six white mushroom sneaking through the night. Right. Turn the nightgown inside out? Not a bad plan, would have meant exposing her fungal flesh only for a moment—but wait. Somebody's compost heap. Buffy whipped off the black plastic covering and wrapped it around herself, capelike. So what if Zorro never smelled like this. Dimmed and aromatic but dashing, she walked on.

Okay, buckle that swash. All she had to do was get to the mall, break in, swing from a chandelier or something, and rescue LeeVon and Emily.

While eluding the cops.

What LeeVon really hated about being a frog, he decided, was feeling so cold and naked all the time. He liked clothes, dammit. Leathers weren't exactly cozy, but they had substance. They had a nice, aromatic, natural armoring quality. Manly. Whereas being a frog wasn't a damn bit manly.

His throat shivered. He squatted in the darkness in a few inches of water at the edge of the pool, keeping to the shadow of one of the boulders, alert for the approach of a bearcat or any other predator; already he had experienced terrifying escapes from a blue fox and a preternaturally nimble raccoon. Shift his perception a tad, he knew, and he would be squatting on the faux-marble edge of a mall fountain, but that would be no safer. People, or most people, were just as dangerous as raccoons to a frog on his own. At least this way there was a chance of a stray minnow. Food.

Either way, there was a chance that Buffy would come back for him.

Buffy. LeeVon's throat throbbed. What was going on with her? Once upon a time, Best Beloved, there was a large and talented woman named Madeleine—but LeeVon knew only the beginning of the story. Once upon a time Madeleine had a missing daughter . . . What's the story, Morning Glory?

Why was he squatting cold, wet, hungry, naked, and frogiform in the darkness of a benighted shopping mall?

LeeVon was a storyteller. Instinctively he knew that things like this happened for a purpose; he had long been conscious of his place as a minor character in a major and inscrutable story that encompassed the whole world of humanity. His talent was to act as a conduit of story; other people, if they had the heart, could find their stories in the books LeeVon ensorcelled with his hands. Sometimes he could help, sometimes he could see what other people needed to know. But he could not seem to help himself. LeeVon did not yet know his own story.

Once upon a time there was a nice enough guy named

LeeVon who—who was gay; did that factor in? Not necessarily. He knew gay people who were loved, who had
true love.

Whereas here he sat cold, starving, all freaking alone.
No one who loved him, no one to kiss him and make him
better.

A nice guy with no goddamn story of his own.

Dammit. Was he sitting in this cold, wet mess of difficulty just because he'd gotten sucked into being a croaker
in Buffy's chorus? Was he supposed to squat here and be
wretched until she came back?

Couldn't think of any other option except to die and
have it done with.

An option that seemed more attractive with every slowly
dripping minute.

Oh, woe. Oh, exceeding unfair misery. Desolation
twisted in LeeVon's belly, surged between his narrow
shoulders, and swelled his throat. He could keep silent no
longer. Like an anorexic green-skinned Job, he cried out to
the god of frogs.

"Grooonk," LeeVon protested. "GROOOONK."

He had never croaked before. It provided a wonderful
release. Moreover, he discovered in moving to a better lo-
cation, one could do it underwater, where it reverberated
interestingly through the ripples of the pool. But even better was to perch on a wet stone, noise pointed toward the
dark dome of sky like a ranine coyote, eyes bugged wide,
and let forth.

"Roooogie," LeeVon lamented. "Roo—grooo—
GROOOOOOONK." To the starless sky.

He had thought that sky was dark. But it was not. It was
serene gray twilight compared to the shadow that now
possessed it.

"GRAAWK!"

The worst thing about wishing is that sometimes you

get what you ask for. The worst thing about crying skyward is that sometimes something answers.

The god of all frogs, or so it seemed to LeeVon, hurtled down upon him.

With its chunky arms and legs spread like a flying squirrel, it plummeted—huge, a black monstrosity rapidly blotting out the sky, appalling. LeeVon caught just a glimpse of its glinting crown and its smoldering golden eyes before he yelped, pissed himself, and fled.

He leaped for a crack between two boulders and wedged himself as far under their bellies as he could. The next instant the megafrog flopped into the pool, sending forth a tidal wave that nearly drowned him.

"Ungrateful newt!" the frog roared. From where LeeVon watched and trembled, it seemed all mouth, a vast, gaping maw unto darkness, the gullet of hell. "Whining salamander! You dare to disturb my rest? Show yourself!"

The god-sized ranine presence was so awful and fearsome that LeeVon wanted to close his eyes, but of course he could not. No eyelids. He had to look. The monster was more like a huge toad than a frog. Squatting in the water, it dominated the fountain and vicinity like a sumo wrestler in a kiddie pool.

It had a golden crown. It had the golden cape of royalty.

"Insolent polliwog!" Its great eyes seared the darkness, searching. "Where is your noise now? Don't you want to croak?"

No, LeeVon most certainly did not want to croak, not in any sense of the word, not anymore. But his whole body was one terrified spasm of trembling. His throat constricted, emitting a terrified ribbet.

Instantly those searing eyes swiveled and found him.

Oh, God. Oh shit oh cloaca doing exactly that oh God. "Mighty one, I'm very very very sorry I bothered you," LeeVon gabbled. Oh, God, was he sorry. He was trembling so violently that all his little facial rings jingled, ethereal, like the fabled ringing of bluebells that lured unwary mortals to a supernatural death. "I didn't mean to. I didn't mean—"

"Silence!" bellowed the mighty one.

LeeVon shut up but couldn't be silent enough. He quaked. He jingled. He was trying so hard to disappear under the boulders that he was bruising himself.

Hard eyes regarded him. "If it were not that you are afflicted with disgusting excrescences," the mighty frog said in harsh and measured tones, "you would be eaten." Then there was a horrible blur—its pale sticky tongue, as long as a spear, shooting through the darkness straight at—

LeeVon screamed.

And damn near fainted. But the tongue didn't quite reach him. The god-frog let out a roar that might have been a laugh and turned its vast back. The next moment, amid a great roiling of water, LeeVon saw it fly up.

It was impossible. That hulk, flying? Yet it flew. The huge thing had little wings—what LeeVon had taken to be a cape was its folded wings. It flew heavily and unnaturally, like a bumblebee. Its flying was a perversion of the graceful flying of frogs without wings, their balletic leaps, their trapeze-artist trajectories, and their sometimes deaths. Flights unto smashed landing. Leaps unto asphalt doom.

LeeVon let out a shivering sigh and extracted himself from his hiding place as gently as he could, trying not to leave too much of his thin green skin behind.

To be a frog was to be always frightened. Even the god of all frogs was just another predator. Already LeeVon's memories of the great ranine presence were fading, his terror was lessening, because such extreme terror would not allow him to survive. LeeVon perched on his wet rock again, watching for a minnow to swim by, settling down to working on another hour or two of survival.

Getting into the mall at 4 A.M. turned out to be not as much of a problem as Buffy had envisioned, simply because the cops were there ahead of her. Searching the place. The main doors to the anchor store hung wide open, guarded by empty cruisers with their flashers going reddy bluey reddy bluey. Buffy walked in, positioned herself in the women's fashion department, wrapped her black plastic inclusively around herself, and became an avant-garde display.

None too soon. Voices coming.

"Probably that damn bird," one of them was saying as a squadron of thick rubber soles tramped past. "A goddamn robin got in somehow, it's nesting on a strut or something. It doesn't fly around at night, but it poops and the motion detectors go crazy."

"Not to speak of the interior decorators."

"And the people who get pooped on."

"Yeah, well, shoot the damn bird, would you?"

"How can we? Fancy glass all over the place. Anyway, shoppers don't like it when Mr. Robin flutters down all bloody. Ruins the ambience."

There was a volley of male laughter. Cops and security guards stood outside the entrance exchanging friendly fire. "At least you guys got here halfway fast this time," one of the security guards said.

"Well, one of the wack trackers got loose from the wacky ward tonight. We thought it might be her."

Their backs were turned. Still wrapped in her black plastic, looking rather like an Iranian woman in a chador, Buffy shuffled quietly away. "Is she dangerous?" somebody was asking.

Ask Prentis.

Once safely around the corner, Buffy let her makeshift cloak fall away from her face and hustled down the mezzanine, past the first fountain, where the giant frog crouched heavily on its pedestal. She glanced up. Odd; the frog's mottled metal body shone wetly, as if it had just been in for a swim.

The sculptor, whoever it was, had made the thing about the same size as the other components of the conceptual triptych, the deer and the princess—which meant that, though deer and girl were the right size for themselves, the frog was the wrong size for a frog. Way too big. Why was it that changing the right size of something should make it loom so? The statue of a deer, life-sized, had seemed sweetly beautiful; the princess, life-sized, likewise—but this frog's oversized, lumpen, wetly shining presence was so disturbing that Buffy stopped and stared.

There was not much light. Shadowy, the frog towered against the glass dome, a squat, gargoyle silhouette topped by the glint of a golden crown. Why hadn't the sculptor understood that frogs should be sleek, not gross and flabby? Leaden, fleshy, massive, it was an ugly statue. Buffy felt as if its murky eyes were watching her.

Jesus. She had no time for this kind of crap. She got herself moving again.

She hustled to the next fountain and crouched by its rim. "LeeVon!" she whispered as loudly as she dared.

"Buffy? Oh, Best Beloved. Thank God." Buffy could not see much—it was dim in the mall despite the security lighting—but she could hear the plash of water as LeeVon swam over to her, sleek, comely, gleaming, all that a frog should be.

"Are you all right?" She held out her hands.

"No, I'm not all right. I'm starving." LeeVon tried to clamber out of the pool and fell back into the water.

"LeeVon!" She grabbed him and cradled him in her

palms, where he crouched and shivered and dripped.

"Starving," he said rapidly but intensely. "It is not a good thing to be a frog with a stud in its tongue, Best Beloved."

"God, I'm stupid. I never thought." Buffy had imagined every other kind of danger for LeeVon—getting stepped on; killed by mall security; captured by some Norman Rockwell-style boy who wanted a frog to thrust all too symbolically at girls—but she hadn't realized he might starve. The omission made her upset with herself. "Pork for brains. Duh. There's no flies in a mall."

"There are, Best Beloved, there are beautiful flies! Dragonflies hovering over the lily pads, lacewings clinging to the rushes, mayflies—but I can't catch them." LeeVon's voice rose deliriously, as if he were crazy with hunger, hallucinating.

Except Buffy knew it was not just a hallucination.

"Shhhh. Ogres on the prowl." In the dim 4 A.M. light she, too, began to be able to see the lily pads, the rushes, and, beyond the fringes of the pool, the clusters of coltslip folded until dawn, the lavender-shadowy forest looming. Quickly, afraid the pillar might somehow disappear if she were not quick, she looked upward for Emily, the princess on the pedestal; was Emily hungry? Could Emily lie down on that narrow plinth and sleep? Was she lonely? Would there be something soft wrapped around her, a quilt, a comforter?

Buffy gasped. The tall pedestal rose empty. She forgot ogres; only shock kept her from shouting. "Emily! She's gone!"

"Is she? I—I can't see that far."

"Yes, she is! There's nothing up there, nothing at all! Where is she?"

"I don't know."

"How can you not know? You were right there all the time."

"I'm a *frog*," LeeVon said, "and I'm starving, and I had a few other things to think about, such as staying alive and not getting eaten by a hedgehog or some goddamn thing."

"But you had to notice how she came down from there!"

"Don't tell me what I had to do." True to the company he was in, LeeVon began to sound hysterical. "I had to dig in the mud for worms, was what I had to do, and then I had to bite the back ends off while the front ends were still burrowing, and then I had to try not to puke. I need *food*, dammit! You want me to pee in your hands?" Buffy could feel him quivering like lime Jell-O.

"All right, okay." At least Emily was down off the pedestal, free. She might be better off.

Crap, no, it was not okay. Buffy was going to have to find the girl all over again. Start all over.

"Goddammit."

"Best Beloved, *please*."

"Okay, chill out." She could feed LeeVon while she was deciding how to start. "Let me see if I can locate the food court." All the vendors would be closed, of course, but even so, a person or a frog ought to be able to scare up something to eat there.

Buffy headed upstairs. Or, more accurately, up trees.

She stowed LeeVon in her bra. Clambering up a huge vine spiraling around an even more massive beech trunk, halfway to the top it occurred to her to be surprised that she was wearing one; since when did she wear a bra under her nightgown? She glanced down at herself and nearly lost her grip. The frog-toting device was a black-sequined bustier that complemented her starry velvet gown. Her smelly plastic cape had somehow turned into a shimmering black cloak that hung in perfumed folds from her shoulders down to her feet. Forget sneakers; her footgear had transmogrified like the rest of her clothing, so that she now wore dainty black leather boots. Yes, dainty, on her size-ten feet.

Voices sounded ahead. And music.

Not cop voices. Not jukebox music. These were voices the color of dark honey. Lute and mandolin music.

LeeVon heard, too. "What the muck?" he croaked.

Lights sifted lavender blue, lavender green through the leaves. Buffy said, "We'd better sneak a peek." Hoisting herself a few more feet upward, she inched her head to where she could see what was going on.

She had attained the canopy of the huge, convoluted trees, yet she found herself standing at the edge of a vaulted hall brightly lit by golden orbs and—people, tall, fair, arrow-straight princes and princesses. Dancing or talking or eating, they themselves illuminated the ballroom with the golden, shimmering faerie glamour that emanated from them, every one, and the fey comeliness that would never grow old. People? But they were fetches, peris, shining eidolons in shining clothing—gleaming gowns streaming down, cerulean, celadon, aubergine, yellow wine; crimson silk tunics taut over broad shoulders; fringed, creamy silk sashes flowing down to brush against hard thighs in lustrous smoke-gray hose. There was too much to see: tall burgundy leather boots; long flaxen and russet and chestnut hair twined with flowers, bittersweet, feathers; stunning bodies, stunning faces—Buffy could not take it all in. And mingled with all the shimmersheen there came to her the aromas of roast suckling pork in crabapple sauce, poached fish with parsley and coriander, chicken simmered in perry, cinnamon rolls, baked quail stuffed with mushrooms and apricots, garlic snails, butter-top bread, strawberries and chocolate—she could not sort it out. Only gradually did she notice the booths lining the sides of the great hall, and the small tables, and the musicians plucking away, and presiding over it all, a personage on a seat elevated above the rest. A golden chair. A throne.

"Oh, for God's sake," she whispered. "The food *court*."

"Will they give me something to eat?" LeeVon quavered. Despite his extremity, he, like Buffy, had been transfixed by the sight of the food court, silent and staring.

"I'm not sure whether we should go in there, dude." Buffy's life had been so screwed at the time a talking frog entered it that she had not been fazed. She had not been totally staggered by all the ramifications since. But looking upon the uncanny court, she knew to her bones, as she had not known before: she was standing at the edge of something she might not be able to handle. That monarch on that throne, majesty of this place that was not a place, ruled by whims that were as sudden and wild as hawk plummet. Buffy remembered the tales of potentates who would get up one day and decide to kill all their children and grow hybrid tea roses instead. What if she failed to curtsy with sufficient grace? What if someone took a dislike to her graying hair, her opinions, her overweight body, her hippie soul? This was what Fay had been talking about: the punishments, the risks.

This was the Realm of Fair Peril.

Buffy told LeeVon softly, "You know as well as I do, all the old tales say that if you eat the food in a place like this, you can never go home again. I don't think—"

Then she saw Adamus.

Ten

$\mathcal{B}$uffy reared up like a warhorse, stepped away from her concealing tree, and strode forward.

How could they all be so different from one another, yet all be so beautiful? They were exquisite. Adamus stood among them, exquisite in his loneliness. Ineluctably he was the shadowed one; something of late-day sadness in his aureate glow had let Buffy pick him out, a hint of patina in his golden hair, darkness under his golden brows, dusky amethyst velvet under his golden tabard. He walked alone, straying from group to group, and even when he stood and exchanged greetings with the others, he gave the sense that he stood apart.

Madeleine Buffmeister Murphy strode toward him with her black cloak lifting to reveal the lambent stars on her midnight velvet gown.

Courtiers' perfect oval faces turned to stare. The crowd parted.

Adamus stood alone.

He was so beautiful, even with clothes on, that Buffy felt her heart thudding. But she hardened her face.

"Great lady," Adamus whispered. He dropped to one knee and bowed his head.

The rest of them, every gorgeous one of them, stood staring, and the lute music faltered to a halt; silence held the great hall in thrall. It had to be the black, glittering gown. Amazing what the right clothes could do.

Or the right accessories. Buffy became aware that there was a live and wriggling frog protruding from her bosom. It was hard to concentrate on the business at hand with that thing squirming between her breasts.

"Great lady," Adamus was pleading, "where is she? Please, where have you taken her? I cannot live without her. I cannot bear it."

Utilizing posture learned in a paramilitary high school phys ed class, Buffy stood majestic (she hoped) but speechless. She had expected princely arrogance of Adamus, not this appeal from the heart.

"Excuse me." LeeVon spoke feebly but with dignity from her cleavage, addressing the court. "Fairies one and all, I am an ensorcelled librarian. Does there happen to be any epicene male among you who would care to kiss me?"

"Lady," Adamus begged.

Buffy found her voice. "You parked her up there on that miserable pedestal!"

"No, I did not, gracious lady! Not of my own will. The way I feel about her—I didn't know it would do that to her. You think I wanted to imprison her? I hate myself. I am going insane."

"Anybody? Please?" LeeVon asked the assembly. "Kiss me and I will renew your overdues. No? Well, then, can somebody get me a French fry?"

Buffy said to Adamus, "You didn't put her on that pedestal, or order it, or intend it?"

"No. Things—things happen around here."

"I see."

"Or a cheese cracker?" LeeVon sounded increasingly desperate.

"Where have you taken her?" Adamus begged again. "Please, I must see her, I must talk with her."

He was an unconscionably handsome young man, yet somehow he was still Addie, her sincere bigmouthed Addie, now no longer obnoxious, only forlorn; Addie in love. She had missed him. And how could she not adore him when he had the good sense to adore Emily? Buffy did not entirely trust him, but she could not remain angry at him. Anyway, she decided, she could use him. She could make him help her find Emily.

"A corn curl?" LeeVon croaked.

Buffy lifted her hands and gently extricated LeeVon from her bustier. "Is it safe for my friend to eat here?" she asked Adamus. "Will eating turn him into one of you?"

"As if I'm not already?" LeeVon yelped before Adamus could reply. "I'm in a fairy tale, for God's sake. I'd rather stay than be dead."

Buffy looked at him.

"Wearing tights would be an improvement," he said.

He seemed quite vehemently sincere. All right, okay. Buffy thrust him at Adamus. "Would you find him something to eat?"

Adamus received LeeVon gently in his hands but stood cradling him without apparent comprehension, looking up at Buffy like a golden-eyed puppy. "Where's Emily?" he whispered.

"I don't know," Buffy told him quietly. "I thought she was with you. Would you get up off the floor and feed that frog, Addie? We've got problems."

"The gay blade in the periwinkle tunic with the tushie slits," Adamus was telling LeeVon, "he's the one you want to approach."

"Ooooh." It was an appreciative sigh with a lot of throat flutter. Apparently LeeVon liked the tushie slits, of which he had a clear view from the table atop which he squatted by Adamus's elbow. Also, he had eaten honey bread and roast suckling pork and spiced apple and several other sorts of goodies and was feeling much better.

"But not in front of the others," Adamus went on. "We're medieval here."

"Yes. This mall is certainly a Grimm place at night."

"Yes, it is. And 'fairy' is a dangerous word. Never use it."

"Okay," said LeeVon meekly. "Thank you."

Sitting opposite Adamus at the small table, Buffy had not eaten, and was listening to this exchange with no more than a quarter of her attention. She was trying to figure out how to find Emily. The first problem, as she analyzed it, was that fundamental information was missing: Emily could have gone back to the "real" world or she could be wandering in the Perilous Realm, and neither Buffy nor Adamus knew which. This initial difficulty might be solved if they could figure out how Emily came to be missing from her pedestal. Had the mall removed her for cleaning or repair? Had someone stolen her? If so, then Buffy needed to search for her daughter in the mundane world. Or had Emily somehow gotten down on her own? Then she was in the Realm of Fair Peril—but the sticking point was, LeeVon could hardly have helped but notice if Emily or anyone else had splashed through his pool, yet he had seen or heard nothing of essence. This had already been discussed. There had been a terrifying blue fox. There had been a terrifyingly nimble raccoon. There had been a consummately terrifying giant frog which Buffy correctly interpreted as the frog-king statue from the neighboring pedestal, but knowing this did not help her. The statues were statues yet themselves as well; so what? It was nothing she didn't already know.

"Addie," Buffy said.

"Yes, great lady?"

"For God's sake, I'm sitting here with frog slime between my boobs, don't call me a great lady. My name's Buffy. Addie, aside from protesting your devotion to my daughter, what else can you tell me?"

"You never let me ride there," Addie said, his golden glance drifting down to Buffy's frontage.

"Huh?"

"Uh, nothing. When I was a frog." With the instincts of a diplomat, Addie kept babbling. "I remember your glass-prison pond not too happily. The night it happened, though, I was in the silver pond. Emily came to me all in star-dark clothing. She kissed me." His face changed, and his voice, quiet to begin with, retreated so low in his throat that Buffy could barely hear him. "Never have I felt such a furor in me, not even when my father betrayed me, not even when my foster father hurled me from the battlements, not even when the Queen of the Perilous Realm placed upon me the brand of her lips. I love Emily, but it is more than that. I am her slave. She brought my soul back to me and carries it in her pocket. She owns me."

"Sounds like he imprinted on her," LeeVon said, "like a goose hatching."

Addie gave him a blank look.

"Okay, but why are you here?" Buffy asked Adamus. "Back to being a handsome prince again, I mean." She was trying not to say fairy tale, fairyland. "Back where they turned you into a frog, right? It seems like the last place you'd want to be."

"It is." Adamus's voice remained very low. "Emily and I, we were happy, thoughtless, we drove fast in the metal chariot, we—I thank you for the clothing, LeeVon." He smiled, acknowledging the frog, but the smile did not dispel the sadness in his eyes. "Black. I like black. We are not allowed to wear it here." His glance touched momentarily on Buffy's black cloak, then drifted away again. "Emily brought me to the mall to buy smallclothes. Calvin Kleins. Then we came to the food booths to eat nachos. Then—I was so happy, so unwary, I was a fool—I think the Queen reached out for us. I am not sure. But here I am again." His lips barely moved, he spoke so softly. "Still a prisoner in the old tale."

Did you kiss Emily again? Did you do more than kiss her?

Probably Buffy would not have asked. But as it happened, she had no chance to ask, for a loud and terrible clangor shook the great hall like a physical calamity—fire, dragons, earthquake, volcanic eruption! "What is it?" Buffy cried, but no one could hear her. Yet no one panicked. The musicians put down their instruments, but no one else moved. Everyone waited. As suddenly as the alarum had begun, it ended.

"An irruption from out there," Adamus told her, gesturing vaguely in the direction of the sky-tinted ceiling, the lavender-green walls. "Your world. But the guards can't see us in here."

"Guards?"

"The ones in blue."

Cops? "But they saw me when I was talking with Emily."

"Perhaps you had not completed the transition. Had your clothes transformed?"

No, they had not. But before Buffy could answer, something garishly golden and familiar, rather like a gilded parsnip, moved at the far end of the hall. Fay walked into the court.

"Oh, I see," Buffy said. She understood what the appalling noise had been. "Mall security alarm." Then her own alarm system began to go off, and her sprinkler system too, drenching her with sweat—because entering after Fay was a six-foot miasma, probably Prentis.

Buffy's first impulse was to run and hide. But pride, along with other priorities, overruled that option. She sat and sweated for only a moment before she got up and strode over to meet Fay, irritably aware that in the clothing hierarchy that seemed to prevail in this place, Fay probably outranked her; Fay wore an elaborate multilayered gold lamé evening ensemble and very large hair. But so what. Buffy demanded, "Is Emily back home?"

"NO SHE IS NOT." Fay seemed a wee bit tad bent out of shape about something. "I beg an audience," she bespoke the court in a tone that did not beg at all.

The silent throng of shining courtiers parted to form a processional aisle leading to the personage seated on the dais. Buffy had not been paying much attention to the golden orbs which illuminated the great hall, but now she saw that they were not suspended from the vaulted ceiling, as she had supposed; rather, they floated, golden bubbles of light drifting in a slow but purposeful pattern on the still air, forming swirls, sunflower whorls, moving mosaics which emanated from the hub, the monarch, the presence on a high golden throne. The smooth-faced alabaster watcher who spoke to no one. The ageless, cool-eyed Queen.

Buffy realized suddenly that the polite move would have been to introduce herself when she came in.

Oops.

In this realm, Miss Manners probably carried a whip. Wondering what the protocol might be now, post-lapse, Buffy stood where she was as Fay sailed up the aisle toward the Queen of the Perilous Realm with Prentis trailing behind her like a smoggy bridal train.

Buffy had never seen anyone in a tight skirt curtsy so low before. In fact, she could not remember when she had ever in her life seen a real person curtsy at all.

"Speak," the Queen said.

Woof?

Fay stood up and spoke, concisely (for Fay) if not eloquently. "Your Majesty, that Murphy person—" Pointing to Buffy. "—has done *this* to my son." Pointing to the cloud of haze standing by her side.

Her Majesty seemed unmoved. "So that is her name, the one in black." Chilly golden eyes turned toward Buffy. "She has not yet been properly introduced. Let her come forward."

Buffy came forward. She knew she would topple on her proboscis if she attempted a curtsy, but she knew she'd better do something obsequious, even though her boobs felt like they were about to ooze out of their bustier. Spreading her cape, she bowed as low as she dared and held it, not sure whether she was allowed to come up for air or say, Hi, I'm Buffy, nice to meet you.

"Madeleine Murphy is a superlative storyteller, your Majesty," said a male voice.

Buffy blinked, then straightened and looked. Adamus? Yes. The prince was standing by her side.

"Really," said the Queen in a voice which, like her perfect face, possessed no texture at all. "She is an entertainer? Yet she wears black? And where are her manners?"

In a voice which sounded as coarse as her hair by comparison with the Queen's, Buffy said, "Sorry, your Majesty. I've been under a lot of stress."

The Queen regarded her with shimmering golden eyes somewhat less warm than the North Star.

"Your Majesty." Fay's constraint gave Buffy an inkling of how much this thousand-year-old monarch was to be feared. "This Murphy person is not only unmannerly but spiteful. Look at my poor son."

Instead, her Majesty looked beautiful and bored, more dangerously so than Emily at her very worst.

"He deserved it," Buffy said. "Anyhow, he's improved this way. He can't talk."

Golden eyes turned on her, somewhat less bored. "You acknowledge the deed?"

"Certainly." Buffy sensed that her best chance was to flaunt her shortcomings. She wore black, which could put her either below or above everyone else here; she had spit in the eye of protocol; she might as well be outrageous and interesting. "Though I did mess up," she added. "I was trying to turn him into a frog."

"Indeed. Why?"

Because she hadn't understood at the time that she could just as easily have turned him into a rutabaga. Well, maybe not. Some words were too long and hard to spell. Buffy decided on a different reason. "Because my daughter ran away with Adamus and Fay wouldn't help me find her and Prentis didn't care. I had to do something."

"Your daughter?" The Queen of Fair Peril stirred like a sleeping snake as she made a connection. "Is that the one I immortalized on top of the pillar because Adamus adored her so?"

For a moment Buffy could not speak. Then she said sweetly between clenched teeth. "You acknowledge the deed?"

"Certainly."

A bone-deep chill of ontological awe kept Buffy from shouting some of her thoughts: witch, bitch, vixen, snake. Abstractions had never worked for Buffy; she had heard of amorality, had no feel for the concept, but face-to-face with embodied amorality, she understood it. She understood it right to the pit of her crawling gut. Some truths can be expressed only in story, and this Queen was what generations of story had made her. So ancient as to be nearly immortal, she was the stone-white bone-white beautiful one without a heart. She did not need to attempt to be evil; evil merely happened when she was in charge, because she cared about nothing anymore.

She's in me. In my mind.

"But where is the little wench now?" the Queen went on in tones of lazy puzzlement. "I seem to have mislaid her."

Buffy could not move or speak, but Adamus folded to his knees. "Greatest Majesty." He bowed his head before the Queen who had left the brand of her lips on his forehead just at the hairline. "Please, Majesty, where have you put her now, where is Emily?" His voice quivered. "I cannot eat for thinking of her."

The Queen actually smiled. "You're funny, Adamus."

Cold old heart. She's there inside me. Archetype.

"I want my son back," Fay begged.

Buffy had never heard tears in her former mother-in-law's voice before. Startled, she turned her head to see Fay's golden mascara melting, running muddily down the gullies of her cheeks.

"I'll put him back," Buffy said. Some which way. She did not yet know how.

"That's a promise. And you always keep your promises, don't you, Madeleine?" Mockery in the Queen's voice told Buffy that she knew otherwise. Of course, dammit. The bitch was in her; she knew everything.

"I'll keep this one." Those soulless golden eyes challenged her. "But I need to find Emily. Will you tell me where she is, Majesty?"

"Assuredly not. What would be the purpose?"

"To restore order."

"Nonsense. What do I care for the order of your little universe?"

Having no answer, Buffy shrugged with a lot more nonchalance than she felt. "Adamus and I will have to find her on our own, then."

The gold of those eyes heated up. "May I remind you that Adamus is *mine, my* little froggy, to amuse me?"

Just a user. Total user.

Just as Emily had said. Once again Buffy could not speak.

She could be me in a thousand years.

The Queen leaned forward on her throne, suddenly interested. "Such a face you are making, you there in your fine black cloak and starry gown. Storyteller, I will make you an offer: tell me a story, and if I am amused by it, we shall see about your daughter."

No ordinary tale would do, Buffy knew. No grade-school ghost story with hand motions and ghoulish voices. She looked around for inspiration, and found herself face-to-unface with the fog that was her ex.

The best and truest stories come from where pain is, she knew.

She said, "Once upon a time there was a handsome young prince named Prentis—"

Three pairs of golden eyes turned upon her in surprise: Fay's, Addie's, and the Queen's. Beyond them, a hundred courtiers had formed a shining ring, listening. Buffy barely saw them. Like them, she was listening for the story to come to her.

"A handsome young prince named Prentis who matriculated at a top-notch institution of higher learning," she continued. "Now, living in a chimney at this college was a grubby sort of cinderella named Buffy. The day she first saw Prentis, her heart jumped right out of her shirt and fell at his feet like a hankie, and he picked it up and absentmindedly stuffed it into his pocket. That was it. From that moment on she adored him. She cleaned herself up and shaved her legs and one thing led to another. After the usual rigors, he asked her to marry him. I will take care of you, he said. And she knew that, according to the plotline, they were supposed to live happily ever after, so she said yes."

Buffy could tell nothing from the Queen's porcelain mask of a face, but all the others were standing silent and attentive. Even the fog seemed focused on her, looming close to her, clearly defined and profoundly still.

"You are my princess now, he said. I will give you everything you need. But he had to get through law school first. So the prince and the princess worked hard. She earned tips and he earned a degree. Then they built a palace together," Buffy said, "and the prince pulled a magic pickle out of his pocket, and the magic pickle made babies, pop, pop, pop, three sweet babies to keep the princess busy and happy. And all was well. And the prince gave his princess a professional decorator and an image consultant and charge cards to pay for many clothes and much hair. And all seemed well.

"But then one day the children grew up and went away to school and the princess had time to look in the mirror. Who is this woman? she said. I don't know her. Where's Buffy? So she went outside to try to find Buffy, and she didn't come home until after suppertime. I don't want you going out like that, the prince said. It isn't safe. So he locked all the doors and took away the keys. Don't worry, he said, I'll bring you food and Prozac and *People* magazine. I'll give you everything you need.

"But I'm a prisoner, the princess cried. Let me go. No, said the prince. I can't have you gadding about and saying whatever you think. I'm going into politics. I'm going to make you princess of Camelot. But I'm not a princess, she cried, I'm not this woman in the mirror, I'm a cinderella. I'm Buffy, I'm grubby, I detest lipstick, I tell stories. You can't make me be beautiful and silent. Then no more kisses from me, he said. I have an image to maintain. And he took his magic pickle elsewhere.''

Buffy took a deep breath. It was getting difficult to maintain her storytelling tone and stance. Adamus stood close to her, too comely for comfort. Prentis loomed. The Queen was watching with a face as smooth and still as a white vase on a mantelpiece.

''Then the unprincess crawled into a chimney and curled up and huddled there, locked into the palace she had helped build, eating much ice cream, and she stayed that way for a long time.

''But one sunny day a little girl came and stood under the window and called, Maddie, Maddie! come out and play in the mud. So the unprincess rose up from her chimney and looked at the sunshine. She had gotten so fat she could not get out the doors even if they would open for her, but she went to the big decorator window and broke the glass. Then she flew out just like a big fat starling.'' Buffy spread her arms, and her black cloak spread with them, and the five-pointed stars shone sharply amid the midnight softness of her velvet gown. ''She landed in a nice gooshy puddle and made herself a little house out of mud and stones and sticks. Then Prentis came running over and said, *What* do you think you're doing? And she said, I'm a witch and you're not. Go away and let me alone, you pompous fool. He said, Don't be silly. Put that stuff away. You need me. I'm the one who takes care of you. I'm the one who's going to pay the alimony. I'm the one who can have my pickle and eat it too and keep giving you everything you need. And she said, All I need is freedom. Go away, you frog.''

In the passion of her narration Buffy swept her arms upward, then blinked, then stared as the fishy-white effluvium that was Prentis swirled, condensed, and took the shape of a huge, squatting frog made of mist, approximately six feet four inches and two hundred twenty pounds, if it had weighed anything at all. Prentis-sized.

Courtiers broke into applause; their clapping was like the ringing of a thousand glass chimes in the wind. Buffy had the presence of mind to take a bow, felt her left breast starting to dive out of her bustier, and hastily covered up with her cloak. Apparently the story was over. Fine; she didn't have a punch line anyway. She said to Fay, "You want to try kissing that?"

"I can't kiss him! I'm his mother. You kiss him."

"Ew." But Buffy had a promise to keep. She approximated her lips to the lips of the fog frog, puckered, and smacked.

A sound like the pealing of golden bells rang out—the Queen's laughter. A solid, slimy, six-foot-four frog sat at the foot of her throne now.

"Ewwwwwwww!" Buffy jumped back. The Queen laughed harder. "Ew!" Buffy scrubbed her mouth with the back of her hand.

Not a bullfrog, this one. Not green. Cream-colored, with a darker marking covering its back, extending from shoulders to hips: a brown X. It was a spring peeper, super-sized.

Buffy sucked in a long breath, then asked Fay, "You want me to try again?"

"Don't let her anywhere near me!" boomed a truly loud voice. "Keep her away from me." The frog quacked just like Prentis.

"Fine by me," Buffy said.

"I'll get somebody else to kiss him," said Fay. "Tempestt can kiss him. Come on, Prentis. Thank you, your Majesty."

As if the Queen had done anything. But Fay bowed to her Majesty, backed away, then turned and swept out with the megafrog hopping after her, spla-THUD, spla-THUD, spla-THUD. Each hop shook the flooring.

Which was, Buffy noticed, made of the living branches of huge trees. A soft pink-and-lavender glow filtered down from behind the golden orbs—no, they were golden leaves now. Dawn was lighting the tinted-glass dome of the sky. Day was on the way.

"Well," said the Queen, "that was most amusing." Facing her, Buffy saw no warmth, only silky merriment. "Quite diverting. Though I must say, I do not entirely understand the story."

"I understand it, your Majesty," Adamus said quietly. "Prison is that which keeps you from being who you are. That's all."

She silenced him with a look of jaded uncomprehension. "Let me think about this matter of the girl, what is her name?" Before either Buffy or Adamus could answer, she gestured dismissal. "Come before me again tomorrow night."

The party was breaking up. Buffy suddenly felt very tired, weary enough to accept the Queen's prevarication. She bowed (keeping her arms folded over her chest) and backed away.

When it was permissible to turn and walk, Adamus walked by her side. "That went not badly at all," he whispered when they had achieved a safe distance from her Majesty. "She could just as readily have turned you into a black toad turd."

Buffy nodded. She knew it was true but no longer cared, she felt so exhausted. "I guess I'll go home and get some rest—no, dammit, the cops are looking for me." It was hard to remember what was happening in that world out there. "I guess I'd better stay here. Take LeeVon and—"

Adamus, she noticed, was looking around anxiously. All the tables were empty, the great hall nearly empty.

"LeeVon?" Buffy asked the hall.

Nobody answered.

"LeeVon? Addie, do you know where he is?"

Adamus shook his head, his fair face pale.

Eleven

The prince in the periwinkle tunic with the tushie slits was standing in a secluded bower, watering the trunk of a tree, when Buffy and Adamus finally found him after several hours of searching. He shrieked and cowered away when he saw Buffy, but it was hard to tell whether his reaction was because of a guilty conscience, because she was a great and fearsome conjuror, or because his weewee was sticking out.

"Have you seen LeeVon?" Buffy demanded.

"Hu-hu-who?"

"LeeVon! My frog!"

"Superlative librarian," Adamus put in. "Green face, tattoos, rings—"

The person in periwinkle had his equipment tucked away now, and turned on them with unexpected vehemence. "I'd dance in hot iron shoes first," he burst out. "I'd roll down a hill in a spiked barrel before I'd kiss that—that slime-pated devil-belch spawn of—"

"So you have seen him! He did ask you!"

"That ringle-jingle serpent on legs! He didn't just ask.

157

He pursued me. He stalked me. He harried me like a green demon. He would not hear me say no. He said—" Periwinkle's voice began to quiver with horror. "He said, Awright, you don't want to kiss me, howsabout I kiss you?"

It sounded as if LeeVon was getting a wee bit tad desperate. "You're lucky he didn't ask you to lay eggs so he could make milt," Buffy said.

"Milady, have mercy," whispered Adamus.

"I guess it's a hetero thing."

"I'm afraid to go to sleep," the courtier whined.

"My sympathies. Where is LeeVon now?"

"He infuriated me." The courtier flushed with defiance, inflated his narrow chest, and glared. "I seized him and hurled him above the treetops."

Buffy saw everything go gray and start to sway. "You—you killed him?"

Hands supported her—Adamus. "Gently, gently," that quiet voice said. "Remember, this is Fair Peril. He may not be killed. Just as likely that he is back in human form."

It was true. It was the insane truth of it that made her want to faint. There was no logic to things—or rather, any probability in this place violated all common sense. Mushrooms might grow wings and fly here, and gold rings turn to rainwater.

"We should be searching for Emily," Adamus said.

But shock still ran through Buffy. She had to get out of this nutty place. She had to. Gray, lavender, periwinkle swam before her eyes; she could not see anything properly . . . then vague whiteness took form around her. Walls. There was a loud, bellicose sound in her ears.

Cops? Buffy cowered.

No. The ranting one was just a large, perturbed man in a plaid flannel shirt and a clashing bandanna. "Lady, would you get the hell out of here?"

"She ain't got a firm hold of her kite string," another voice said. "We oughta call security."

Urinals on the wall. Three distressingly normal-looking males faced her. Adamus was nowhere to be seen. "I'm back in the mall?" Buffy whispered.

"This is the men's room, for God's sake. Would you get the hell out?"

She exited hastily, noticing that something stank—it was, she realized, her. There she stood wrapped in smelly black plastic in the main concourse of the Mall Tifarious, with quite a few people looking at her.

She ditched the plastic in a trash container and scuttled in her nightgown toward the nearest exit and outside. Amazing, the energy jolt a good rush of adrenaline can produce, even in a person who hasn't eaten or slept. Flannel flapping, clutching wallet and keys in one hand, Buffy ran for her car—

It wasn't there.

Yes, this was the right parking lot. Yes, this was the right row. No, the car wasn't there.

Buffy wondered briefly whether her Escort could have kissed a frog-eyed Sprite and run off. Then she started giggling. Actually, the cops probably had her car, giggle, giggle, giggle. Here she was wandering around the mall parking lot in her nightgown; her daughter, who did a damn good statue imitation, was missing somewhere in Fair Peril; she had contributed to making her favorite librarian first an amphibian and then a guided missile; now her car was gone? It seemed hilarious. Giggle giggle GIGGLE at the thought of calling the cops to report her vehicle missing, along with LeeVon. Damn cops had probably grabbed the car because they were looking for her. Crazy woman in nightgown giggling in the parking lot at ten in the morning, giggle giggle ye ha ha snort. Emily's Probe was gone too. They had probably towed it—

Emily's—car—was—gone?

Buffy stopped giggling with a gasp, about-faced, and thundered back into the mall to find a phone. She dialed Prentis's number. The Trophy Wife answered.

"Hi, Pestt, this is Buffy. Has—"

"You have the colossal nerve calling here!" Tempestt sounded just a teensy smidgen overwrought. "After what you've done!"

"Yeah, well, has Emily—"

"Big wet frog tracks all over the carpeting!" Tempestt yelled, tearful. "I don't know how I'm ever supposed to get them out."

Prentis was home, evidently. "Did you kiss him?"

Tempestt's voice shrilled to a new level of hysteria. "That's personal! Why do you want to know?"

"Just curious."

"That's incredibly rude!"

In other words, she hadn't kissed him. She couldn't deal with it. Prentis would have to take his pickle-puss elsewhere. "Has Emily come home?"

"Emily? Who cares about Emily!"

Nobody but me, evidently. "Is she *home*?"

"*NO*, she's not home. How can you ask such things when my husband—"

Buffy hung up and stalked down the mall and bought herself a cup of coffee and a soft pretzel. There was nothing like complete nutrition to keep a person going, and evidently she was going to have to keep going for a while longer. She headed toward the mall office, passing all three fountains and all three pedestals on her way. The winged stag, she noticed, was gone—interesting but unsurprising, as she herself had seen it fly. The princess with the garland of golden roses and the star on her forehead was still missing. But the frog king was still squatting sullenly up there.

" 'Scuse me," Buffy bespoke the horse-faced woman at the mall-office desk. "Can you tell me what's happened to two of the statues?"

The woman was staring at her instead of answering her. The people at the pretzel stand had stared at her too. People she had passed as she was walking, likewise. Buffy concluded that her nightgown was not being perceived as a fashion statement.

"The statues on the pedestals in the fountains," she said in read-my-lips tones. "Where are they?"

"Missing," the woman said.

"Missing? As in, somebody stole them?"

"Looks like." Only the woman's mouth had moved. The rest of her equine personage was still rigid with staring.

Next question. "Is there a place around here where I can grab a nap?" There had to be a quiet corner somewhere.

The woman's glassy eyes widened to the limit of their sockets. "You're not to sleep in the mall! There's a homeless shelter—"

"I'm not homeless!" Why would this appearance-challenged person think she was homeless? Just because she was dressed rather casually? Hadn't shampooed her hair in a few days? Was getting a bit skanky?

"Then you should go home and *get a bath* and some sleep, shouldn't you?"

Buffy expressed her exasperation with a sigh and headed out. As she paused outside the door, trying to think what to do next, she heard the woman call to somebody else in the office, "It's getting screwier around here every day. Did you see the woman with the monster frog on a leash?"

Homeless, baloney. But phew, Buffy had to admit that Essence of Body Odor was going to linger on the air after she was gone. She headed toward a john to take a sponge bath. Make that a paper-towel bath. The plan, insofar as she had one, was to stay at the Mall Tifarious, get some sleep somehow—there had to be storage areas where they kept the naked and dismembered mannequins, the seasonal displays; Buffy pictured herself napping with the Easter Bunny—and then she would start looking for Emily again. But as she walked toward the rest rooms, her tired brain farted out a notion and she veered into one of those nature-and-ecology whoa-green-is-expensive stores. Her nightgown, aside from being overdue for a wash, was not suitable garb for public places. But she needed a starry, starry garment in order to do transfrogrifications. Maybe there would be one in here.

There wasn't. There were jigsaw puzzles depicting the constellations, but no starry T-shirts. The T-shirts had koalas and flamingos and coatimundis on them. So much for that idea. Very tired, too tired to think, Buffy stood and stared dazedly around the store.

Something on one of the display tables caught her eye; she toddled over there. Under garish wooden parrots hanging from the ceiling, amid hand-up-the-ass endangered-species puppets, amid rubber moose and plastic mongooses and metal make-a-noise cicadas, amid all the tacky envirokitsch reared a carved snake made out of some sort of white stone, alabaster or white jade or something, a museum-quality sculpture with graceful lines and a lifted head, a white snake looking back at her.

Carved stone, yet its golden eyes seemed alive.

"You were there," Buffy whispered to it.

She was tired, so tired, exhausted, drifting. The cloth on the display table fluttered like leaves. "There! There!" a parrot squawked from overhead.

Buffy whispered. "You were there that day. Do you know where my daughter is?"

Yes, the white snake did. The white snake knew. Except that his forked black tongue flickered out, his mouth did not move, but Buffy heard as if he had spoken inside her head. Or rather, she did not hear—the snake's preverbal reptilian language was not her language—but she sensed a wordless affirmation. *Yes, certainly, I am the white snake. Of course I know.*

"Tell me! Where is she?"

Barely changing position, nevertheless the snake was slowly gathering, coiling, rippling, flexing, clenching his muscle in the lazy way of a strong, confident serpent. His upraised head swayed in languid negation. *Nah. No. Don't feel like it.*

Like a child who has been hauled around a shopping mall way too long, Buffy could have cried. "Tell me!" Her whisper flipped into a yell. "Why won't you tell me?"

Why should I? I am the white snake. How have you deserved my help?

She knew she had been unmannerly. She knew the tales and their number-one rule: speak politely to everyone and everything until you know for sure who or what it is. The arrogant older son, the bitchy stepmother, the haughty queen, they always forgot the rule and always got the business. But Buffy could not stop. She danced in red-hot-iron frustration, she writhed in spiked-barrel despair. She screamed. Her hands shot out to seize the white snake and wring the truth out of him.

She never touched him, of course. He bit her.

The ballista that had hurled frightened young Adamus from the battlements could not have been more spring-loaded, more sudden. Before Buffy knew what was happening, fangs pierced her hand and withdrew. She looked down on two ruby-red pearls of blood. Tiny pearls—but within her she could feel the bite slithering its way through her veins, chill, huge, an enormity.

Punissshment, the white snake told her, turning his lithe, indifferent back and sliding away.

* * *

Buffy knew she was supposed to die. She just did not know how or how soon.

Everything changed very quickly.

Everything was moving. Wooden parrots flew up with frightened cries and disappeared—quite literally disappeared. The mall was disappearing—or transmallgrifying. Instead of glass-domed ceiling and glass storefronts, Buffy saw glass walls closing in. Fountains puddled around her feet. To get out of the water she jumped up an oversized step and stood on top of a large, dank, reddish-brown platform—brick?

Before she could think, her footing shook and there was a sound like mountains grinding together. Cowering, she looked up as the roof, or top, whatever it was, lifted off. A giant face peered down, seemingly from the sky, a face gargantuan beyond anything she had ever seen or imagined. If God had nose hair and wore a dirty baseball hat, then this was God.

A hand the size of fate came down. Buffy wanted to run yet froze like a terrified rabbit; the only parts of her that seemed able to move were her bladder and her bowels, spewing away her self-respect as the hand seized her between thumb and forefinger and lifted her right up through where the roof should have been. Close to fainting, Buffy shut her eyes and hung in that coarse-skinned grip, much too far above the ground, dripping. "Now, here's a fat little stinker," the voice of the God-ogre said, booming and distant, so huge that she could barely catch the words between the deep echoes in the dome of the sky. "Good for bass. You put the hook in here—" A fingertip threatened to cave in her face. "—and you bring it out here." He nudged her side; Buffy felt ribs scream. "Tie one leg to the shank but let the other one loose so she keeps wiggling."

"Wait," Buffy whispered. Then she managed to open her eyes and say it louder. "WAIT!" she yelled. "I'm not bait!" She looked down at herself—yes, it was her, all right, feet kicking in wet sneakers, legs sticking out pale and unlovely from under her soiled nightgown, wallet and keys, those apodictic proofs of her sanity and humanity, clutched so tightly that her hand was going white. "You're making a mistake!"

The baseball-hatted giant did not seem to hear her at all. "Uh-huh," the other one was saying, his voice flat, uninterested in being taught how to bait a hook for bass. "I'll take her. Box her up."

The—other—one?

That flat, quaking voice—no. It couldn't be. Panicked, Buffy looked—it was hard to make sense of the immensity of these personages as big as sky, it was like finding coherence in the clouds, but—the inside of the little white box felt awfully familiar, though Buffy had never been imprisoned in a Chinese takeout container before. Funny, how the inside of a pristinely white box could look black in the absence of light. It was him, all right.

"Prentis!" she cried.

The box swayed, throwing her from side to side, as he carried it by the wire handle. Either he didn't hear her or he wasn't hearing her.

"Prentis, please! What are you doing with me?"

No answer, only a jarring thunk as he set the box down, then vehicular vibrations. They were in his car now. Going somewhere.

It was like one of those Mafia movies. *Where are you taking me?*

No. It was worse. Far worse. On her hands and knees in the corner of the box, Buffy puked up her soft pretzel, she felt so sick with fear, carsick, seasick, airsick, nauseated in zero gravity; which way was up? How/when had she become fish bait while remaining the same size? Did Prentis know the prisoner in his little white box was her? Did he have plans specifically for her, maybe to sink the hook a bit more viciously than necessary? Or did he think she was a bug or something? Everything would have been more bearable if she had just understood what was going on. Whether she was going to live or die.

No, actually, it might not have been more bearable.

She tried shouting again. "Where are you taking me?"

No answer. Trying to stand up, she was thrown to her belly as he veered into a driveway or something. The car stopped.

Buffy stayed where she was, lying down. A good move—the box swayed wildly as he carried it. She heard the snick of a doorknob turning, felt the lurch as he stepped inside. Thunk, the box shook again as he set it down.

"Did you get a nice one, honey?" asked an older woman's throaty voice.

"Sure, Mom." Prentis sounded weary and supercilious.

Mom? *Fay?* Once more Buffy's bowels spasmed, but there was nothing left in her to let go.

Fay said, "Prentis, dear, your tone of voice. I'm only trying to help."

"Yeah, whatever."

"Better put it in the aquarium so it doesn't die before we're ready. This may take a while."

The box swooped up, opened to let in a glare of disorienting light, careened over, and dumped Buffy with a splash into shallow, stale water. Did Prentis know it was his ex-wife he was dumping—again? Moot point. A shock worse than the chill of the water kept Buffy sitting where she was, mouth open but not functioning to speak: she was in her own aquarium, looking out at the interior of her own messy bungalow, her own kitchen, where Fay and

Prentis were sitting at her plastic-covered table.

"Coffee, hon?" Fay offered. Fay was always so sweet to Prentis that it made Buffy's teeth hurt. And the more his mother courted him, the more he closed her out.

"No thanks."

Fay rose to get herself a cup, banging cupboard doors one after another. "Can't find anything but dirt. This place is a swamp." Splendiferously aureate as always, Fay provided enough reflective surface to light up every speck— okay, in Buffy's case, it was more like clumps—every lurking lump of filth. Finally locating a coffee mug, she eyed it suspiciously and made a sour face. "That Murphy person never did keep anything clean."

Being called "that Murphy person" roused Buffy from her waterlogged daze. "Hey!" She struggled to stand up, her nightgown sodden and streaming. "Get your claws off my stuff!"

Neither Fay nor Prentis heard her, of course. "Can we just get on with it?" Prentis grumbled.

Fay sat down with her coffee. "You can't hurry this book." It lay open on the table; she might have been scanning it for some time. Now she picked it up in both hands, balancing the base of its hefty spine on the table. Big book. Big green book. Buffy did not have to look closely to know: *Batracheios.*

In Fay's hands the green cover seemed to turn golden, like green leaves turning golden in late-day sunlight. Standing in the glass prison, looking on, Buffy shivered with cold.

"I've been looking all morning," Fay said in tones of mild annoyance, "and I still can't find where Emily might have gone if she ran off with a frog."

"What's it matter," Prentis said. "She'll come back when she wants to. She likes her car, and we've got her car. She likes her clothes, and we've got her clothes. Tell you one thing, it's a lot more peaceful now she's not in the house."

"YOU COCK-UP!" Buffy yelled hot and loud as a volcano—but they couldn't hear. They'd never been able to hear, neither of them, what she was really trying to say. Prentis, sitting there, no health-club pose when he was around his mom, just being his lumpen, jowly self—Buffy wanted to bite him and give him rabies. She wanted to chew his nose off.

But his mother put down the book and gazed at him solicitously. "Emily made it hard for you and Tempestt?"

Prentis just gave her a look.

"It's frustrating when you're a new couple," Fay said.

"Just shut up and find me an answer, would you, Mom?"

"Well, I need to know what kind of—"

"I just want Tempestt to get more interested in me and less in the goddamn money!"

Buffy sank down to sit on rotting wood, weak with exhaustion and astonishment. Neediness, in Prentis? Truth, in Prentis?

Silence, as Fay flipped slowly through *Batracheios*. Prentis jiggled his leg.

Fay beamed, as befitted an ormolu presence. "Here we go. This ought to do it. Okay, first you're supposed to take your frog and drive pins into it."

Buffy started to shake.

"That's supposed to make your beloved feel pangs of love," Fay continued with no apparent levity. "Then, when it's stuck full of pins, you're supposed to bury it alive. Then after six weeks you're supposed to come back and dig it up and it's supposed to be dead and decayed and there's a little bone like a hook. You're supposed to hook that on your beloved someplace, like on her belt or something, and that's supposed to do the trick. Okay?"

"Sure, whatever."

"Fine. Where's Murphy keep her pins?" Fay laid the book down. "Where's her sewing basket?" On golden spike heels she clicked into the next room. Hunched in a corner of the aquarium and shaking, Buffy could hear her moving things around in there, searching. Sewing basket, what did Fay think this was, a nunnery? Buffy hadn't owned a sewing basket in years, but she knew exactly where there were some straight pins, in an orange juice can along with three slowly petrifying pencils, a few thumbtacks, and some paper clips, in plain sight on the kitchen windowsill, and she prayed Fay wouldn't think to look there.

"This place is a *cesspool*!" Fay called from the next room. "Prentis, do you know where she—"

He bawled back, "How the hell would I know! Just find something, Mom, wouldja?"

Something dark and desperate in his voice made Buffy start to scrabble and claw at the glass walls of her prison, even though she knew she could not possibly escape.

Fay moved on toward the bedroom. "I suppose we could use a brooch or something from her jewelry box, if I can figure out where *that* might be—"

"God's sake, Mom, just skip the pins and come on!"

Prentis had always been impatient, and Buffy had never previously found this trait the least bit attractive in him. Now, however, she stopped clawing at the walls and whispered, "Bless you, Prentis!" Skipping the pins sounded like a wonderful idea.

Rooting in the bedroom, where there might—oh, God, please don't let her notice them—there might be a few pins under all the junk on the dresser, Fay called, "Just give me a minute!"

"Buffy might waltz in here any minute!"

"Not likely." Fay spoke to soothe. There, there.

"Who says? We don't know where she is!"

"I'm right bloody here!" Buffy shrieked, but of course they didn't hear. Might as well talk to trees. They kept on bickering.

"Whose idea was it to do this here?"

"Look, we couldn't do it no place where people might see!" Prentis's grammar always fell apart when he got himself exercised. "Wouldja come on?"

"Murphy is miles away from here. May I remind you that she doesn't have her car anymore."

"*Mom*," Prentis bellowed, "all I need is the goddamn bone. Just come *on*!"

Fay minced back into the kitchen, disapproving. "I thought you wanted Tempestt to love you."

"Not if she's gonna pang at me. I hate it when women pang. Goddamn pain in the ass. Just grab something and let's bury this frog and get out of here."

"Well, get it out of the aquarium, then."

Buffy scrambled around as much as she could, with bitterly unsatisfactory results; despite her best effort, they had no trouble catching her. "I'm a person, damn it!" How could they look at her and think she was a frog? A frog wouldn't be wearing a disintegrating nightgown. A frog would have done a better job of giving them a hard time. "I'm human!" Kiss me, I'll be human, I promise. I'll be a princess, I'll be good . . . screw that. Why should being human or not matter? What they were willing to do to an inoffensive frog was unthinkable. "You can't do this to me!" She tried to bite. Her teeth could not penetrate Prentis's fat fingers. "Gimme an F—" But she knew right away it was no use. A little filthy, squirming thing couldn't do spells worth squat. No presence. Not appropriately garbed.

They put her into the white box with its familiar feel of imprisonment, carried her out to the back yard, got a shovel from the cellarway, and buried her.

Buried her.

This, too, felt awfully familiar. I can deal with this some-how, Buffy kept telling herself as the dirt thudded down, shaking her cardboard coffin, shutting her into a blackness more absolute than any she had ever seen, so black the white snake could have been in there with her and she wouldn't have known. I can deal with this—it's better than pins. I can deal . . . The hell she could. She screamed. Screamed, feeling the box shudder and flex; any moment it could collapse, she could be crushed under the weight of too much heavy, uncaring earth. If not that, then she would die of suffocation. There wasn't enough air. She must not scream. She screamed anyway.

"Help me!" she screamed. "Somebody, somebody help me!"

Nobody did, of course. She thought briefly, crazily, of Addie. But he was so far away he might as well have been a golden dream.

What was the name of this white nightmare?

Punissshment.

When her throat closed and she could not scream any longer, she sank down and panted, and maybe the air was getting bad already—or maybe she was just very, very tired. She lapsed onto the bottom of the box. Cold. Soggy cold. She curled, fetal, and imagined that the white snake was burrowing to crawl in there with her, but she didn't even care. After a while she stopped noticing the blackness anymore.

Twelve

*I*t was like being woken up from a very bad sleep, except that the person with the panicky voice was not merely joggling her but seemed to be trying to haul her up by the arms. Resisting, Buffy thrashed, bumping against something damp and sticky, then opened her eyes to find herself nose to a wall of dirt. Even before she remembered, she screamed. A rush of adrenaline sent her scrambling out of her open grave. "Addie, they—" But the sight of his beautiful, frightened face undid her. She sobbed and clawed at the grass. Adamus gathered her up gingerly, as if he were trying to hold a big mess of dirty laundry together, and she bawled on his shoulder.

"They—no matter how loud I yelled, they—" Crying kept her from saying much.

"The white snake gave you a poison dream," Addie told her gently.

"But—it was real!" Quaking with sobs, Buffy turned her head against his shoulder to look down into the hole she had just crawled out of. It was quite deep and quite real.

Dirt was mounded all around. She could feel the stickiness of dirt all over her.

"Of course it was real. You are the storyteller."

"But—" The hole in her backyard, the grave—it was a six-foot rectangle, maybe more than six feet. Not the right size. Or rather, how had it gotten to be the right size? Or how had she? Buffy wailed, "I don't damn understand!"

"Shhhh."

"It was *not* all in my mind!"

"I am real," Addie said, holding her. "I am in your mind. I have been real in people's minds for a thousand years."

"They were—they were giants!"

"Yes. I saw."

Buffy managed to stop most of her bleating and shuddering and gulping, then pulled back and looked at him. Day was over, darkness falling; he shone like water in the twilight. More quietly she said, "Addie. What are you doing here?"

He looked not at her, but past her. "I saw the giants pick you up." His voice had gone very low. "I could not fight them, but I—I tried to follow. I could not run fast enough. Then—I did not know where else to look for you, so I came here, I saw. It took me far too long to dig you out." His golden eyes turned to her, wincing, wet. "I thought you would be dead."

Quite unequivocally, he had saved her life. There he knelt in her backyard, all besmirched with dirt, her snot and tears matting his velvet tunic. "I'm humbly grateful," she said, her voice thick; it had been a long time since she had said anything so sincerely. "But I mean—I'm the one who put you in that fish tank, made you wear that awful tux—why are you here?"

"Oh." He understood. "Because I am a prince from out

of the primal Pool." He gave her a wisp of a smile, but there was sadness in his voice now. "You shape me, my lady."

He was a prince, all right. "That's why you saved me?"

"You are the storyteller. I am what you want me to be." Now his eyes were dry, wry, bleak. "I think you are mixing me up with the brave woodcutter, my lady, or the wandering soldier." His smile turned into a wince. "We fairy-tale princes don't usually get to be heroes. We don't do much. We are golden trophies, we wait for a taker. Look at me." Bitterness. "Lollygagging around the court, crying for Emily, instead of questing forth to find her."

He flung his head back like an impatient colt and got up, holding out his hands to help her do the same. Implications astounded her. She could not stand without swaying. She could not think of what to say to him.

"Change the story," he said, so quietly the words came and went like a breath, a breeze in sere golden grass. "Please. I need to find her."

"But—I—"

"I think you want to keep me for yourself."

It was so level and selfless and true that she cried out, "If storytelling can make it so, then why can't I just find her?"

"Because we are all trapped in my story. Make a new story."

She shook her head; she could not think or comprehend; she reeled like a drunk as she tried to walk. In the house, she grabbed the sugar bowl with shaking hands and gulped from it like a dog.

"We must return to Fair Peril soon," Adamus said. "You must appear again before the Queen."

"Oh, Jesus." She had, of course, utterly forgotten. She wanted to scream with weariness but knew she had to go. Had to keep going. Had to find Emily. She mumbled, "I'd better get cleaned up." Even the magic of Fair Peril might not be sufficient to transform her filthy self into something presentable at court.

Walking a little more strongly since her sugar fix, she went and showered, leaving her starry, starry nightgown on the bedroom floor with a sense of finality; with sudden intuitive certainty she knew she didn't want to turn any more people into frogs or fogs or even rutabagas, not ever again. She would take her chances. She would risk being her unmagical self. After her shower, feeling more fit to cope, she dressed in blue jeans, a chambray shirt, her newest, whitest, cushiest tube socks, and white sneakers. Padding out to the kitchen again, she pulled on a purple windbreaker, grabbed a box of graham crackers from the cereal cupboard, and asked Addie, "You want anything to eat?"

"No, thank you." God, was he gorgeous. It seemed inconceivable that any male so gorgeous should be there in her kitchen, sitting at her table.

You want to keep me for yourself.

She tried to keep her thoughts, not to mention her feelings, from showing in her face. "Okay, let's boogie."

"I beg your pardon?"

"Let's go."

She left the house door unlocked. No clue to where her wallet and keys were, proofs of sanity and humanity; so what. No car, either. They walked. Buffy munched graham crackers. Between streetlamps Adamus looked at the sky.

He said, "The nights are very different in your realm."

"You sure you don't want something to eat?" Buffy had munched an entire packet of grahams and still felt hungry.

He shook his head. "I cannot see the stars."

"Too much light."

"Yes. The sky is full of a haze like milk smeared on black glass. You people have chased back the night and many of the old demons along with it." He sounded uncertain. "No trolls here."

"Yes, there are. We grow our own." Home-grown trolls sounded both safer and scarier to her. She peered at Adamus, seeing him clearly by his own glimmering sheen. What was going on in his head? He sounded wistful. She asked, "You want trolls?"

"No. I mostly just want the velvet sky. And the stars." Looking up, as if it were the same thing he said very softly, "I want Emily."

As if it were a reasonable question Buffy asked, "Why?"

His perfect head swiveled; he looked at her blankly. "Pardon?"

"Why do you want her, Addie? Really?" She had cried in his arms; perhaps for that reason she was now able to ask, not at all harshly, "Have you coupled with her?"

He merely stared, though not as if offended. He did not answer.

Buffy said, "I don't want that for her. Not yet. She's too young. A child bride." She said, "That's what my mother was. A child bride. Got pregnant and married my father when she was only fourteen. Not old enough to stick up for herself. She might as well have been a slave." Her voice was gentle, almost tender. "Is that what you want for Emily? Is that what you want Emily for? Addie?"

"I—" He faltered to a halt and stood facing her under the lavender glow of one of those tall, looming streetlamps they call cobra lamps. So softly she could barely hear him, he said, "I just want somebody to—" His voice hitched, but he got the word out. "To love me. That's all."

Buffy found that she had to turn away or she would have bawled on his shoulder some more. She walked on, and he walked beside her.

Silence. She could not look at him. She could not face his neediness; it would have meant facing her own.

She could not say it. She was not as brave as he was, or as honest.

She had to say it.

She tried three times. Finally her mouth obeyed her and formed the words, though she could not quite say the most dangerous word, the *l* word. "That's all I want too," she said. "The same thing."

Emily lay asleep and dreaming that she was still on the damn pedestal. From a pedestal you can see far, far, you can see clearly, but you cannot do a godforsaken thing. She could see the thin, bone-white, hook-shaped form of her grandmother out on the benighted lawn of the nursing home, picking at the dirt of the world, picking at the dirt, picking at the dirt. She wanted to tell her, It's all right, stop, rest; but she could not. Even if she had been kneeling at Grandmother's creaky, knobby feet, she would not have been able to tell her. Or rather, she could have said the words, but Grandmother would not have been able to hear her.

From the pedestal she could see Adamus weeping, and her heart beat like wings, and she wanted like fire to put her arms around him, but she could not reach him. She could not comfort him.

From the pedestal she could see her mother searching, searching for her, hardly crying at all but searching night and day. Her heart hovered like a hummingbird, watching. Could it be that her mother loved her?

Could it be that her mother, who searched, loved her better than her prince, who wept?

If only she could decide, Emily knew in her dream, then she would be able to call out. But meanwhile, she could only watch. There was Mother getting closer, Mother with her coarse no-style hair, Mother in a T-shirt and jeans not big enough to hide her bulges, Mother in those awful, dorky shoes. Mother looking in all the wrong places. Emily had to decide. If she could really believe that her mother loved her, she would call out, Here I am! She would cry, Mother, here I am!

The problem was . . . calling out was not enough. It was not fair that she could do nothing, nothing, except call out.

And even if she called . . . would her mother hear her?

Yes . . . no . . . Her heart's wild beating woke her up.

Her eyes snapped wide open, saw a pale attenuated heart floating in the night: the breast of a bird perched above her. Her rapid breathing slowed down as the scents of mint and timothy comforted her. It had been only a dream. She was not on the pedestal any longer. Her pounding heart calmed down. She lay in a nest of grasses at the edge of a forest meadow, with friends slumbering all around her.

Emily closed her eyes again but knew she was not likely to go back to sleep.

These creatures . . . they had saved her, they were beautiful, they were kind to her, and their kindness should have been enough. She felt ungrateful that it was not. Was anything in life ever going to be enough for her?

She wanted someone to love her, that was all. She really just wanted someone to love her.

Buffy wanted to walk fast, but her body wanted to walk very slowly, if at all. Because she had to struggle along, it was after midnight before she and Adamus reached the mall.

The plan, insofar as there was a plan, was to break in somehow, run for the food court when the alarms went off, and hope for a quick and easy transition into the realm of Fair Peril.

But none of this was necessary.

The main doors once again stood open. Police cars once

again were parked outside with their flashers going. This time the cops and the security guards were outside as well, on the mall apron, fully preoccupied. They had all formed a knot around the youngest, newest rookie cop, to whom they were listening dubiously.

"It came up out of the goddamn fountain," he was insisting. "The middle fountain. I'd just walked past and I heard this splish-splash jingle-jingle and I turned around and there it was."

Assessing the situation from behind the nearest cruiser, with Adamus crouching by her side, Buffy barely restrained a squeak of joy.

"And it was like a frog," said one of the cops in carefully neutral tones.

"Like a real skinny goddamn frog, except it walked on its hind legs and I swear to God it was six feet tall. And it had some kind of goddamn satanic tattoos on its arms, and it was full of rings."

"Rings on its fingers?"

"No, dammit, nose rings all over the place, here and here and here and here." The youngster was indicating sites on his own anatomy, the others were watching him carefully, and Buffy and Addie quietly slipped toward the door. "It came bouncing up to me—"

"Clothing?" asked a cop with a notebook, businesslike.

"What the hell would a frog be wearing clothes for? It had big webbed feet. It left water all over the floor."

Buffy and Addie were crouching inside the mall doors now.

"It came up to me kind of hopping on its hind feet, and I was so goddamn freaked I never moved. It stuck its wet hands on me. I damn near shit my pants."

"It assaulted you?" The cop with the notebook maintained a severely professional tone.

"It, um, it was trying to, um, stick its face in my face."

"It *what*?" Forget the professional tone.

"It, uh, it requested me to kiss it."

"It *talked*?"

One of the older cops growled, "Why the hell shouldn't a pervert in a frog suit talk?"

"It wasn't a frog suit!"

"Green latex or something."

Another cop put in, "Those fountains are only about a foot deep. How could something that big come up out of one?"

"Look, I know what I saw! It wasn't a guy in a frog suit, either. For one thing, it didn't have no dick—"

This was getting entirely too engrossing; time to move on. Buffy touched Adamus on his arm. Abandoning the young cop to his fate, the two of them headed into the penetralia of the Mall Tifarious. As soon as she dared, Buffy called softly, "LeeVon!"

"Suppose it's a golem?" Adamus whispered.

"It's a golem, okay, a golem with a tattoo of a really well-hung Mowgli on its butt." Having no dick had to be rough on a guy turned into a frog, Buffy realized, especially this guy. That, and being hurled through the air by the pissed-off object of his affections. Why hadn't the impact turned him human, like in the fairy tale? Why had it only worked halfway, turning him into a human-sized frog? Maybe Periwinkle was bi. "LeeVon!"

"Best Beloved!" With a ring-jingle and a mighty flapping of wet feet on vinyl tile, LeeVon came kangaroo-hopping out of the shadows. He shimmered greenly—it was hard for Buffy to tell whether he was shinily, froggily wet or slick with otherworldly glamour. Tall and entirely too thin, he caromed up to them.

"Oh, poor LeeVon!" Buffy was so relieved to see him alive that she hugged him, which was a mistake that cost her truly weird dreams on occasion for the rest of her life.

She had just hugged a six-foot frog. He was indeed wet. His green skin pressed obscenely soft and tacky against her cheek. His body squished like no human body. She could feel his baggy throat pulsing.

"Best Beloved, Best Beloved!" His voice a croaky sob, he hugged her back. "Buffy, you have to help me. If they don't kill me soon, I will starve to death."

"Food court," Buffy said. Or—was it because he had eaten the midnight food of that court that LeeVon was still a frog?

"No! Take me to the Pony Ride, please, now, quickly!"

Buffy stepped back from him and eyed him, trying to work out the logistics. "I don't have a car," she said, not to refuse him, just thinking aloud. But he thought she was going to refuse him. Agonized, he bounced in place, ringing like a wind chime.

"Best Beloved, *please!*"

"The Queen is expecting us," Adamus interjected, similarly thoughtful. "She gets surly if she is kept waiting."

"You go," Buffy said to Adamus, having made up her mind what she had to do. "Stall her or something. And, Addie, can you give LeeVon your clothes?"

"*What?*"

"He gave you his once upon a time."

Adamus winced, impaled on a point of honor. "My lady, mercy," he begged.

"I don't need clothes," LeeVon put in.

"Yes, you do." In the dark, with clothes to cover his shiny green nakedness, LeeVon just might be able to make it to the Pony Ride without causing a panic and bringing out the National Guard. "Adamus, do it."

Prince Adamus d'Aurca swallowed hard and started pulling off his tunic. "Very well." He handed LeeVon the tunic and began extricating himself from his hose. "But surely he can go to this place by himself, milady. The Queen—"

Buffy said, "I'm not a lady. I'm a mobile disaster area and I'm to blame that he's in this fix. And I let him down once already." These were things LeeVon was too kind to say. "I'd better go with him. Tell the Queen that I'm keeping a promise."

Then she found it hard to leave, for, standing there in his smallclothes, Adamus looked too vulnerable and all too sweetly flesh and too beautiful, like a strong, sleek golden colt, and too much the prince of her dreams.

"Stop that," Buffy said.

"Stop what?"

"Enchanting me. I'm going. Addie . . ." She did not know what to say to him. She did not dare to name the emotion she was feeling, though it trembled in her voice.

With a great clang the mall security alarm went off. Instantly Adamus blinked out like a firefly, gone as if he had never stood there golden and gorgeous and half naked, while Buffy and LeeVon ran and leaped, respectively, for the door.

"Hang on to my arm," Buffy told LeeVon, "and try to walk like a human."

LeeVon obliged. The side street along which they were promenading was romantically ill-lit, and it wasn't every evening that Buffy got to go strolling with a date in a velvet tunic, and LeeVon's legs looked quite nice in Addie's hose with the feet hacked open to accommodate LeeVon's huge webbies. Still, Buffy hoped no one was watching.

"You walk like a drunk."

"I can't see where I'm going. My eyes are on the wrong side of my head." Upright, with his snout pointing heavenward, LeeVon perforce goggled back the way he had come, but this did not seem to trouble him. "Just get me there, Best Beloved, and I'll be okay. Something has happened."

"No duh. A lot has happened."

But LeeVon did not seem to be interested in hearing her story. Rather, he was intent on his own. "Hanging around in fountains can get kind of perilous at intervals, but it still gives a person plenty of time to think," he said. "I got to considering, Why was I just waiting to be found, to be rescued? I mean, in general. I mean, my whole goddamn life. I thought, What would Kipling think of me? If Kipling were writing me, you can bet your sweet ass I wouldn't be hanging around waiting for somebody to kiss me. If nobody wanted to kiss me, well, I'd just fricking find somebody. Get a little proactive. Be the kisser instead of the kissee."

"Sounds good," Buffy said automatically, because LeeVon had that excited tone people get sometimes when life starts to make sense or they have just had a really good bowel movement. But then she started to think. "Uh, LeeVon," she said gently, "you tried that with Periwinkle, right?"

"Absolutely."

"And the cute cop at the mall?"

"Certainly. Your point being?"

"You got hurled above the treetops and you got an entire police squadron called out on your account."

"So?"

"What if some guy in the bar decides to clean your clock?"

"Oh. Goodness. I can't risk that. Forget what I said; I'll just stay a frog for the rest of my life."

Sarcasm didn't become LeeVon, but Buffy had to admit he had a point. She said nothing.

"I can't see where I'm going at all." His tone changed suddenly, becoming gentle and cheerful, almost tender. "Is it sensible for me to trust you to lead me, Buffmeister?"

"Hell, no."

"Yet here we are. It reminds me of those touchy-feely games we played in college where people led you around blindfolded."

"We're almost there." Buffy could hear Madonna's "Vogue" throbbing ahead.

"Help me, Best Beloved. I'm fainting with hunger."

He wobbled into the Pony Ride on her arm. Buffy hesitated, disoriented by darkness, strobe flashes, too many male bodies pumping and posing; she caught MTV-style glimpses of butt cheeks flexing below really minimalist cutoff shorts, of cocks enticingly delineated by tight athleticwear, of torsos bobbing with arms in the air, bare washboard bellies rubbing. She stood and stared, but LeeVon—and this was the guy who liked them young and cute—LeeVon scarcely bothered to glance at the dancers at all, crouching like an amphibious pointer and tugging her straight toward the food.

"Jesus jumpin' on the water!" gasped a male barfly as LeeVon entered his limited range of focus.

"What kind of queer *is* that?" agreed the guy next to him.

"You see it too?"

"I wish I didn't."

"Jesus some more, what's that with him?" The barfly's drunken attention had turned to Buffy. "Nice falsies, dude," he called to her. "But get serious, wouldja? Perm the hair and try some makeup."

Good God. Probably the guy wanted her to shave her legs, too. "Get a *life*," Buffy complained, but her critic didn't hear her. He was gawking at LeeVon, who had reached the tray of buffalo wings on the counter and was throwing them down himself one per second, bones and all.

"Jesus washin' feet," he said in awed tones. "Somebody bring that green guy some beer."

LeeVon glugged down the bowl of ranch dressing instead, then paused in his ravenings long enough to peer with one golden rolling eye. "Kiss me," he croaked, "and I'll turn into a librarian."

The male barfly squeaked and fled toward the loo. "I'm drunk, right?" appealed the other guy, a very presentable (in Buffy's opinion) young blond. "Somebody tell me I'm just real, real drunk."

"You're nice and drunk." LeeVon advanced, steady now since he had eaten, handsomely puffed and erectile. "Haven't seen you in here before, have I."

"Uh, no."

"Let's dance."

"Uh, me?" The man shrank against the bar. Tall, handsomely palomino, and well hung, with a banana-curled ponytail—he was no competition for Adamus, of course, but undeniably young and cute. Buffy wouldn't have minded having him for herself. LeeVon's type?

"I am an ensorcelled librarian," LeeVon told him.

"Uh, okay, green dude. You want to talk about it?"

"No," LeeVon said throatily. "Talk is cheap." Buffy had never seen him so masterful. Fair Peril might have done something for him. "Dance with me." He maneuvered his chosen partner toward the floor.

Buffy's attention strayed to the few buffalo wings LeeVon had left on the tray. Chewing greasily on one, she turned her head to see how LeeVon was doing but found herself staring instead at a face at the far end of the bar, caught by its hard gaze aimed back at her, an alabaster oval face. Sitting there arrow-straight and solitary, the man—man?—but so much was surreal that it seemed unimportant whether it was a man or a woman, more important that the purple cape hung regal from slim, square shoulders, a flash of gold showed at the base of a fine throat, dark hair flowed free, the hard white face confronted Buffy, perfect and familiar and strange.

"Drink, girlie?" a drawling voice invited. The bartender. The kind of place this was, probably he called everybody girlie.

Buffy shook her head but asked, "Who's that?"

The bartender approximated the focus of her stare. "Her?" His voice lost its drawl and became soft and wary. "That's the Queen. You know. The Queen."

Buffy didn't know. Somewhere behind the music she was hearing strange noises, far, high noises that made her think of sky, wild geese flying perhaps, or wind. Then she wasn't hearing the music at all, just the inside of her head, swoosh, as if her brain were going down the drain. Peripherally she saw LeeVon dancing as only a six-foot, long-legged, balletic frog could dance, great leaps of blind faith, trusting his blond partner to keep him from hurting himself. And his partner seemed to be doing that—but she did not know whether the man was drunk enough to kiss him. She did not know where Addie was, or whether he was all right. She did not know where her daughter was. She was not sure she knew *who* her daughter was. She felt so drunk on fatigue and sugar that she was giddily unsure of her own name. Buffles? Maddie-lin? Maddie?

But she knew, as a flash of gold glared in those fine eyes, as a white hand lifted and beckoned at her, she knew that it was as the prince had said: the Queen was pretty damn pissed at her.

"No," she whispered. She had to stay a bit, to see whether LeeVon—

But "No" was the wrong thing to say. The glittering eyes flared like fire, the white hand flexed. Buffy wanted to scream but couldn't as she felt herself whirling away into darkness.

Thirteen

$\mathcal{I}$n silk and velvet LeeVon leaped, LeeVon vogued, LeeVon danced, jingling like a great green tambourine, and his attention was all for the partner who guided him by the hands, whose presence he sensed just inches from the taut, tender skin of his belly; the world he saw, behind him and upside down and wildly in motion, was like a video that accompanied the music, the dancing, the partner. It was a lushly atmospheric video—the dim, smoky room, dusky wood and tawny lights, starry display of glass behind the bar, the people, the half-naked men and the woman in the cloak and the woman in blue jeans, all ebbing and flowing to the rhythm of the music; he would remember it forever, what he had seen on this most important of all nights, yet it did not concern him.

LeeVon saw Buffy disappear and kept right on dancing. On his own again. Just as she was once again on her own in her story.

This, then, LeeVon dared to think it . . . this was his story.

His story.

All of this suffering, being turned into a frog and dragged around and thrown around and starving . . . it was for some purpose.

The music was thumping, pulsing, pounding like his dancing heels, his dancing heart. With a titanic effort LeeVon jackknifed his head forward, creasing his throat, to look at his partner.

The blond young man stared back at him in fascination and terror. Lovely, those wide gray eyes shaded by long toast-colored lashes. Lovely, those grave brown brows, that high forehead, the shining hair pulled back. LeeVon had never before noticed a young man's eyes. Typically, he had been paying more attention to other parts. But this dancing partner was special, different, dancing arrow-straight, head high, brave gaze despite his fear, ponytail swinging—something about him reminded LeeVon of a character from Kipling, or maybe from Robert Louis Stevenson, some adventurous lad with the ponytail, the shining hair, the high forehead over sweet eyes, couldn't think which boy, which book, maybe *Alice in Wonderland*—

"Kiss me," LeeVon said, his voice issuing as a strangled croak from his constricted throat.

The dance went on, yet everything seemed to slow down. The young man's lips parted, moving wordlessly. LeeVon felt his soul hanging upon the softening of that Cupid's-bow mouth; he could have died that way and withered into a hook of bone hung on this darling's pocket. Yet he knew that the soft stirring of those delectable lips was not for him. Not yet.

He begged, "Kiss me. Please."

The young man moved his mouth again and this time managed to get a word out. "Why?"

"Because . . ." To help me, to turn me human so I can get on with my life, so I can go back to being LeeVon the librarian . . . but as he thought it, with a soulquake, an interior cataclysm ten on the Richter scale, LeeVon realized that it was not enough. Not nearly enough, just to go back to being what he was before. His story wanted more. Demanded far more.

The floor seemed to shift under his feet. He could not dance any longer.

Because I want someone to love me.

God oh Jesus oh God, he wanted, wanted, wanted to be loved and not lonely anymore. He had reached through his pride to truth, that was something ... but no, it got worse. Oh God oh God of mercy, he wanted—this lover whose name he did not yet know. This one, this brave, grave, blond dancing partner, this gray-eyed ponytailed prince, and no other.

The dance was drawing to a close. There was not much time.

Say it, then.

And he would have said it. He had found his way past pride. He could tell the truth.

Kiss me. Do this for me. Love me.

But—his own aching need—it was true, but it was the wrong truth for the story.

LeeVon of all people knew: the happy ending had to be earned. Always.

All around him, couples were going off to get a drink. He stood a green, silent grotesque on the dance floor. The one who could save him stood facing him, gray gaze steady upon him, waiting for an answer. How much longer would he wait?

LeeVon had not thought there could be anything more difficult to confess than this: *because I want someone to love me.* But there was one thing more difficult. And even more deeply true.

He got his wide, slimy mouth moving and said it.

LeeVon said, "Because I will love you." He thought of

Adamus, of how Adamus felt about Emily as he said it, and he knew he had reached the bottom line. Seemingly on their own, his sticky, splay-fingered hands lifted, reaching toward the other, though not presuming to touch. Hoarsely he said, "Because I will adore you and cherish you. Maybe you won't care for me; it won't matter. I'll love you like a mother. Take it or leave it."

His could-be true love gawked at him, mouth softening again, this time in astonishment. And terror. Understandably terror. Either it would happen—or he would go out the door into the night and LeeVon would never see him again. It was up to him.

I don't even know his name.

LeeVon lowered his tacky green hands and waited.

Buffy did not think she had moved, but there was no longer any Pony Ride. No LeeVon, no cute blond guy, and no men, cute or otherwise, dancing in suggestive clothing. Neither was there any court this time, with lambent men dancing in tights. No lute music, no courtiers, no Prince Adamus to help out. No golden orbs of light, no lavender walls, no up and no down. Just scared self and the Queen—alight with incandescent rage.

"You stood me up!"

"No. I—Majesty, I beg your pardon." I plead your pardon, I grovel your pardon, I toady your pardon. Buffy actually attempted a curtsy, which in a black place of no up and no down necessarily failed. She babbled, "I was just running a little late."

"You—stood—me—up!"

"I had to keep a promise, your Majesty! I had to help a friend!"

"Friend? You dare to speak to me of a friend? What of me? What of your daughter?" The curled white hand lifted to do God knew what to her, maybe send her into orbit, and even though she knew that the Queen's outraged concern for Emily was wholly a convenience of the moment, Buffy felt terrible. For just that moment she felt guilty enough to accept her punishment.

She had no thoughts of escape; she felt only a strange empathy. In utter submission she whispered, "Once upon a time there was a cold old queen."

The white hand hovered in black-ice nothingness. Buffy watched the hand, the white, angry face—yet it was not that cold old Queen of Fair Peril of whom she spoke.

"There was a cold old queen who had a warm young daughter," she said. "The queen loved her daughter as well as she was able, which was not very well. And the queen said to her daughter, Come, let us go down to the river, let us catch a shining fish for you.

"The daughter loved her mother the cold old queen as well as she was able, which was not very well. She loved other things more. She loved the leaping of deer and she loved the flying of birds and she loved animals, all animals. Still, because she loved her mother as well as she was able, she walked with her mother down to the river to catch a shining fish."

The Queen of Fair Peril had lowered her hand. Out of her porcelain face her golden eyes steadily watched the story unfolding on Buffy's face and on the storm-colored air.

"At the edge of the river a frog sat waiting with his heart pulsing in his throat. The queen's stare upon him made him unable to leap away. A few steps, then the queen crouched and imprisoned him in her hand. Now, she said to her daughter, with this fat frog as bait we shall catch you the greatest of shining fish. She stood up, and in her other hand she seized the fishhook and prepared to thrust it through the frog.

"No, the daughter cried, don't. Don't use the frog so.

"But we are going to catch you a shining fish.

"I don't want a shining fish! Please, let the frog go. Thus the warm young daughter begged for the life of the frog. But the queen was stubborn in her cold old heart and would not grant it to her. *My* frog, the queen said. She readied the hook again, and seeing it coming, the frog screamed like a human child. So the daughter snatched the frog out of her mother's hands and ran away.

"Because she had disobeyed her mother, she ran far, far away with the frog in her hands. She ran across the river and into the other kingdom.

"Then the frog said to her, Princess, thank you for saving me. For in the other kingdom the frog could speak to her. I will grant you three wishes, the frog told her. For in the other kingdom the frog had that power.

"Now, the princess was warm of heart, but she was also young and foolish. So she wished for a golden star on her forehead and a garland of golden roses around her neck and for the frog to be her playmate and companion and love her forever."

Buffy closed her eyes and waited for the rest of the story to come to her. She had to trust that the Queen would wait with her. The blackness around her reminded her of having been buried and made her sweat. Closing her eyes let her think better. Less black.

"The cold old queen cried out for her daughter," she said slowly. "She cried out, I have been a fool. She cried out, I have made my daughter run away from me. I must find my warm young princess daughter. And she followed her. She followed the princess across the river of shining fish into the other kingdom.

"She searched for her beautiful daughter who had run away with a frog. She searched for fair hair and wide eyes and a winsome face and a sweet voice. She had caught no shining fish, so she went hungry. She asked the hedgehogs,

Have you seen my beautiful daughter? But they only looked at her with their silly faces and shook their heads. She asked the deer, Have you seen her? But the deer only flagged their white tails at her and leaped away. She asked the parrots in the trees, Have you seen my beautiful daughter? And the parrots told her, Look down. She looked down, and at her feet was a puddle of muck, and there in the mud sat a slimy, potbellied frog with a golden star on its forehead and a wreath of golden roses around its neck. The frog looked at her with sullied golden eyes and cried out to her, Mama. Mama! I only wanted him to love me.

"The queen looked down and felt her cold old heart catch fire with sorrow. Then the queen crouched and picked up the little mud-brown frog tenderly in her hands and kissed it. With its slime on her hands and its stench in her face, she kissed it again and again. Little by little, her kisses gave her princess daughter back to her. And she hugged her and kissed her yet again and took her home across the river."

Buffy opened her eyes and ended the story there and was silent. The Queen of Fair Peril looked silently back at her, floating on—no longer blackness. The two of them seemed to be drifting in the midst of a fiery magenta sunrise.

"I understand most of it," the Queen said judiciously, "but what were the shining fish?"

In Fair Peril, everything was itself and also something else—but that did not mean Buffy had to understand. Besides, floating without footing was making her queasy. And irritable. "I have no idea, your Majesty."

"Huh." The Queen gave her a measuring look. "I suppose you don't understand soul cake, either."

"Sorry, no, I don't."

"You storytellers, you are foolhardy, you tell tales the

way angels sing, without understanding. Do you at least understand that the river is a form of the Pool?"

"Uh, yes." Buffy was ashamed to admit otherwise. Anyway, there was something about water, something linking all waters. She had sensed that.

"Very well." The Queen's steady eyes held no more expression than a pair of golden rings through which the black depths of the universe showed. The Queen said, "It is a good story. The Queen said, "If you go to the white snake and bespeak it nicely this time, perchance it will tell you where Emily is."

"Look, I swear to God," the young man was begging the attendant on duty in the wacky ward, "you gotta give me back my uniform and let me out of here. It really was a six-foot frog. It really did come up out of the fountain. Why would I be saying something that crazy if it wasn't true?"

The attendant did not want to listen to this. The attendant was sweating. The attendant just wanted this guy, this cop, probably an ex-cop now, to take his soap and his towel and shut up.

But he didn't shut up. He pleaded with great sincerity. "Listen, you got to give me back my uniform and my gun. Maybe it's some kind of alien invasion, and I'm the only one who can do anything about it because I'm the only one who goddamn believes me."

The attendant said, "Look, just save it for the doc and get in the shower." He didn't say it too hard, because he had a neurotic respect for authority and it wasn't a good idea to make a cop mad, not even a stripped-down cop who was probably never going to work again, a cop who had spent the night in the loopy room. The attendant was sweating and starting to shake, not because the cop was gaga but because he was afraid the cop was going to say "frog" again and he bloody hated that word "frog." He hated the word, he hated Kermit, cartoon frogs, T-shirts with pictures of frogs on them, pocket frogs, frogs that went a-courtin', fairy-tale frogs, real frogs, frogs inclusive. HEHATEDFROGS HEHATEDHEHATED HEHATEDFROGS! The cop better by damn not say "frog" anymore. Aside from that, the attendant was sweating and shaking because they had put the cop in the wacky ward and he, the attendant, felt pretty sure that the cop was as sane as he was. Either they were the only two *compos mentis* people in a crazy world or they were both over a green, croaking edge they hadn't even seen coming. The only difference between him and this cop was that he, the attendant, didn't have the guts to say anything.

And it had better stay that way. So the cop had better not say "frog" again.

The cop was so frustrated he was attacking the bed now, pounding it with his fists. The attendant pulled out his keys to lock the door on him for the time being. The attendant tightly gripped his keys, because keys were sanity. Keys were the only thing that kept him from being the same as the cop.

Pounding the bed, the cop yelled, "Fricking frog!" The cop yelled, "Fricking fracking freaking big FROG!"

The attendant threw the keys at him. The attendant screamed. Screamed. They were coming, the authority figures, the white-coated doctors on duty, he could hear the running feet, but he could not see anything except green, and he could not stop screaming.

The Queen of Fair Peril lifted her white hand in a gesture of dismissal, and that was the last Buffy saw of her. Magenta sunrise spun around and she felt herself falling through a distance much greater than she liked. Her arms shot out in a monkeylike reflex and her mouth opened to scream, but she sputtered instead. Soaked, drenched, soggy, sopping wet, wet, wet. She was goddamn underwater. Kicking hard, she surfaced and discovered that she was drippily back in the Mall freaking Tifarious. The Queen had plunged her into one of the fountains.

Except it was not a fountain, of course. Deep. A pool. She was in Fair Peril, and from rocks at the edge, a bearcat's round, fuzzy face peered at her.

Laboriously, struggling to stay afloat in her waterlogged clothing, Buffy swam toward shore. But as soon as she got within six feet of the edge, the bearcat lifted its adorable whiskers and snarled at her.

"Oh, for God's sake." Treading water, Buffy studied the bearcat uncertainly. Bearcats, plural. Several of them. They were cute animals, but big. Like her, cute and big, right? And look at all the damage she had done. Buffy swiveled and tried for shore in a different direction.

Just as her hand reached for the rocks, an excessively large hedgehog appeared upon them with an expression of great decision upon its geeky concave face. It swelled to a sudden forbidding prickliness, and Buffy retreated.

She was beginning to get it. "Guys," she pleaded, "I need to get out of here! I'm not a goddamn amphibian; I'll—*blub*!" Already, getting tired, she was going under. Was the Queen trying to drown her? Panic gave her kick enough to surface again and hastily slough off her sneakers; the socks went with them. Panting, then holding her breath as she ducked beneath the surface of the water, she wrestled with her heavy jeans and got them off. Her waterlogged shirtsleeves dragged at her arms. She yanked the shirt open, ripping buttons, and got rid of it.

Trapped in deep water, naked except for cotton panties (probably with stains on them or holes in them, a disgrace and a scandal, just as her mother had always feared) and industrial-strength bra, half-naked and vulnerable, all wet,

Buffy felt—not frantic, as would have seemed appropriate, but suddenly and illogically light and lucid and free.

Free. It was like those times way back when she was a little girl and took off her dress and ran around the neighborhood. Or took everything off and sat in the grass and sang. Back before anybody had yet succeeded in making her ashamed of her body, though already poor Mama was working on it.

Mama. Back before anything, there was Mother. Cradled in the watery embrace of the pool, Buffy did not care that the bearcat had snarled at her; she could swim forever, and she wanted to. Lolling at her ease, she smiled up at the lavender sky.

All in due time she rolled over, put her face in the water, and looked for a shining fish.

It was wonderful down there. The deep, limpid water magnified the round coppery pebbles seeming to swim on the bottom, the waverings of lime-green, feathery waterweed, the flickerings of minnows. Snails clustered on boulders, pewter spirals that left pewter squiggles of slime. A turtle lazed past, bubbles trailing off the yellow-rimmed scales of its shell. The turtle had ponderous clawed feet that paddled lightly for such a heavy thing. Wonderful, that something so shelly, lumbering, cumbersome, could swim so—so much like a certain middle-aged woman. Or a fat bearcat, or a seal. Heavy and lumbering on land, lithe in water, free of the weight of self.

Her clothes were not down there anywhere. Sneakers, jeans, shirt had simply disappeared. Buffy didn't care. They would have looked all wrong smothering the plumy green waterweed, clunked down amid the shimmering pebbles and the snails.

Buffy came up for air and noticed the feathery waverings of reflected forest on the pool's surface, the silver flickerings of ripples. Again she put her face beneath the rumpled surface of the water. This time she saw a shining fish. She saw tadpoles clustered in a belly of sunlight. She saw the yellow-footed underside of a duck. She saw the hair on her own arms white and wavering and feathery with bubbles. Lifting her head for air again, she saw in the scintillations on the water the white snake wrinkling away from her.

She followed.

Paddling like a turtle, kicking like a frog, splashing like a walrus, she followed to the central island where the tall, empty pedestal stood. Odd; had the island been there before? She hadn't seen it when she had been thrashing around, about to drown. Not that it would have mattered; there were guardians on the boulders of the island too. A black-crowned night heron stood with swordlike beak at the ready. A badger glowered, flexing its Schwarzenegger shoulders, sharpening its massive claws on the rock. A skunk basked like a black-and-white flower. More animals ringed the place: sable and ermine, an egret, a black jaguarundi. All made way as the white snake glided ashore and passed between them to the base of the pedestal. All watched—and from the water Buffy watched raptly—as the white snake flowed in a milky spiral up the tall wheat-colored shaft and coiled itself into a perfectly symmetrical truncated cone, its head at the apex, atop the plinth.

Buffy came ashore.

For the first time in her life sorry that she was wearing Fruit of the Loom instead of Victoria's Secret, she clambered onto the island, streaming like a porpoise. The guardians let her pass, as she had known they must, for the white snake awaited her. He awaited her, the immaculate serpent on his throne.

Barefoot, she walked up the rough slope and bowed herself into a properly obsequious lump at the base of the pedestal.

Conjuror woman. You are supposed to be dead. As before, the dry, black-tongued voice sounded directly inside her head.

"I know it." She kept her head down and did not look at him. A breeze blew; snaky sensations tickled her skin. Her bra and panties, she noticed without caring, had grown lustrous watery streamers of silver-gold veiling; she was crouching there in a glittery silk belly-dancing outfit, with her embonpoint billowing out all over it. Lord. What did this snake want from her? Too late she realized that she had sounded abrupt; she should have called him "Your Snakiness" or something. What was the proper mode of address for a supernatural ophidian? She did not know. Good grief, what use was a public school education, anyway?

You have great power.

Was he offended? Buffy could not tell from that dry, uninflected, incorporeal voice.

Where is your stellated gown?

She lifted her head. "I left it behind."

Brave of you. Or foolish.

"Yes." Buffy tilted her head far back to look, seeing little but that frightening blunt head atop the white circinate mound of coils, those cold golden eyes. The white snake was much, much bigger than she remembered. She had to force herself to speak. Her voice came out a grainy whisper. "Please tell me, where is my daughter?"

Why should I?

He did not deny that he knew. But then again, why should he deny anything?

How have you deserved my help?

It was a farce, of course. Buffy had gone to Sunday school; she knew that the idea of praying was not to deserve. The concept of praying, petitioning, begging, pleading, boon-craving, sucking up, was not to earn anything, but to confess oneself undeserving and thereby toady the tyrant, deity, lord, politician, suckee into such spasms of ego gratification that he felt like giving you what you wanted. It was a joke. A game.

Yet—Buffy felt a chilly sense that in Fair Peril it might not be a game. She whispered, "So far I've gotten by on telling stories."

Suppose I don't want to hear a story. Why should I divulge anything to you?

"Because I need to find Emily."

You need? I am not concerned with what you need.

"But—she might be hungry. . . ." "Hungry" was the least of Buffy's fears for her daughter. In all-too-vivid fast-forward sequence, as if watching the movie preview from hell, Buffy imagined Emily starved, imprisoned, abused, molested, tortured, and it was as if a wasp the size of a poodle had stung her—no way could she whisper anymore. She rose up on her hind feet like a rearing stallion. She shouted, "Doesn't anybody but me goddamn care? She's just a girl, a child. She might be cold. She might be hurt. She might not be eating right. Her asthma might be acting up. Some cretin might be taking advantage of her." She knew that this was the white snake, she knew it would be wise to bespeak him softly, but she could not. If her life depended on it, which it very well might, she could not be ladylike any longer. She bellowed, "This is EMILY damn it my DAUGHTER my BABY my CHILD and I want to know, WHERE IS SHE? WHAT HAS HAPPENED TO HER?" Buffy shouted so loud that the guardian birds flew up with craking cries, the otters and bearcats splashed into the water. "IS SHE OKAY? IS SHE HAPPY? WHERE IS MY LITTLE GIRL?"

Ssssilence! The white snake convulsed under the impact of her shouting, his perfectly coiled symmetry destroyed. His anterior half rippled down over the edge of the plinth and swayed tautly in air with his tumid corpse-colored head thrust toward her, his black tongue flickering nearly in her face.

Buffy knew that he meant to bite her if she went on. And this time he would make the punissshment stick. She knew it.

But she could not stop. To stop would have been to be a lost soul, a toy, a squatting frog like Adamus, not Buffy, not Madeleine. She roared, "I DON'T CARE WHAT HAPPENS TO ME! NOBODY BETTER DAMN MAKE EMILY CRY!"

Sssorrow, the snake promised, pulling back like a fist to strike.

Like angel bells from on high, a blonde young voice called, "Mom!"

Bullheaded as Buffy was feeling, the white snake probably could not have made her flinch away. But that voice jerked her around like a golden chain. "EMILY!" Where was she, where was Emily? Stumbling back, frantically looking, Buffy did not even notice that the white snake jabbed at her and missed.

"Mom! Mommy!"

The voice came from the sky. The wise-eyed stag flew in on eagle wings. And riding on his back, gowned in samite and hanging on to his antlers like they were a steering wheel, was—

"Emily! EMILY!" Tears flooded Buffy's face so that she could barely see to avoid the rocks as she ran toward her daughter.

Fourteen

*P*risoner.

Walking between lavender trees, Adamus realized that his present circumstances—garments of velvet and gold, magical food to eat, mystical woods for the wandering— he realized that the luxury of his non-life would not have seemed like durance vile to most people, and the realization did not comfort him. Most people would have traded places with him, and most people were fools. They did not understand: waiting, tortured by hope, was prison. Excruciating boredom was prison. Prison was his inability to go, to do, to act.

He talked to the trees. "Emily," he whispered. Thinking of her—*Where is she?*—tightened invisible chains around his chest, making him moan. He wanted to go forth, find her, save her, be her love, her hero, but he could do nothing. The storyteller had not yet changed the story. To be a fairy-tale prince was to wait, like a doll swinging from a vendor's stall, until someone or something reached out and snatched you.

And even then, what followed might not be pleasant.

Adamus felt quite sure the Queen was not done with him. Ye gods and little fishes, he had come before her in small-clothes, and then he had given her Buffy's message, which had sent her shooting off in a fury, galloping away in her chariot of air. Probably, having dealt with Buffy, she was just now contemplating his condign punishment.

Buffy, I'm sorry. I warned you.

The storyteller had not yet changed the story, and probably now she never would.

Emily's mother.

"Emily . . ."

Chains tightened again, threatened to make him sob. With shackles on him no one could see, Prince Adamus d'Aurca walked deep into the mystical woods. No one could see the chains, but they hurt like real steel. He still had his pride; he wanted to be far from anybody, alone with his misery.

Aimlessly walking, he found a pretty forest glade full of statuary—a long, straight, shady glade—and he wandered down it, his footfalls soft and silent in wildflowers as thick as a carpet. Great beeches towered on each side, their silver trunks softly gleaming, their leaves rustling overhead, translucent, golden, though not with autumn. To either side stood white marble ruins, columns and cornices in pale arcades beneath the beeches, and the shafts of the columns were sometimes fluted pillars but more often white presences, caryatids and telamones, stone youths and maidens half naked beneath carved draperies. Beautiful youths, lovely maidens. Adamus walked on with slow steps and looked at them with some curiosity. He had thought he knew all of Fair Peril, but this was not a place he had ever been before.

Buffy shrieked, "Emily!" She could not seem to stop her unseemly noise, Emily, Emily, Emily! and the tears brightening everything to a wavering watery glory. Oh God oh joy oh God—but could this be the real Emily, this warm princess, hugging her? Hugging her with utter abandonment of adolescent dignity? Looking back at her with a starry light in those midnight-blue eyes?

Emily scanned her. *"Mom,"* she said, "what are you doing in that outfit?"

It was the real Emily, all right. Buffy laughed with teary relief and hugged her again. "Sweetie, I've been going crazy. Are you okay? Has anybody been bothering you? Have you been eating?"

"Mom, I'm fine." But Emily said it with none of the usual teenage scorn.

"Are you sure?"

"Yes! I'm okay-fine-copacetic.. Mom, meet Stott." Emily placed her hand lightly on the bearded neck of the stag standing next to her, near the pool's edge; the three of them stood well down the rocky slope from the pedestal. "He's a dear."

"I can see that."

Emily rolled her lovely eyes. "No, I mean, he really is a sweetheart. He came flying down and got me off that pedestal. Then the white snake . . ." Emily turned toward the serpent in question, who was lying atop the pedestal in sulky disarray and did not acknowledge. "The white snake gave me something to eat, and now I can understand what the birds are saying. They've been telling me how you— telling me how you've been looking for me and everything." Emily's indigo gaze was steady, but her voice wavered. "I never really understood before."

"Understood?"

"That—you really do love me."

Buffy wanted to shout, OF COURSE I DO! But she couldn't say a word. Her heart had gone hot and full, like her eyes. All she could do was reach out. Emily's hand embraced hers.

"The birds told me."

"Good." Buffy finally found her voice, though it was a husky whisper. "The birds are right. Can we get you home now?"

But Emily wasn't listening. She turned toward the white snake again. Evidently it had spoken to her; her expression had gone flat and fierce. "Why doesn't somebody ask me what *I* want for a change!" she yelled.

"Don't shout." The golden-winged, golden-antlered stag spoke up suddenly. "Noise exacerbates it."

Startled, Buffy asked him, "Are you an ensorcelled something-or-other?"

"No, just a talking coat rack."

With her voice reined in but passionate, Emily was saying to the white snake, "This being a princess sucks. It's like I'm a toy, a gilded Barbie doll, a trophy for somebody's shelf. I get moved here, I get moved there, I don't have a life. You've got me, Stott's got me, Adamus wants me, Mom wants me back. When is somebody going to ask me what *I* want?"

It was so simple, so eminently feminist, yet so sublimely unthought-of that Buffy stood with her mouth sagging open in an uncouth way. Emily—Emily didn't want to be a princess?

Emily didn't necessarily want to fling herself into a princely embrace?

Maybe Emily was not a child after all?

Maybe Emily didn't need to be rescued?

"You're just a stuffed puppet or something in the real world," Emily was saying to the white snake. "All Mom and I have to do is go back where we came from."

At which point Buffy would be a woman in nothing but her underwear standing in a fountain in a public mall, but who cared. She asked Emily humbly, "Is that what you want to do?"

"Yes." But Emily looked at her with troubled dark eyes. "No. I mean, not yet. First we have to help Adamus."

At the end of the forest glade, the Queen awaited him.

At first, wretched and wandering and unwary, he had thought it was just another white marble statue, an imposing one, a seated goddess, and he would look at her when he got there. Then—her stony stillness did not change, but he felt her eyes on him and he knew.

His face showed his shock. He could not help it. And he should have known, curse everything, he should have known—he had thought it was his wayward feet bringing him here, when all the time it was her voiceless bidding.

There was nothing he could do but walk up to her and kneel before her and bow his head.

"So. Adamus, my frog," the Queen greeted him, and her voice was not unpleasant—but that meant only danger. "My little princeling who wants to be mortal, you have come to face the music."

He dared to look up at her, to look her in the face, because he no longer cared what happened to him. "Your most puissant Majesty," he said, his voice low but steady, "I crave your pardon."

"What, for coming before me half naked?" She smiled. Then Adamus began to feel truly afraid, for it was almost a wistful smile, it rendered that hard face almost tender, and thereby signaled extreme danger. "Seeing you in your smalls was not so hard for me to bear, Adamus. You may recall, we established some time ago that I would like to see you in less than smallclothes, and in my bedchamber. And that I would like to do more than just look at you."

Terror turned him wooden. He could not speak.

"Surely you did not think my desires had changed in

the passing of a mere thousand years, Adamus? I am the Queen. I do not change. And I want you for my very own."

He could not speak, but he shook his head. No.

"No?" The word issued from her white mouth soft and light, like snow.

He shook his head again.

"I will command you one more time, Adamus: come to me."

"No." Adamus suddenly found his voice. "No. Do what you will to me, my Queen, but no. You cannot make me love you."

Silence. All around, the statues watched and listened in rigid silence.

The Queen no longer smiled. She spoke in a voice hushed and cold, like snow. "There are few things anyone can deny me, Adamus."

Few, but he knew his body to be one of them. In that one way she could not own him. His back straightened, his head lifted a fraction of an inch, because perhaps he had a soul after all.

"And," she went on, "there is nothing that anyone can deny me without consequence."

"Turn me to a frog again if you must," he said. "I care not." Sometimes he almost missed the watery beauty and peril of being a frog.

"No." The Queen's chilly golden gaze looked not at him any longer but past him—not a good sign. "No, that would be too easy, Adamus." Her stare swerved back to him again and held him as if her two white hands had cupped his face. "We have established that I want you. And we have established that you deny me."

Once again he could not move or speak. He merely stared back at her. But she knew the answer.

"Well, then," she said, "you cannot deny me my vicarious pleasure."

"Help Adamus?" Buffy did not understand. Was Addie in trouble? He hadn't been rendered ranine again, had he?

But there was no time to talk, because the white snake was becoming, as Stott had pointed out, exacerbated. Rearing up, standing almost on its pointed tail, straight as a white broom handle atop the dais, it glared down in a way that made Buffy realize how cold a belly dancer's costume was and wonder briefly, unreasoningly, whether the serpent could fly at Emily like a white spear through the air. There seemed to be no such thing as a safe distance. That chalky snake-face and those flat golden eyes made her think of the Queen.

"Um, see ya, your Hissiness," Emily sang, taking a step back. "Stott," she asked her stag between her teeth as she presented a gleaming smile to the white snake, "can you carry Mom too?"

"No," Buffy answered for him. She knew she was big enough to break him in half. "Go, you two. I'll meet you on the other side." She plunged into the pool.

> *Mother, may I go in to swim?*
> *Yes, my darling daughter.*
> *Hang your clothes on yonder limb*
> *But don't go near the water.*

That was the way the annoying old rhyme went. Crazily, Buffy found it singsonging through her head, though she had not thought of it since she had put the picture books away.

Who was the mother and who was the daughter here? Something had changed. Instead of being liquid light, this time the water seemed made of limpid darkness. Spangles of pewtery silver and coppery gold starred the bottom. It was like swimming through an inverted nighttime sky. Yet when her head broke the surface, Buffy found the Forest Multifarious still awash in lilac daylight.

Sculling like a turtle, she swam to the edge. This time she had help with the pertinacious hedgehog. Stott prodded it aside with his antlers as Buffy clambered out of the pool, then turned to look back at the dimpling water. Maybe it was something about the slant of light. Always before, she had noticed golden circles, shining fish, she had looked into clear water, but this time—though the pool was no less clear—it cloaked itself in surface. It was a dark, rippling mirror. She could see only reflections. Rocks. Stott. Herself.

No. Adamus, shadowy, looking back at her.

What was it LeeVon had called these pools?

She turned around to ask somebody what was going on, and saw the stag nuzzling Emily flush on the lips.

All logical thoughts were shocked out of Buffy. She knew she should not have been so taken aback, she knew Emily was a big girl now, she knew this was a place where everything was itself and something else—nevertheless, she stood speechless and gawking as Stott concluded his farewell. The stag lowered his head away from Emily's, bowed to one foreknee, then straightened and flew away. In her lavender samite gown, Emily looked after him until he disappeared over the treetops.

Buffy stood dripping and staring at her daughter. Yes, Emily, you may go in to swim. Yes, you may go near the water.

Yes—though the thought staggered her—you may even dive in. Though preferably not while your mother is watching.

"Well," she said softly, "you have grown up."

Emily turned and smiled. Then for some reason Emily hugged her again.

"You're getting yourself all soggy."

Emily nodded. "At first I thought it would be fun," she said.

"Getting yourself soggy?"

"Going with Adamus. Being a cinderella or whatever. A princess." Emily turned and started to lead the way toward the food court. "But then—that stupid pedestal—and the Queen is a real pain."

"No kidding."

"Yeah. I had to go to the stag party just to get away from her."

"*Stag party?*"

"Lighten up, Mom, it wasn't like that. Stott and his friends are nice." Emily added over her shoulder, "But I don't want to stay with them, either."

"Either?"

"The birds have been telling me about cages. I don't want to belong to somebody like that. I don't want to belong to Adamus or Daddy or you or Stott or anybody. I want to belong to myself, that's all, at least for starters. Be somebody. Do something." Emily looked back at Buffy, who was lagging behind her. "What, I haven't a clue. I haven't had enough time to think about it." Emily frowned. "You're limping."

"I stubbed my toe." Walking through a jungle was not the best option for bare feet.

"You need shoes. And something to wear that covers more of you."

"True." It was so undeniably true that Buffy took no offense. "How do we go about—"

"This is a *mall*, Mom. We go to a *store*."

The familiar scorn, the familiar Emily, made Buffy smile. "I don't have my wallet."

"I've got my charge card."

"Of course. What was I thinking?" As if anything, even alternate realities and Prince Charming himself, could ever separate Emily from her VISA Gold Card.

"Come on." Emily took Buffy by the hand.

It felt so right, to be mothered by this daughter. Tamely Buffy allowed herself to be led, but she said, "You know they'll call the cops. I'm going to be standing there in my underwear."

"As far as I can figure . . ." Emily looked around, gauging their position, then wrinkled her lovely nose. "We're in Sears." She sighed and shrugged, acknowledging that Sears, however uncool, would do. "We'll grab you a muu-muu or something quick. One of those ugly chenille things. Cover you up. Then we can get you some shoes and get back here."

Of such seemingly inconsequential decisions, such innocent detours, are very bad days made.

The Frog King wore a golden cape. Perhaps it had been wings once, but it was not wings any longer; such a gross being did not deserve wings. It was the shoulder trappings of royalty, nothing more. The Frog King wore a golden cape, and the Frog King wore a golden crown. Erect, with his meaty thighs bulging, the Frog King stood six feet tall or more. From his lowly position, kneeling on the ground, Adamus looked up at the Frog King as he had once looked up at someone in a cape, someone in a crown, someone far taller and bulkier than he was, long, long ago.

The Frog King looked down on him and laughed. There was nothing human about the Frog King's massive verdigris face with its immense smirking mouth—yet Adamus knew that laugh. He remembered that laugh; even after a thousand years, one does not forget one's childhood. That laugh had often preceded a thrashing.

Adamus whispered, "Father."

"Look at the big eyes," the Frog King remarked to the Queen. "Like two big jelly eggs. He always was a pitiful little polliwog."

Do with him what you like. I have the hammer and the anvil still to make better ones than he.

Adamus surged to his feet, his teeth clenched. He wanted to shout, roar, rage, but passion choked him; he managed only a single word. "Betrayer!"

The Frog King knocked him to the ground with a single clout of a green fist. With the breath walloped out of him, Adamus could not speak, lay struggling to get up. The Frog King bellowed with laughter.

"Blind mudpuppy!" he boomed, laughing. "You finally recognize your sire, do you?"

Adamus sat up, gasping like a fish, finding just enough breath to pant, "You're—no father—of mine."

"I'm not? I am, though." In an instant like a flash of lightning the Frog King stopped laughing, crouched, and thrust his great mushroom of a head toward Adamus. He roared with bulldog vehemence, "You think you can disown me? You can't. I'm in you. I disowned you first."

Adamus rose only to his knees. "You're a frog. You're a frog in a crown and a clown suit."

Somebody laughed again, but this time it was the Queen, laughing like bluebells pealing.

The Frog King rolled his tarnished eyes toward her as she laughed. He said nothing to her, but cuffed Adamus on the side of the head; Adamus stolidly withstood the blow. The Frog King barked at him, "You toadlet, who are you to tell me what I am? I am the Frog King, that's one thing, and I am Daddy, that is the other. I'm every mad bad Daddy, and you know what?" He ogled Adamus fiercely. "You want love, don't you, you puppy? Forget love. Whatever you want, I will take away. If you love something, it's mine. What Daddy wants, Daddy gets."

Sears itself, remarkably, worked out a lot better than Buffy had expected. After the transition, she found herself near the dressing rooms. She was able to duck straight into one without attracting the attention of anyone likely to call the police. Emily went and purchased a truly hideous caftan and brought it to her there. "Is this your revenge for something I've done?" Buffy inquired, putting it on over her belly-dancing getup.

"Just come on. Shoe department."

Emily's sense of urgency had to do with Adamus, Buffy decided as she grabbed herself a pair of canvas slip-ons. "Explain to me what's going on with Addie."

"It's the Queen," Emily said, heading toward a cashier with the shoes.

"Well, what else is new."

But Emily never got to explain any further, because a large napiform dazzlement darted from behind a Totes display and grabbed her by the elbow.

"Grandma!" Emily gasped.

Buffy was too startled to move or think anything but, Damn, should have known Fay shopped at Sears.

Gripping a white sweatshirt with puffy glitter trim in one hand and Emily in the other, Fay snapped, "Emily! Where do you think you're going? Everybody's waiting for you!"

Hardly the way to greet one's long-lost granddaughter. Standing there quite flat of bare feet, Buffy blurted out, "What do you mean? What's going on?"

"You!" Fay wheeled on her, showing remarkable athleticism and presence of mind for a woman her age; in the same peevish movement she swung her massive gilded purse. She didn't even let go of Emily or drop her new sweatshirt to do it. Her elbow whipped around, and mass times acceleration equals force or maybe it had something to do with angular leverage but who cared, the effect being the same whatever you called it, which was that the purse being pendulous upon Fay's arm whipped around like an absolute sonuvabitch and conked Buffy on her head and shoulder hard enough to make her see stars. Buffy did not fall, but she definitely felt the store floor shifting under her feet as she gazed in fascination at the special effects. Lichen-colored splashes. Exploding celadon glass. Green-white fireworks starry-starry on a black flannel background, shades of her discarded nightgown. She could hear Fay scolding at her, but she couldn't talk back. She couldn't move. She couldn't see.

"Bad bad bad bad bad!" Fay was barking. "Ungrateful cow! Did she tell you what she did to your father?" This last was apparently aimed at Emily.

Emily said, "Let go, Grandma, you're hurting my arm."

Hard to tell star-dazzle from Fay-scintillation, but Buffy could see enough now to tell that Fay did not let go of Emily's arm. Rather, Fay started propelling her granddaughter toward an exit. "Move, young lady, you're late. They're all waiting."

"Who? Waiting for what?"

"Your guests, Emily! Not to speak of your bridegroom. Your wedding!"

Emily's mouth softened into childish bewilderment. Being hustled out, she looked back over her shoulder at her mother for help, her dark eyes wide.

With a struggle as if tearing loose from concrete, Buffy started forward. "No!" she shouted. "Let go of her!"

"Slug! Twerp! You don't tell me what to do!" The purse of doom struck again, harder this time. Buffy saw fireballs and volcanoes now, not just stars. She could not move or speak as Fay led Emily away.

Fifteen

With an effort sharp enough to make her scream, Buffy broke free from her purse-induced paralysis and got herself moving.

"Emily?" Oh, dear God. "Emily!"

The canvas slip-ons the girl had been about to buy for Buffy lay in an inadequate trail, as if Hansel and Gretel had had only two size-ten bread crumbs, one for the accessories aisle, one for the store entrance, or as if a really megapod Cinderella had lost both slippers this time.

"Emily!"

Buffy knew damn well it was already too late, but she could not seem to stop calling. "Emily?" She thundered out into the mall. No Emily there, either. "Emily . . ." Damn. Tears. Buffy's head hurt as if a thousand Fays were still whamming it, ached almost worse than her heart, but she knew she had to stop crying and think. Do something. Fast. "Stott? Anybody?" She looked down the mall; all the pedestals were empty. Everybody had gone to the wedding but her.

Emily's wedding? Could Fay be serious?

Cold prickles in her palms told Buffy that yes, indeed, Fay could.

Next question: wedding to whom, or what? Adamus, one would assume. Yet—could one assume anything?

Only one thing seemed certain: Emily was in peril.

In Fair Peril.

And Buffy couldn't get there to help her. She could not seem to make the transition. Wide awake, in a panic, she saw only the bright banalities of the Mall Tifarious— kitschy coffee mugs, rock star T-shirts, key chains—she could not conceptualize the other reality. It was terrifying, like that time when she was a child coming home from summer camp on the train and her parents had told her to meet them in front of the station, and she waited and waited, looking out at the parking lot, the cars, the road, where was her family, where were the people who were supposed to love her, they had forgotten her, disowned her, moved someplace else while she was gone—and everything looked familiar, parking, cars, road, yet queasily strange, until at desperate last she had set off with suitcase in hand to walk home and the streets were ordinary-looking yet strange, nothing seemed right. A large man in a white collar had stopped her, questioned her, escorted her back to the train station and showed her: two fronts, two parking lots, two roads, mirror images, almost identical—but her family was not there in front of the othergates door, either. They had gone home, she was too late . . . The damn mall felt that same way, like a waking, heartbreaking nightmare monument to her own stupidity. If she could just understand, if she could just see whatever it was she wasn't seeing, just fight free of the mind-set and *see*—

"Bridal shop," she muttered, and with bare feet flapping on the flooring and caftan snapping around her thighs, she set off.

Bridal shop. Maybe seeing the white gowns, maybe

thinking of Emily, the child bride, all dressed in lacy white, white as death, maybe then she would be able to find her way to Fair Peril.

But a score of ranked television screens confronted her now. Big screens. Some sort of entertainment store. Desperately urgent, Buffy could not stop, but—on every single screen her ex confronted her.

"Prentis."

Only this could make the day more surreal than it was already: thirty or more super-sized Prentises were talking with their giant wet, lippy mouths choreographed like that snarkiest of all sports, synchronized swimming. Multifarious Prentises. The effect was so mesmerizing that Buffy slowed to a halt and stood watching too many Prentises with fascination, as if Fay had whacked her over the head again. It was a live broadcast, some talk show; evidently Prentis had managed to get himself defrogged. Perhaps Tempestt had done her kissy duty after all. Buffy was so upset she could not follow what Prentis was saying, but she gathered that he was exhorting and being sincere; promising to cut taxes, probably. Back in the frog race. How dreary to be somebody, how dreary to be Prentis frog, telling his name the livelong June to the admiring public bog. Prentis was the real frog king. He and Tempestt had gotten married at a froggie resort under a froggie moon in June. But it wasn't June bride time again already, was it? It couldn't be June yet. Where was the bridal shop? But maybe it didn't matter. Everything seemed hazy. Starting to fade. Transition.

Oh, please, let it happen. Calm down. Breathe. Lamaze, help me now. Breathe. Again. Breathe.

As if she were seeing the too-many Prentises through a fly's eyes with many facets, Buffy watched as he loomed, shifted like a kaleidoscope, and turned into—okay. God bless America. There was a Prentis-sized frog talking to her, quacking something about family values.

It was like being trapped by a boor at a cocktail party. Buffy dodged past him quite rudely. He didn't matter. She had to find Emily.

But he seized her by the hair and yanked her back to face him again. "How dare you, wench." And his voice was dank and stony and nothing like Prentis's voice. "Attend when I speak to you." His murky eye froze her. Then she saw, how could she not have seen it before? The terrifying serried crown perched above that eye.

And she remembered that she had seen the third pedestal empty. And she knew she was up against an untried peril here. The Frog King.

"No," Adamus said to the Queen, still kneeling before her. All parts of him ached from holding that position, except his lower legs, which had lost all feeling. He had been kneeling for hours. Seemed like years. About a thousand years.

"You shall do as I say." The Queen's voice cracked like a whip, stinging him; spear-straight and stiff with wrath, she kept her regal seat, but Adamus felt the fiery impact of her anger, not for the first time, across his shoulders.

"No. I cannot." The words were like river stones, settled, worn smooth of all passion by many repetitions.

Death, the Queen threatened. The word, a whisper, a breath, a siffilation, sounded right inside his head. She had that power.

The cold old witch. Adamus lifted his head to look at her. There she sat in her ermine cloak on her white-stone woodland throne, quite simply being what she was, with not even a gravedigger's understanding of why he couldn't just be what he was, too. Could no one understand? Adamus cried out, "I cannot do that to her! You think I'm a fool? She would never marry me of her own free will; I know her. She's a wise child, she's her mother's daughter, she would never throw away her freedom just to serve some fairy tale. And even if she would, I would not do that to her. She is young and beautiful and I love her."

Golden leaves rustled overhead, silver beeches sighing like a presence. "You would rather be one of them?" The Queen raised her fierce porcelain hand and pointed at the ranks of marble columns that flanked her throne, at telamones, caryatids, stone youths and maidens looking on with dead eyes, bearing their forever load with everyoung, lifeless bodies. "You think you are the first? Behold. Other young fools who thought they would be human and have free will."

Then Adamus began to breathe hard, knowing that each sweet breath might be his last, and he flexed his feet to drive away the stony feeling; pain surged through him instead, bowing his head—but pain was better than not feeling, than not being. Pain proved that he was not an automaton. Not just a boy doll for the Queen to play with. Not just a golden trophy waiting on the shelf.

Not entirely a Prince of Fair Peril.

Pain—but there was too much pain. Too much struggle against too heavy a weight of history, story upon story upon story. The storyteller had to be dead. Otherwise, why had she not yet changed the story? But she had not, he could tell she had not, and now she never would; there was no hope for him. He was still the Prince. The weight of his golden fate lay upon him like a slab of granite.

"You shall do it," the Queen said.

"No," Adamus whispered, but he knew he would not be able to hold out much longer.

"Let me go!" Buffy tore free of the Frog King's grip and lunged away from him. He was loathsome. He had called her wench. And now that she had been irredeemably rude to him, he could go milt himself. He didn't matter.

Behind him in the lavender forest, waiting at the end of an aisle of beeches, stood a young woman in a white lace dress.

"Emily?" Buffy ran to her. "Emily! What's happening? Are you okay?"

She smiled but did not answer. It was Emily, yet—not Emily. Emily's indigo eyes, Emily's creamy skin, Emily's face, but—this was someone who would eat flowers, if she ate anything at all. A star of gold glimmered on her forehead. Her hands, curled like ivory rose petals, did not move. Her white dress floated as crisp and ethereal as starlight, without a single redeeming smear of chocolate on it.

Worst of all, her VISA Gold Card lay abandoned on the grass at her feet. Not Emily.

This was the Princess.

Puffing and pompous, in green suit and fishbelly-white waistcoat, walking humanwise, the Frog King lurched up to them. "Begone, beldam," he commanded Buffy, "or I will put you on my enemies list." Then he turned his back on her. To the Princess he offered his arm. She smiled a soulless, docile smile and placed her dainty hand in the bight of his thick green elbow.

Somewhere, lute music played. Emily and the frog wheeled and began their promenade down the aisle.

"No!" Buffy shouted. The Frog King did not turn his head. Neither did Emily. "No, it's not right!" She shouted again, louder. But no one paid any attention to her or her noise, just like when they used to get mad and shut Maddie in the closet, and that had to be because she was a bad person, she had always been a bad person, she did not count. She was living inside an Anne Sexton poem and her guilts were being catalogued. "Emily, don't marry that thing! Kill it!" Take a knife and chop up frog. Frog has no nerves. Frog is as old as a cockroach. Frog is—father's genitals.

Father. Was it Prentis?

Oh, nausea. At the feel of frog the touch-me-nots explode like electric slugs. Slime will have him. Slime has made him a house. He says: Kiss me. Kiss me.

Buffy felt so sick she could not move.

At the golden end of the silver beech aisle, the wedding party stood ceremonially ranked under an archway of golden roses. Buffy saw that ormolu ogress, Fay, holding a huge bouquet of exceedingly phallic calla lilies and showing her gleaming teeth in a smile. She saw Stott posing like a lawn guardian. She saw, amid miscellaneous courtiers, some bearcats and ferrets and a carefully groomed hedgehog or two. At the exact geometric center of the silent arrangement, straight and severely symmetrical and taller than the others, the Queen of Fair Peril waited to officiate.

On the Frog King's arm, Emily—or this automaton called Emily, this plaster Princess, this articulated trophy—walked down the aisle on a carpet of heather and saxifrage to stand in front of the Queen.

"No!" Buffy leaped out of her trance of horror like a deer, took one running stride, stomped on the hem of her—gown; her caftan was now a heavy gown larded with gaudery, as befitted the mother of the bride—pitched forward, and fell flat in the loamy aisle. Struggling up, lavished with dirt, she did not take time to brush herself off but yanked her skirt above her unlovely knees and sprinted forward to—well, to do something. Somebody had to do something. What, she didn't know.

"Choose," the Queen's hard white voice was saying to someone as Buffy ran forward.

"Mercy, O my Queen." The voice was so soft and strained with pain that she didn't recognize it.

"No. I have been more than patient and merciful. Choose now. Obey, or be stone."

Buffy saw him then, saw his shoulders quivering as he knelt before the Queen, and the shock stopped her in midstride. She stood halfway up the aisle, panting, mostly with emotion.

He did not speak, but lifted his head and turned it to look behind him.

Adamus.

His pale, taut face was turned not toward her but toward Emily, or the docile creature called Emily, standing there on the arm of the Frog King. Adamus looked, and the Frog King glowered back at him, but Emily only smiled her brainwashed smile, and Buffy saw Adamus wince as if he had been struck.

Then he turned his shadowed eyes to her, the storyteller.

He looked at her, and she could not think what to say to him, what to do. As if she had never seen him before, she stood startled and doltish in the presence of Prince Adamus d'Aurca's supernatural perfection, the thoughtless balletic beauty of his long thighs in their tight white hose, the slim wedge of his torso under its velvet tunic, his strong shoulders, his wide, wild mouth. His pagan cheekbones and temples and brows. The brand of his Queen's lips a romantic, never-healing wound on his forehead. His wide golden eyes pooled with black.

Pooled deep with despair.

He looked at her for a harsh moment, then turned away from her and back to the Queen. In an empty, wintry voice he said, "I will do it."

Off in the goldengrove somewhere, a bird gave a melancholy cry.

"Very well," said the Queen of Fair Peril, blasé. "You may live, then, Adamus, to carry on with your function." She raised one hand in a kindly, dismissive gesture to the

Frog King. "Very well, Batracheios, we shall not be need-ing you after all."

The Frog King bowed his hulking bulk. "I give this Prin-cess to be married to this Prince," he said in a bullfrog's throaty roar. "And I crave vengeance for the insolence of an interloper in our midst."

"Later," said the Queen. "Let the nuptials proceed."

Batracheios stepped back. Adamus rose and took the bridegroom's place.

Buffy wobbled on her feet with a sort of cowardly relief. Sometimes you take what breaks you can get. Adamus would be kind to Emily; of that much she felt sure. Far better that Emily should be given to Adamus than to that horrible Frog King. Besides, Adamus was so beautiful—if he married Emily, that would mean Buffy would get to see him. It would keep him around. It would be a kind of vicarious way of having him for herself.

Fine. Good. Buffy felt shaky and stone-bone-weary; maybe she could just sit down and watch her daughter's wedding? Emily had walked down the aisle on her father's arm, in a sense. Emily was to be married to a prince with kind and beautiful eyes. It was the fairy-tale ending; why fight it?

Courtiers, deer, frog, hedgehogs looked on. So did the statues. Many statues of young and beautiful youths and maidens stood watching with blind stone eyes. Adamus and Emily, just as young and beautiful, seemed only mar-ginally more alive.

With the look of a trapped wild thing, Adamus faced Emily and reached for her hands. As automatically as if he had pressed a switch, she lifted them and placed them in his.

Why fight it?

Buffy found herself choking back a sob.

Why fight it? Because coiling inside her, coiling and stir-

ring and swelling and hissing like stormwind and stinging
her heart with thunderbolt rage was a wild black emotion
of which she did not yet know the name. As wild and
black and bleak as the wintery anguish in Prince Adamus's
eyes.

Adamus. He had looked at her, then turned away. *Betrayer*, that look had said.

She had failed him.

He gave up. He gave up on me.

Addie. Her Addie.

"Let the nuptials proceed," the Queen was saying.
"Adamus and Emily, repeat after me—"

"No," Buffy whispered. She knew the name of the black
snake inside her now. It was despair. Or desperation.

It was knowing it was all her own goddamn fault.

Her. Being a jerk.

Her problem.

Her brain farting.

"*NO!*" she shouted, and she strode forward.

In his modest third-floor apartment, LeeVon stood quite
seriously holding both of the blond young man's hands
and looking into his beautiful eyes.

It was a nice apartment for a librarian. Lots of built-in
bookshelves, good lighting, a window nook, a pleasant
bird-chirpy yard to look down into. Friendly junk lying
around: a working model of a roller coaster, a 3-D puzzle
of the City of Oz, a ceramic bust of Kipling. Escher posters
on the walls. Newspapers piled on the kitchen table, magazines in the bathroom, books everywhere else. LeeVon
felt quite happy to be back in his own apartment, almost
as happy as he was to be back in human form. But both
of those happinesses put together did not equal the happiness he felt about the blond young man, whose ponytail
was undone at this moment so that his hair hung in a most

appealingly tousled fashion around his bare shoulders.

"Richard," LeeVon said, for that was the young man's name, "you have to understand, what I said—I meant it."

"I know," Richard said almost in a whisper. LeeVon loved the youthful tremor in his voice. He loved the delight and alarm in his gray eyes. He loved his thick, tawny eyelashes. He loved everything about him.

He said, "I've imprinted on you just like a goose. Which I resemble in other ways, actually. I'm silly about you."

"I think I could learn to like that."

"You're free, you know," LeeVon said, knowing with a pang of joy that he himself was no longer free. That was the secret, to be willing to risk. Give away freedom for a chance at—this. "Free to go, free to come back whenever." But LeeVon did not let go of his hands.

Richard shrugged his bare shoulders, an act LeeVon watched with appreciation. Richard said, "What if I just hang around?"

"Even better."

"Okay."

"I want to marry you."

Richard smiled. "They're not about to let us do that."

"Stupid laws. What's the big problem with a marriage of equals? Let us not to the marriage of true minds admit impediment."

"Who said that?"

"I just did."

"No, I mean, who said it before?"

"How should I know? I'm just a librarian. Children's. Romance is not in my department. Velvet's not my usual scene." LeeVon found himself anxious to correct any possible misconceptions. "I'm more into leather."

"Leather is the coolest, man."

LeeVon felt warmth swelling in his chest and a loopy

smile growing on his face. He moved closer. But then he winced. "Ow."

"What's the matter?"

"Sudden headache." He flinched as it intensified. "Buffy's shouting somewhere."

"Buffy? Who's Buffy?"

"A friend. One of those people who makes you wonder why you need enemies." Having been turned into a frog was a consideration that kept LeeVon from worrying much about what was going on with Buffy at this point. He was home again, and she had her own story to pursue and he, blessedly, had his. "We happen to share a collective unconscious. Ow." LeeVon was forced to let go of Richard's hands and rub his own head. "Ow, she's loud. Damn. I wish she'd get over it, whatever it is, and shut up."

"NO!" Buffy strode forward. "NO, IT'S NOT FREAKING RIGHT!" She shoved her large self between Adamus and Emily, neither of whom resisted her. Emily turned bland eyes toward her; Adamus, tormented ones. "WHAT HAVE YOU DONE WITH MY DAUGHTER?" Buffy demanded of the Queen.

"Silence, you insolent fool." The Queen spoke with the perilous patience of a middle-school teacher. "Don't you see her? Right beside you?"

"Murphy, you jerk, shut up!" Fay shrilled at the same time.

"Buffy," Adamus whispered, "help. Change the story."

Buffy listened only to Addie, turning to him. "What's going on? What's happened to Emily?"

"She's trapped in happily-ever-after, just like I am."

There wasn't a whole lot of time to think, to sort it out. Fay had relinquished her bouquet of calla lilies in favor of her fearsome handbag and was advancing; the Queen of Fair Peril was growing exacerbated, her face stretching taller and narrower and more like a white snake every moment; Buffy looked to Stott to see if he might help, but the stag stood ornamental and useless, like Emily.

The hedgehogs were rattling their quills.

The sky was darkening. A rising wind rustled the beech leaves.

The Frog King's mouth opened as wide as the maw of hell, and he started to laugh.

Buffy roared, "ONCE UPON A TIME!"

Everything stopped. The ormolu ogress stood with her golden weapon upraised; the white snake coiled rigid where the face of the Queen had been; Adamus stood like a gallant statue, as if he had stopped breathing. Silence hung like mist in a spiderweb. The Realm of Fair Peril stopped because Buffy had spoken words of consummate power. In the Perilous Realm, the greatest power is that of the storyteller. For only in story is there life.

And death. The storyteller's is the greatest power, and the greatest peril: the storyteller faces the terrors of the mind. Anne Sexton had killed herself.

"Once upon a time," Buffy said more quietly, "there was a real world. And in this real world ordinary people lived."

She fingered the dirt clinging to her bodice as she spoke.

"One of these ordinary people was a middle-aged woman named—named Madeleine," she said. "Maddie. And hoo boy, was Maddie mad. Pissed off. Ticked. Bummed, peeved, sore, miffed, nose out of joint, disgruntled. She was mad because she was getting fat and wrinkly and old. She was mad because somebody was supposed to love her and nobody did. Her mother was supposed to love her, but she got Alzheimer's. Her husband was supposed to love her, but he got himself a gold-plated, midlife replacement wife instead. Her daughter was supposed to love her, but her daughter preferred Daddy. So Maddie found somebody to love her. Somebody young and cute who adored her and would do anything for her. Kind of a private friend, a secret playmate. Maddie had an animus, and Maddie called him Addie."

For the first time, Emily's velvet-blue eyes focused on Buffy. Emily started listening.

"Addie," Buffy said. "Adam, swimming in the dark pool of her mind like a frog in a well." Everything in that well was itself and something else. "Swimming in the black, starry water of her dreams like a soulmate in her womb. Addie, her animus, her man. Everything she would have liked to be if she had been born a boy instead of a girl. Just like a hundred thousand thousand dreamers before her, Maddie made him golden and beautiful and ardent and a prince."

The Queen—or the white snake, for the Queen was herself and that serpent as well—the white one listened rigidly, her golden eyes cold on Buffy, gelid. How far, Buffy wondered, could she interlope; how much ownership of Adamus could she claim before the Queen of Fair Peril struck like a white whip, a white snake, a lightning bolt smiting her down?

Too bad for the Queen. Understanding the Queen all too well, Buffy said, "Addie was the mirror, mirror she kept in thrall to tell her she was beautiful. Gold-framed trophy on the wall. Mirror, mirror with no soul of its own." She paused. The Queen stood like white crystalline poison, Lot's wife on drugs, but too bad for her and too bad for Buffy; the story was coming alive, the storytelling was as irreversible as parturition, had to go on. Screw the Queen. Buffy shifted her attention to Emily.

Emily, gazing back at her, all dressed in white, gloved, corseted, far too tame; Buffy remembered the real-world Emily. Buffy said, "So everything was hunky-dory for a brief while. But then there was the daughter. There's always a daughter, isn't there, when there's a pissed-off, get-ting-older woman looking for a reassuring mirror? The daughter was, of course, a rosebud just opening, dewy-new and beautiful and rebellious and thoughtlessly cruel, a mirror to tell her mother she was ugly. And Maddie hated her as much as she hated herself, but loved her more." More than she loved herself; far more than she hated her. And, thank the love and the hatred, Emily was beginning to respond. Blue vexation flared in her eyes. Her rosebud mouth opened just a little, as if she wanted to rebut or interrupt, though she did not.

"The daughter's name was Emily," Buffy went on. "And Emily also swam in Maddie's dreams, for just like a hun-dred thousand thousand dreaming mothers before her, Maddie had made a rosebud of a girl into a golden prin-cess. So how was Addie to help falling in love with her, when Maddie loved her so much? Of course the Princess had to meet the Prince. Of course Mother Maddie had to be the wicked witch who tried to keep them apart. Of course they had to hate her, and of course they had to kiss. Of course they had to run away together and leave her all alone.

"Then all the mirrors turned their faces to the walls, and Maddie lived in a dark, dark house. She might as well have been buried in a grave."

Adamus regarded her steadily with a troubled, waiting gaze.

"Buried alive," Buffy said, keeping it very quiet, very level. "It's enough to drive a person crazy. So she cried out. She called out for someone to help her, save her, love her. She screamed for her prince to come. And someone came, but it was a stranger dressed all in white. He had kind eyes. He took her away to his white mansion with many rooms and spoke to her gently and offered her pills to stop her crying. His big house was a genteel place where everyone said please and thank you, but there were locks on the doors and bars on the windows and Maddie could not get out.

"She stood at the window and looked at the sky, where starlings were flying. I am a prisoner, she cried to the starlings. I am a prisoner, she cried to her prince, come set me free. And from far away far far dark inside her, Addie cried out in answer, I am a prisoner more truly than you are. La Belle Dame Sans Merci has me in thrall. Cold old queen, you own me.

"Maddie did not want to listen. She looked at the sky, where sparrows were flying. I am a prisoner, she cried to the sparrows. I am a prisoner, she cried to her daughter. Emily, come back, comfort me. But from far away far far dark inside her, Emily cried out in answer, I am a princess now. I am more of a prisoner than you are. Here I starve on my pedestal. Cold old queen, you own me.

"Maddie looked at the sky, where frogs were flying. There is no one to help me, she cried. Story of my life. A white snake flew past her window on golden wings. We are all prisoners, it said to her. We are the stories we tell, it said to her. Change the story.

"So she bent her mind upon the bars and broke through them and went forth to look for her daughter."

"Mother," Emily whispered.

Buffy looked at her daughter. Emily looked back with liquid eyes, deep eyes like midnight pools mirroring the stars. Buffy reached out and hugged her.

"Mom, Mom, Mommy!" Emily returned the hug, then stiffened. "Ew, Mom." She pulled away. "You're all dirt."

It felt so good Buffy could have bawled. She forbore to hug Emily anymore, but cried, "You're back!"

There was an irritable siffilation of white scutes as the most crucial personage in the audience stirred. "Ssssilence," the snake-queen hissed.

"No." Buffy turned to face her, trying not to show her fear. "The story is not over; it is still going on. I am Maddie. I am here to set my daughter free."

"What about me?" Adamus whispered, his exquisite face taut.

"Of course you, Addie. Especially you. If you are sure you want to be mortal and real."

"I am certain."

The snake-queen reared up like a cobra, speaking so vehemently that her black forked tongue rattled her starched lace collar. "These are my subjects! My chattels! My playthings, my froggies, my pets! How dare you encroach? You shall not take them from me!"

"How could I, your puissant Majesty?" Buffy said quietly. "But I have come to set them free from *me*."

"Sssstoryteller—"

"Maddie journeyed far, far dark inward," Buffy said to Adamus, to Emily. "And she found her animus and her princess daughter, and she spoke with them. And she said, I do not own you anymore. Live your own stories now. Love each other if you want to, but only if you want to. Cleave to each other if you want to, or go your own ways if you want to. Be free of my dreams for you. Be free of my dreams for us. I will dream for myself now. I will tell new stories. I will no longer attempt to use you. I will not constrain you to love me. I will learn to live on my own, I will be as free as a wild goose on the wind, and I will always love you."

There was a crash of stone and a crackle of glass; cornices fell down, and the tinted dome overhead spiderwebbed and burst apart; the rainbow shards flew like doves. Caryatids and telamones cried out like the donkeys of God, flung off their burdens, and began to dance. Beech leaves turned to butterflies. Stott bugled. Adamus threw back his head and shouted a wordless yawp of joy.

The white queen shrieked and coiled to strike.

"ONCE UPON A TIME," Buffy bellowed. "THERE WAS A REAL WORLD."

Adamus grabbed Buffy's hand and Emily's hand just in time as, with a thunder roar like the sky pouring in and a starry blackness and a whirling vertigo, quiddity imploded upon them.

Sixteen

*I*t was not one of those slip-in-slip-out-again transitions to which Buffy was becoming accustomed. This moment between realities was noisy, violent, and felt quite final. Fair Peril had tried to swallow her, but was spitting her out instead.

Then quiddity steadied, and there was a profound prismatic silence.

Buffy opened her eyes. She and Emily and Adamus were standing in the ornamental-plasterwork store, under the pallid and incurious gazes of gargoyles and horses and Venuses and cocky Davids and paunchy eunuchs and steatopygic cherubs perched on sconces, and entirely too many plaster-framed Art Nouveau mirrors.

"Ew!" Emily complained. "I hate this place. Everything's icky white in here." She headed out toward the mall mezzanine.

Looking around him wide-eyed, Adamus followed. Heads turned; shoppers stared at him. Even if he had not been wearing an amethyst velvet tunic with gold embroidery, white silk tights, and dove-colored doeskin boots, people would have been staring at him, because he was too eerily beautiful to be real, as if he were a living, moving publicity still with all his pixels Scitexed. "What is he, some soap opera dude?" Buffy heard somebody ask somebody else.

"Prithee, Princess Emily," Adamus whispered. He sounded frightened.

Emily turned to him. She wore a rumpled white shirt from the Gap, jeans, sandals. Just a normal teenager, which was to say, supremely beautiful—to her mother. With no such delusions concerning herself, Buffy was flapping along in bare feet and her hideous caftan.

"I'm not a princess," Emily told Adamus gently.

"I—I know that, but—" He looked around as if something might be stalking up behind him, a harpy, a doomster, a snake. His hand reached out to her yet faltered in midair, a lost thing.

"But he's still a prince," Buffy said in a low voice, stopping beside Emily. "He's having trouble with the transition." Perhaps never in his millennium of existence, Buffy realized, had Adamus made a full transition. As a frog, he had talked, he had still been Prince Adamus. In her experience his princely garb had never changed, whichever world he walked in. Always he had felt the unseen chains of the cold old Queen around him. Now they were gone.

Freedom can be terrifying.

His shadowed gaze turned to her, so intense that the golden rings of his irises seemed to pulse. "Milady, please. Help me."

"How, Addie?"

He seemed not able to say, but stood with his lips parted, his breathing ragged. Buffy saw his shoulders trembling.

Emily saw it too. "Mom, do something!"

"Like *what*?"

Adamus's otherworldly face was so pale and translucent that Buffy could see the white, winglike angles of his lovely cheekbones, the blood pumping dark in his temples, the Queen's mark on his forehead pulsing to the same panicky drumbeat.

That raw mark. How could she have done such a thing, putting her brand on him?

Impulsively Buffy stepped toward him, captured his head gently between her hands—the texture of that golden hair between her fingers, hot and silky as sunlight, was like nothing else she had ever felt—and drew him toward her so that he bowed his head. Just because it was the motherly thing to do—to make it better—she kissed the red mark on his forehead.

She felt the change before she saw it, through her hands. There was a jolt, like electricity, or a twinge, and then the texture of his hair was just—hair. As satisfactory and normal as a horse's mane. Buffy's startled hands let go of him, and she stepped back, wide-eyed. The mark was gone from his forehead. Utterly gone. So was the sheen of golden glamour. So was his eerie, extravagant beauty. And so was his fear. A freckle-faced young hazel-eyed man looked back at her, quizzical, as if to say, What the hell are you doing, lady?

"Addie?" Buffy whispered.

Yes, it was him, all right. In some ineffable way Buffy recognized the clownish mouth that was quirking into a smile. Only a person who had once been a frog could own such a droll mouth. But other than that, he was just a nice-looking kid, nothing special. A few pimples. Hair the same khaki color as his eyes. He wore a faded purplish chambray shirt, blue jeans, running shoes that had probably been white once upon a time.

He said, "Did I ask you to kiss me?"

"Uh, no, not really." Hastily Buffy stepped back, al-

though there had been no tinge of challenge or rebuke in
his tone, just bemused inquiry.

In the same polite, bewildered way, he inquired, "What
did you call me? Addie?"

Buffy nodded.

"Is that my name? Do you know me?"

Buffy's mouth sagged open and stayed that way; she
couldn't say a word. Beside her stood Emily, similarly in-
capacitated.

Addie—or this new creature based on Addie—could see
that they were flabbergasted. "I guess I'm being a dork,"
he said cheerfully. "See, I can't remember. Don't know
where I am. Don't know how I got here, and—" A sudden
wide, whimsical smile. "And I sure don't know why I feel
so good, 'cause I ought to be upset, shouldn't I? Considering that I can't remember a blame thing."

Emily got her mouth moving first. "But you do feel
okay?"

His smile, unbelievably, spread yet wider. "I feel *fantab-
ulous*."

"Then maybe not remembering is better."

"Maybe." He shrugged, looking around him happily,
taking in the bright sights of the mall like a child at a
carnival. "So, do I know you people?"

"I'm Emily, and this is my mother."

He offered his hand to Buffy. "Nice to meet you, Mrs.—
uh—"

"Murphy." Buffy managed to get herself functioning,
though her voice croaked. She shook his hand. "Buffy
Murphy."

Emily put in, "You're, um, you're my boyfriend."

That smile of his would have lit up a dark winter night
and warmed it too. "Really?"

"Um, yes."

"You look way too sexy to have a boyfriend named Addie."

"Adam," Emily said. She reached around him with easy familiarity and pulled a wallet from his back jeans pocket. She opened it and showed him his driver's license. "There. Adam Prinz. See?"

"Hey!" He regarded his own unflattering mug shot with huge satisfaction. "There I am. And there's my birthday. And that's my address, right?"

Peeking at the address, Buffy saw that it was hers. "Hoo boy," she said.

"Right," Emily said. "C'mon, we were just heading there. Right, Mom?"

"I released him," Buffy said, "and now I get to rehabilitate him, is that it?"

"Don't ask me, Mom." Emily rolled her eyes and started walking. Her putative boyfriend followed. Sweet kid. Buffy barefooted along rapidly in her hideous caftan, watching Addie from behind as he gazed all around him. More than sweet; he was an innocent, like a newborn. And he had the right attitude. It was not a half-bad world, really, with sunshine sifting down through the tinted-glass domes and a robin flying around. It looked like the thing was nesting on one of the pedestals. Oh, goodness. Oh, wow. It was a *wonderful* world; the damn bird was nesting in the frog king's crown, pooping on his fat verdigris face. Hallelujah, there was justice in the universe.

"You've lost weight, Mom," Emily remarked.

The kind tone, the smile, the compliment, from Emily, felt so wonderful Buffy could barely speak.

"Thanks," she managed. "Good."

"Huh?" Adam turned in surprise. "What's good?"

"I've lost weight."

"But—" His mouth faltered and his hazel eyes lost focus as he struggled to chase down what he wanted to say.

"But—why do you want to lose weight? I mean, back in the—" He looked disoriented, almost frightened, but he struggled on. "In the Middle Ages, or, like, you know, the Renaissance, women were supposed to be big, you know? Like you." He blushed and looked down at the floor.

With force and clarity as if a white snake had bitten her, Buffy did know. She knew several things at once. She knew that Adam almost remembered but did not quite remember that he had been Adamus d'Aurca, a Prince of Fair Peril, a thousand years old instead of eighteen. She knew that he almost remembered but did not quite remember that he had been Addie, her frog and her pet. She knew with an exaltation of her heart that she had been beautiful to him.

She knew that he had loved her.

She knew that his almost-memories would quickly fade.

She knew that it was better that way.

"Adam," she said firmly, "you're quite right. I'm big and I'm gorgeous."

Adam threw back his head and laughed. His just-born joy rang through the mall like golden bells. People turned their heads to smile at him.

"Gonna take that boy in hand," Buffy said to Emily or anybody who happened to be willing to listen. "Gonna take that boy home and feed him soul cake."

Bent like a fishhook, Mom shuffled across the nursing-home lawn, her hands dragging the grass like grappling tackle. "Must get it done," she droned. "Must get it done."

"Mrs. Murphy!"

But the poor child all gussied up in white was as worn out with this nasty world as she was. Young innocent dressed in white like a bride for the slaughter. Zipping up old men's flies for them. The poor little white lamb wouldn't come after her right away. Stayed sitting on the patio with the old poopieheads.

"Mrs. Murphy! Don't go so close to the road!"

It was time. Mom's hands, as brown and gnarled as tree roots, rose up suddenly like praying mantis claws. Like a turtle, Mom lifted her head to peer out from under her hunchback, scanning the unimagined distances across the street. Recklessly she lurched forward, forcing her feet to accelerate until her thick-soled oxford shoes were shuffling double time, swishing her cotton skirt.

"Mrs. MURPHY!" The nurse's voice rose to a shriek.

"Enough is enough," Mom panted as she labored at top speed off the edge of the lawn, onto territory unexplored, the sidewalk. "Enough is enough."

"Stop her!" the nurse yelled as something whizzed by— a boy on a bicycle. But he could not stop her. His rude stare and his churlish comment did not faze her; his trajectory dangerously close to her did not interrupt her progress. The nurse came running—Mom could hear the silly young thing's screaming drawing nearer, but did not look. No time. Had to keep the feet moving, one a weenie length ahead of the other, then the other a weenie length in front again. Keep moving. She had to get there.

"Almost there. Almost there. Almost there."

She could see it just a few feet ahead, the cliff, the edge of the conceivable world, painted yellow because there was no parking here, near the corner. The curb.

"MRS. MURPHY!"

The sheepie-white nuisance was almost upon her. Mom ignored her, turning her face to the street. Against her straining cheeks Mom could feel the hot winds as the many-colored lightnings flashed up and down that abyss; she could hear them roar. But she was not afraid. Rather, her lumpy old heart was pounding loudly with excitement. For a turtle in the spring it is time, or for a frog, and for her also it was time to cross to the other side.

She never hesitated. It is of no use to tread carefully when it is time to cross. Never breaking the rhythm of her escape, she moved her right oxford forward its condign six inches. Its heavy toe caught in the crack betweeen the curb and the sidewalk. Mom pitched forward.

Then there were screechings, and then a lot of windy noise and many bright lights. But no pain, absolutely none. Not that she would have minded pain. Not at all. But it was nice this way. Mom listened to the whirling winds and watched the colorful lights and smiled. She had done it. Finally she had done it. She had run away.

Was she across? She didn't really know. But no matter what happened now, she was free. She was free. She would never have to listen to him again.

Buffy barged in singing, "Fairy *tales* can come *true*, it can happen to you, if you're *Jung* at heart. . . ."

"Stop it," LeeVon complained. "Quiet in the library."

With a flourish, she laid upon his desk the green-covered book she was returning. "I don't need this any-more," she said not very quietly. "Hey. Have you heard the latest spooky story the kids are telling? About the web-footed bouncing, jingling monster lurking Grendel-like in the fountains at the mall?"

LeeVon said starchily, "No, I have *not*."

"I understand they just released that poor cop from the wacky ward last week."

"*Stop* it, Best Beloved." LeeVon squeezed his head in his hands, disarranging his black leather, bunny-studded headband. "Not everybody cherishes these contretemps as gleefully as you seem to."

"It's just that I'm feeling so much better." Buffy perched her large blue-jeaned posterior on the edge of his desk and spoke more gently. "So are you ever going to tell me all about that guy who kissed you?"

"No, I am not going to tell you." Suddenly as smug as she was, LeeVon looked up at her and smiled; like ethereal angel laughter, his facial rings chimed. "His name is Richard. Draw your own conclusions. I will tell you that I still haven't gotten my bike back."

"I haven't located my car, either. And I'm out of a job. And my insurance doesn't cover the wacky ward. Isn't the collective unconscious fun?"

"Sure. Absolutely. It's a blast. How's Emily?"

"Good. Emily's terrific." Buffy smiled hugely just at the thought of Emily. "She's a lot more connected than she used to be. We're a lot closer." Buffy's smile grew bemused. "She won't talk about what happened, though."

LeeVon understood instantly. "Good for Emily," he declared. "Neither will I."

"Spoilsports."

"Sane persons, that's all." Firmly LeeVon moved the conversation onward. "How about Addie? Are he and Emily still an item?"

"I'm not sure." Buffy's smile shifted into a minor key. "Did I tell you?" Of course she hadn't told him. It had just been decided. But she was trying to be casual. "Addie's moving out."

"Oh?" His eyebrows levitated.

"Yeah. Soon."

"Did he find his own place?"

"Not exactly."

LeeVon sat waiting for the rest of it.

"He's going looking," Buffy said.

"I take it you are not speaking of apartment hunting?"

"You take it correctly. I visualize him as heading west. Riding into the sunset."

"He's on a sort of Prinzly quest?"

"Exactly. He wants to find out who he is."

"Ah."

"He's not unhappy," Buffy added. "He hasn't been un-happy at all, just curious. Interested. And now he's down-right excited."

"Good."

"I just hope he won't be disappointed."

"He won't." LeeVon sounded quite certain. "Tell him to come here first, for a guidebook."

"Like heck I will."

"But you should. He will find out all he needs to know if he does. Maybe not quite the way he expects, but it will happen. You found out who you are, didn't you, Maddie?"

"Huh," Buffy said.

Emily told no one about Fair Peril, but it was on her mind all the time like a theme song. She hugged it to her-self like a good secret, like when she was a child and she had found a place under the lilac bush in the backyard where there were truly blue stones. No one but her was allowed there. Certain places were precious. They were personal. Fair Peril was that kind of place. None of her mother's business—not because it was bad, but because it was beautiful. She pondered Fair Peril in her heart, but she did not miss it, because it was still with her.

Adam was going away, but he would still be with her.

The night he told her, she took the news gravely, but knew that her heart was not broken. Yes, she realized, talk-ing it over with a stuffed armadillo late that evening, yes, she would miss Adam—but true comrades know that they will meet again. Besides, she had things to do. A new job, in the Express store, that required lots of clothes. Scads of reading to do for Advanced Placement. Swimming parties to get ready for. In addition to all of which, she and her girlfriends were collecting fuzzy stickers in their sticker albums while they plotted the overthrow of the Western world.

Still . . . this time of night, when Prentis and Tempestt wanted her out of their way . . . it would be nice to have somebody to talk to besides a stuffed armadillo.

Emily smiled suddenly and reached for her phone.

"Hi, Mommy. Did I wake you up? No, nothing's wrong. I was just thinking, you're really going to miss Adam, aren't you? Yeah, so am I. Listen, after he goes away, could I move in with you? Would you like that? You sure? Good. So would I."

"So, any idea at all where you're going?" Buffy asked Adam as the kid settled into the used Mustang that had gone on her MasterCard. He needed a haircut, but she refrained from mentioning it, only noticing silently that his drab hair protruded messily from under his Pittsburgh Pirates baseball cap. He had jammed the thing on his head either to hide the fact that he needed a shampoo or to prevent her from kissing him, or simply because he habitually wore a baseball cap indoors and out. Along with stonewashed jeans, slang, wallet, and driver's license, Adam had come equipped with a complete complement of male teenage attitudes. And with charm. And more than enough testosterone. And a good heart.

He had come with everything but memories.

She had known him only for a few weeks, and now he was going.

She stood by the car with arms folded. Adam said with his usual immense cheer, "I got no clue," but then he looked at her, and his smile dislimned into an unusual seriousness. He sat without starting the car, gazing intently at her.

He was, Madeleine knew, a test she had to undergo, administered to her by whatever devious storyteller was in charge of these things. So far, she had passed. He had lived in her house and she had been a friend and a mother to him, nothing more. She had not competed with her daughter for his time or his affection. She had not courted him, she had not made him feel that he was indebted to her, she had not constrained him to love her, she had not constrained his heart in any way. She had set him free, and she was letting him go.

Gazing at her, he said slowly, "I think I'll be heading toward water. A lake, a wild river, maybe one of the oceans, I don't know." His hazel eyes shifted focus to look far beyond her, still intent. "There's something about water," he said very softly. "I don't know. I think it would be cool to get down in the water. Look up at the surface like at a sky all different glass colors."

He hesitated and glanced at her to see if she understood at all. She did; she understood more than he knew. She nodded at him to go on.

"Look up at the surface, look down at the bottom," he said, his gaze slipping away from her again. "Slugs and stuff. Swim around down there. Sneak up behind a fish or something. Sneak up under a duck and goose it. Or maybe you're the one with something after you, maybe there's something bigger than you down there. Maybe at night. Might be scary. But maybe the fish shine at night. I think it would be beautiful." He glanced at her almost as if looking for her approval. "I think I gotta find the right lake or whatever and then I want to learn to dive. Be a frogman or whatever."

Buffy tried to keep most of what she was feeling from showing in her face. He did not know he was remembering the beauty and peril of being a frog; he thought he was sharing a dream with her. And in that he was no different than anyone. How do any of us know where our dreams come from?

She said, "Let me know when you find it."

"I will."

"Keep in touch."

"Yeah. That too." Now he was focused on her again, looking up at her from the driver's seat. Quite abruptly, he said, "You saved me from something, didn't you?"

She stood gulping air like a fish. Oh, God. His first memory was of her kissing his forehead; he was not stupid, he had to wonder, he had to know there were things she was not telling him. But so far, he hadn't pressed her for answers—

He still didn't. He said quietly, thoughtfully, "I was so damn happy to be—just to be. Still am. Happy like a hog in mud. I think—whatever came before—must have been pretty awful. I think maybe I better not know. Better not remember."

Buffy succeeded in shutting her mouth. She nodded and stood back.

"Well, I'm outta here." He adjusted the mirror.

"You going to say good-bye to Emily?"

"Did. Last night." He leaned forward and started the car. "It's not like I'm not gonna be back," he added, eyes on the road. "Heck, you two couldn't fight me off with a stick."

God bless him, he made her smile. Then he looked straight at her with that loopy grin of his as wide as sky, with happiness warm in his ordinary eyes. "See ya," he said, and he lead-footed the gas and roared away.

Buffy watched after him until he was out of sight, which didn't take long, the way he drove. She sighed. Just like always. Give a kid a soul, then let go.

She hardly ever heard from the other two, Curtis and Marjorie.

Emily was coming to live with her, God bless sweet Emily, her phone call had been the best surprise in a long time—but Emily would grow up, too. Soon. Emily would leave.

I'm gonna be completely on my own.

Slowly Buffy began to smile. The smile warmed and widened and grew into a grin, because a new idea was tickling her cortex and tingling its way toward her brain stem: she was going to be completely on her own, and for the first time in her life, she was going to like it.

Once she had said that all she wanted was for somebody to love her.

Well, by damn, somebody did. And that somebody was the one person she would always live with.

Grinning, Buffy started to hum. Humming, she headed down the street, thumping along in her old sneakers, jeans swishing between her thighs. Taking a walk. Making a new story.